LUNCH LADIES

LUNCH LADIES

A novel

JODI
THOMPSON
CARR

Poetic references are to *The Road Not Taken*, and *Birches*, both written by Robert Frost and first published in 1915.

Published by CENTURY HOUSE PRESS. Printed in the United States of America.

Character sketches by Zoe Mitchell.

Design by Damonza.

ISBN 979-8-9915682-1-0

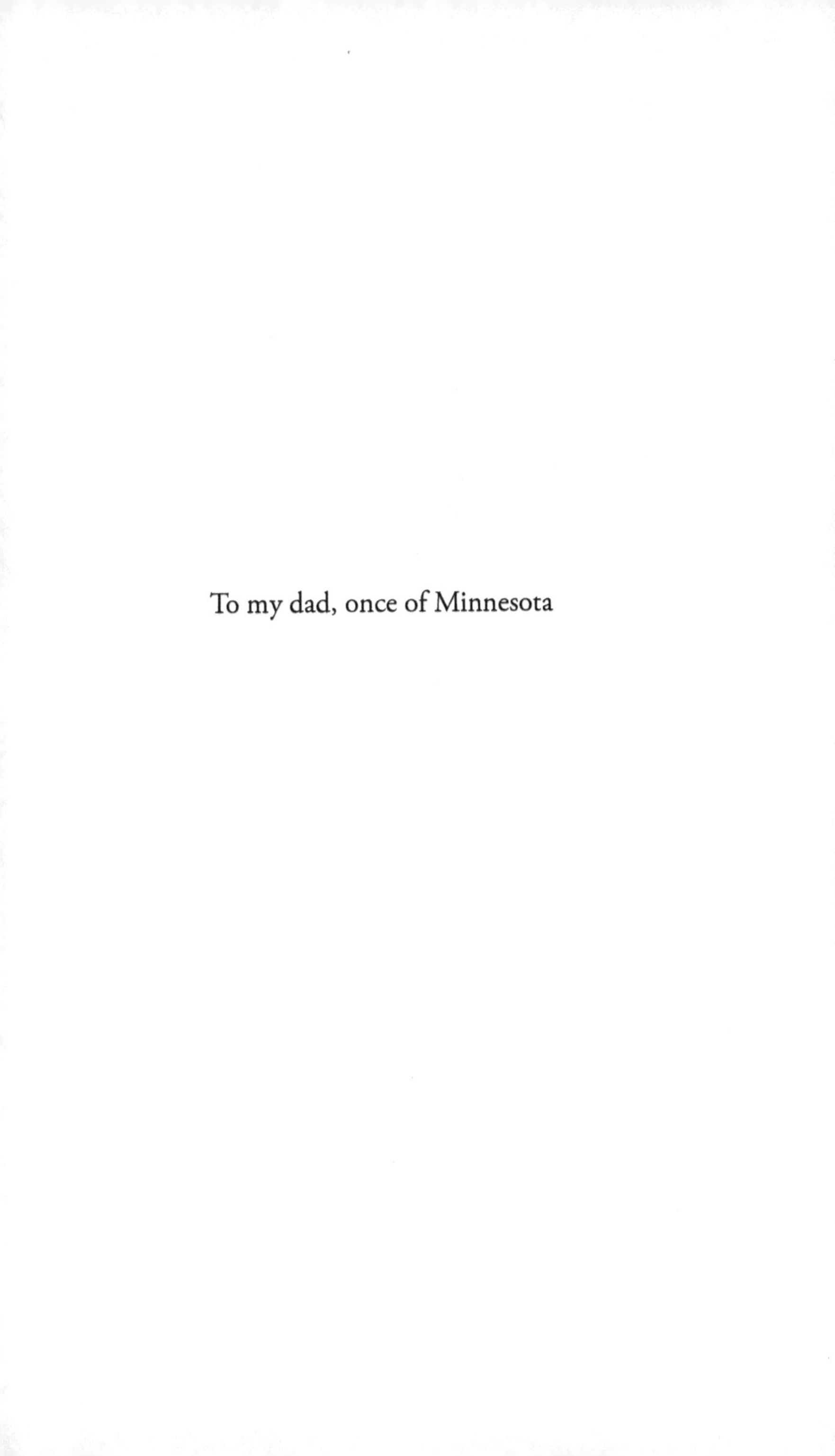

To my dad, once of Minnesota

PROLOGUE

WELCOME TO HANLEY, Minnesota. Work-a-day, not too flashy. A pleasant park along the Mississippi River. Farms and lakes on the outskirts of town – as far as the eye can see. Tidy, respectable houses – mostly on the small side. Home to just about everything a town could need: Denny's, Burger Bill's, Piggly Wiggly, the Come On Over Pub, Larsen's Corner Grocery, and Doubles and Bubbles Hardware. Schools, stores, churches, banks, an animal shelter, two laundromats, a nursing home, and a hospital scattered about in locations that generally make sense. A lovely downtown with a proud Center Street where Hanley will celebrate the bicentennial, come July.

Occasionally folks depart, never to return, or to return too late. But most have called Hanley home for generations. Why would they leave? Some look no farther than their own backyards. Some are up to their necks in everyone else's business. Among them are the lunch ladies: Crystal, Coralene, and Sheila. Through the tools of their trade, the lunch ladies are represented here in the company of their families, friends, and co-workers; with the people who died and left them; and the people who died and didn't.

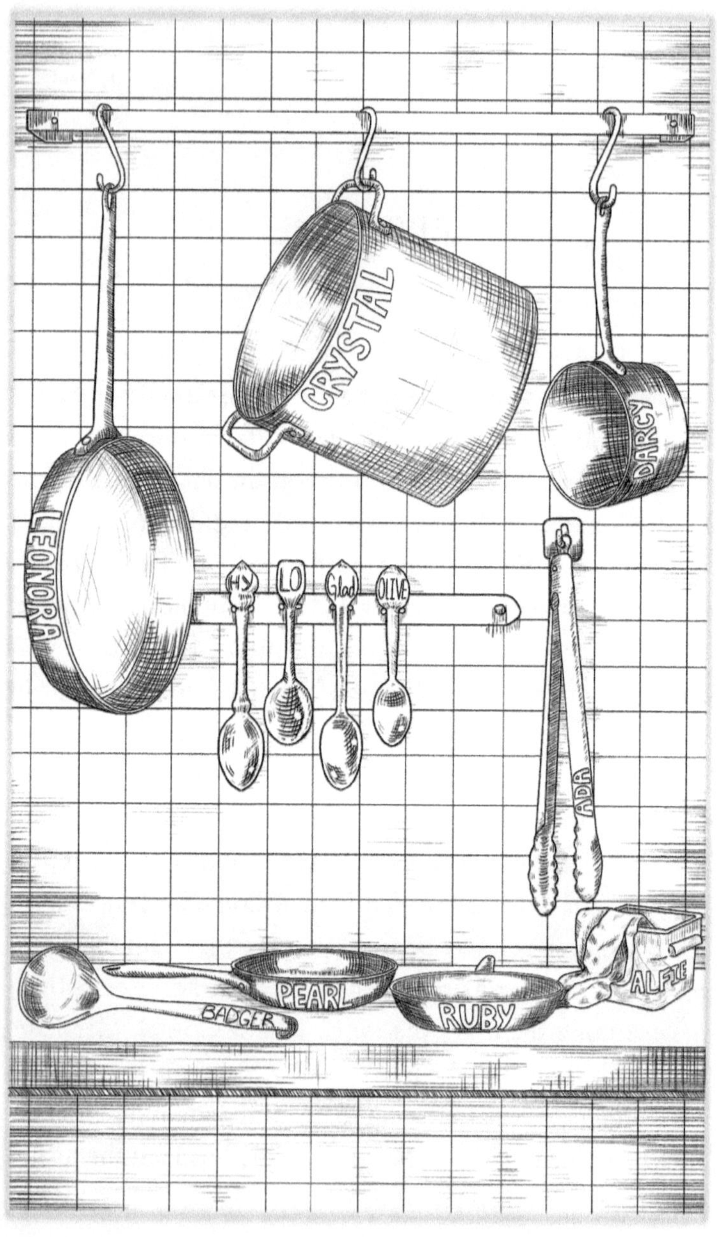

CRYSTAL
DARCY
LEONORA
HY
LO
Glad
OLIVE
ADA
PEARL
RUBY
ALFIE
BADGER

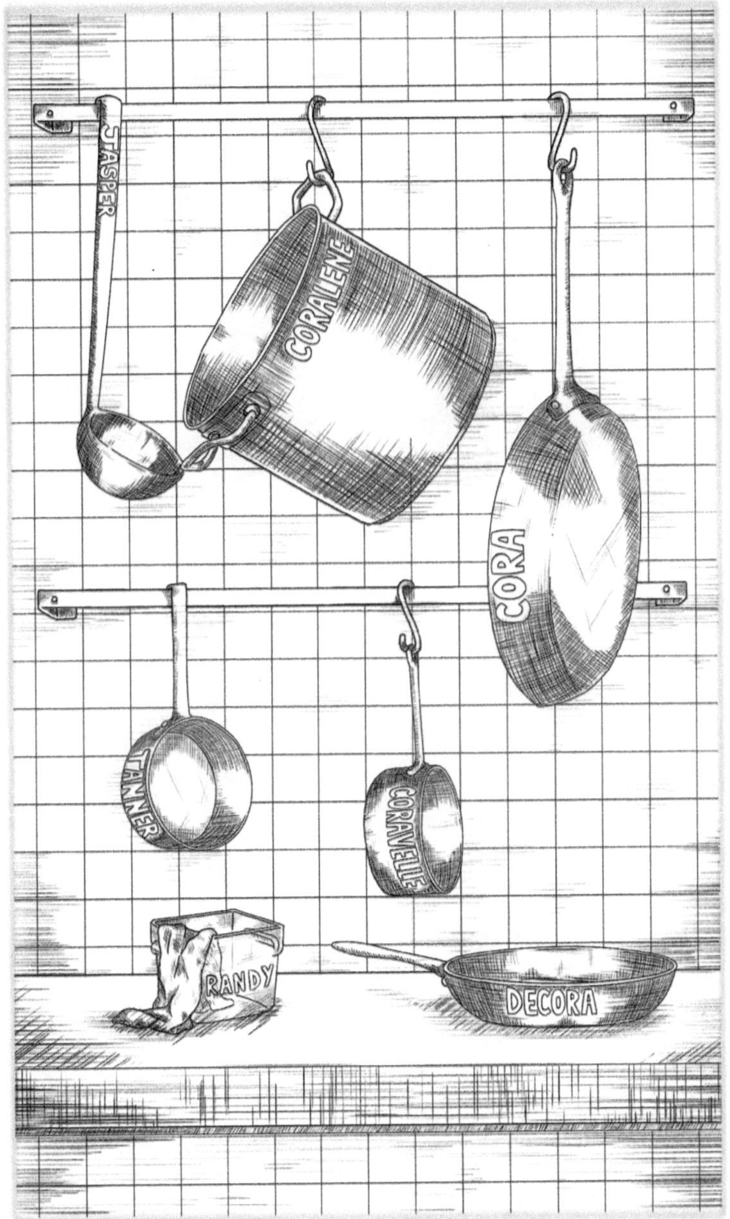

JASPER
CORALENE
CORA
TANNER
CORAVELLE
RANDY
DECORA

TOM
LEXIE
SHEILA
CONNIE
EVELYN

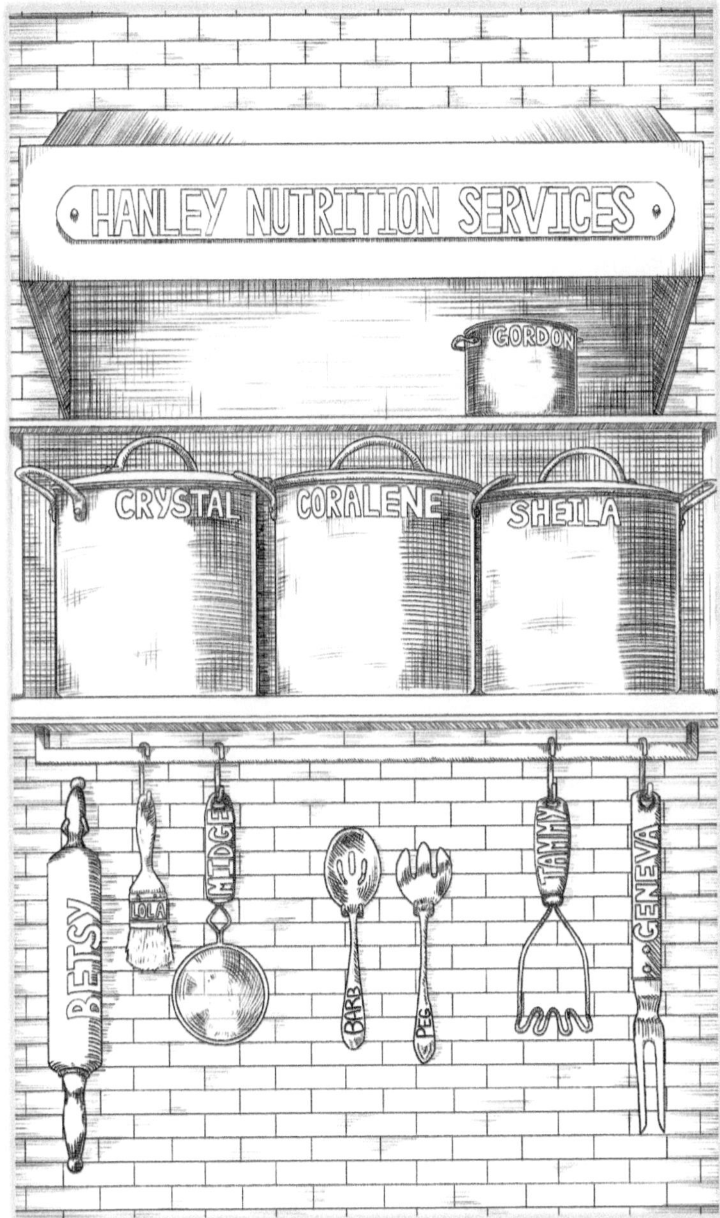

HANLEY NUTRITION SERVICES
GORDON
CRYSTAL
CORALENE
SHEILA
BETSY
LOLA
MIDGE
BARB
PEG
TAMMY
GENEVA

PART ONE

"Everyone starts in a different place, takes a different road, you know? And they might end up in a spot that's not what they wanted. Only some of us get lucky. So you got to remember that most of the time, most of the folks, are doing the best they know how to do."

BADGER DANIELS
1893-1928

CHAPTER ONE

CRYSTAL

FRIDAY, FEBRUARY 27, 1976

SEVERAL OBITUARIES IN Sunday's *Hanley Herald* had caught Crystal's eye. She'd chosen Roger Squirrel's:

Roger Remington Squirrel, October 2, 1915 to February 20, 1976. Born in Wendell, Minnesota to Albert Matthew Squirrel and Evelyn Marie (nee Johnson) Squirrel. Roger is survived by his mother Evelyn and his sisters Yvette (Edwin) Gatesman and Annabelle Squirrel. Roger moved to Hanley, Minnesota upon graduation from high school and subsequently served two years in the United States Army before returning to complete a college degree in business. Roger was a successful salesman and entrepreneur and founded Squirrel Furniture and Design, the largest furniture store in town. In his free time, he enjoyed gardening, reading, and playing bridge. Roger was a well-respected colleague, mentor, renaissance man, and friend to all. Services will be held on Saturday, February 28, 1976 at 2:00 at the Blessed Rest Chapel of the Woodlawn Cemetery.

~ ~ ~

Crystal hoped she'd found the perfect match for Roger Squirrel in the lady sitting beside her on the park bench. Crystal thought of this as *her* bench. It was close to the river, with a view of the Wisconsin shoreline. The wood on the stretch between Crystal and the lady had lost most of its green paint, one tiny chip at a time. But it was dry, and as viable an outdoor seat as one was going to find in February.

The lady appeared serene. Serene would be good, maybe even contemplative. Roger had likely been a contemplative fellow. The lady wore a thick black coat. Some kind of fake fur. Thank God, Crystal thought. She hated real fur. Who did that? Animal skins? How did the animal die in the first place? She didn't want to know. Well, she did, but she didn't.

Fake-fur-black-coat lady was holding a paperback: *Every Night, Josephine!*, by Jacqueline Susann. Crystal remembered her grandmother saying it was the only "clean" Jacqueline Susann. How would Grandma know *that*? Did they talk about this? Grandma and the ladies from the hospital guild? Who read the dirty ones?

Fake-fur-black-coat lady had short white hair. Cotton-ball white. Ivory Soap white. As Crystal had crossed the street into the park, approaching the bench from behind, the hair had struck Crystal as distinctive. Stylish. On closer examination it was straight as a needle. Pointy, and short.

On her lap, fake-fur-black-coat lady held a shapeless blue knitted hat. She wore green gloves. Why would she pair a black coat with green gloves? And a blue hat? The hat was royal blue, not navy, which might be mistaken for black. Royal blue. With black? No. Just, no. Jacqueline Kennedy Onassis would've had the perfect hat; it might've sported a bow. Although Jackie O would have worn fur. And she would not be sitting on a park bench in Minnesota.

Shoes, Crystal told herself; check the shoes. Oh dear God, they were brown. And scuffed. Rather than being stylish, fake-fur-black-coat lady was ho-hum. Worse than ho-hum. She was a mess.

The decision was made. Fake-fur-black-coat lady was not a match for Roger Squirrel. Poor man. He must've been teased mercilessly as a boy. But Roger had not been ho-hum, and he had definitely not been a mess. His obituary photo had shown him in an open-neck shirt and a cardigan. Probably a fisherman's sweater like Crystal's father wore when Crystal was young.

Crystal glanced side to side. Always best to double-check. Her purse was on her shoulder, where shoulder purses belong. The remains of her lunch – an apple core and the crusts of a peanut butter sandwich – were in the brown paper bag in her purse. Her gloves were on her hands, where gloves belong. She had not brought a hat.

As Crystal pushed herself up off the bench, fake-fur-black-coat lady also moved, standing up smoothly. No exertion. Well, poorly fashioned women could still move gracefully.

A man approached from the path by the river, walking

across the ice-crusted grass. He was tallish. He smiled as he closed in; he had beautiful teeth. He wore a trench coat over what Crystal knew would be a fashionable sport jacket that matched those perfectly creased brown slacks. His loafers shined. His shirt was white. His tie appeared sufficiently wide to be fashionable.

He was Clark Kent, but older. Yep, an aging Clark Kent. Fake-fur-black-coat lady stepped toward him and they kissed. Briefly, but still.

What in the name of Pete was Clark doing with dowdy fake-fur-black-coat lady? Crystal hadn't even named her; it hadn't been worth the effort. Clark should be matched with Rosalie Cecile (nee Taylor) Ward. Rosalie's obituary had also been in Sunday's paper, one column over from Roger Squirrel's:

Our Rosalie passed away peacefully on February 19, 1976, her family by her side. Called to her heavenly home, Rosalie left behind the misery that had cursed the last year of her life. Rosalie was born to Eugene Taylor and Maud Victoria (nee Grant) Taylor in Burlington, Vermont on April 12, 1935. Rosalie was the youngest of Eugene and Maud's seven children. She was preceded in death by her parents and her brother, Jacob Joseph Taylor, who died at age five when crushed by a falling maple tree. Rosalie married her true love, Richard Wallace Ward, when she was seventeen. Richard and Rosalie's daughter Emily Rose was born October 1, 1952. Tragically, Rosalie lost both Richard and Emily Rose when the car Richard was driving was struck by a train. A widow at eighteen, Rosalie lived out her life on her family's farm, tending to her nieces and nephews until she succumbed to lung cancer at age forty-one. She will be missed. No services at the family's request. Cremated remains will be interred locally.

Banishing further thoughts of Clark Kent and fake-fur-black-coat lady, and without either of them acknowledging her departure, Crystal ambled back up the grass and across Northeast Second Street. Her lunch break was over. Pulling open the heavy front door, she dug a tissue from her coat pocket. The transition into the overly warm hallways of the former school always made her nose run.

Crystal returned to her desk, ruminating on the Roger misstep. She'd held Roger to the end of the week, figured she'd enjoy a quick win, have Saturday off, and be ready when the new set of obituaries hit the newspaper on Sunday. Rosalie would be easier to match than Roger was proving to be. She'd missed her chance with Clark Kent, but Crystal was optimistic. She'd take care of Rosalie's match on the bus ride home.

~ ~ ~

Crystal chose from the living, just as she chose from the dead. On Sundays, she rescued travelers from the obituary page in the *Hanley Herald*. Over the week, she found them suitable companions: someone whose living spirit could support a dying one as it made its way. Companions needed to be caring. Travelers needed care. No one needed to know.

Crystal knew what it was to be lonely; she'd been alone since she was thirteen. True, her grandmother would frame it differently. Not without compassion, Grandma would speak of the "hurdle," the "challenge," the "heartbreak" that their family had endured. She'd declare that Crystal had never been alone. Thing was, Crystal would be the one to know, and what she hoped more than anything, was that back in August 1948 – when she'd lost her mother – someone else had been doing this job, which she, Crystal, had recently taken on.

~ ~ ~

At 5:00, Crystal straightened her desk – leaving Gordon's memo unread – and put on her coat.

Gordon Hund was an idiot. He'd been assigned to manage the Hanley School District's lunch department, and he behaved as if he knew what it meant to do a job such as theirs. He didn't have a clue. Crystal, Coralene, and Sheila were the ones doing what needed to be done. If schoolchildren across Hanley had had to rely on Gordon for a hot meal, they would've been shit out of luck.

When Crystal was still a lunch lady at Hastings Elementary, there'd been talk of having lunch ladies start answering phones, shelving books in the library, even putting little squirts on the right buses after school. Something about efficiencies, making the most of taxpayer dollars, and all other sorts of baloney. After much too much hubbub, three lunch ladies from across the district – Crystal, Coralene, and Sheila – had been promoted. Now they were responsible for ordering, scheduling, equipment repairs – the whole shebang. Instead of cooks at the schools planning menus and making sure they had the goods, Crystal now decided such things. For the elementary schools anyway, which were all Crystal cared about. As for elementary cooks left behind? Last Crystal had heard, when they finished serving lunch, they grabbed their whistles and followed the kids outside to watch them skin their knees on the playground.

There were rumors aplenty on how it was that Gordon had been brought in to manage all this. Even so, Crystal had been willing to consider how he'd fit as a companion for one of her lonely travelers. But no. He was no more suited to what Crystal was trying to do than fake-fur-black-coat lady had been. Crystal had seen that light quickly and avoided a match between Gordon and Leticia Arlene Brewsberry. She'd found someone else for Leticia: an older fellow who worked in the produce department at the Piggly Wiggly.

Gordon wore short-sleeve shirts and poorly tied ties. He came to the office in a windbreaker, which looked silly but was preferable to pasty arms emerging from half sleeves like twigs off a birch tree. *Get a complete shirt, Gordon; we know you can afford it. Get a real shirt.*

Gordon described their work as "Nutrition Services." Good God. Swat that fly dead. They were the lunch department. They'd all been lunch ladies, who had been reassigned to this school-turned-office building to ensure that the kids, all those wonderful kids, got a tasty hot meal promptly at noon, five days a week.

Heading for the door at 5:00, Crystal paused to wait as Coralene put on her coat so they could walk out together.

"Good day?" Coralene asked, offering Crystal the pained half-smile of a middle-aged woman.

"Good enough," Crystal replied, presenting her own version, which, like Coralene's, showed no teeth.

Coralene's last lunch lady assignment had been at one of Hanley's two junior high schools. Now she was in this office, making sure all those smelly, noisy teenagers-in-training were well-fed.

Coralene was a large woman, nearly as large as Crystal. After moving to her office job, Coralene had shed the white lunch-lady dresses and black aprons in favor of polyester pantsuits. Today's pantsuit was yellow and it was, Crystal thought, a lovely shade, framed by Coralene's dark-brown skin. The pants of Coralene's suit had a seam down the front. It gave them a tad bit of structure, which was wise. The jacket had a pointed collar and squared shoulders. Coralene wore a boldly flowered blouse underneath, which was worthy of the outfit. The jacket was long, eight buttons was Crystal's guess, and it extended to the knees of the matching yellow pants, serving to acceptably cover Coralene's ample behind.

The #17 bus appeared right on time; Crystal and Coralene climbed the three steps. It would take precisely twenty minutes to reach Crystal's stop. Twenty minutes would be more than enough time to find someone for Rosalie.

The two women always sat across the aisle from each other, close to the front. Should the bus fill, they might need to share their seats with strangers, but when it came to bus riding, bulk was an asset. Few other passengers attempted to squeeze into the seats next to Crystal and Coralene's respective windows. Should someone approach, each woman would swing her legs into the aisle, making it clear that if the interloping passenger really wanted to take a load off, said passenger would need to shimmy between the women and the seats in front of them – only to find that the spot by the window was no longer a full seat. Not even close.

Few other riders braved what some knew from experience would be required to get those window seats next to Crystal or Coralene. Most only needed to glance in their direction to get the idea. Because really? Who would be stupid enough to mess with a lunch lady?

Today's bus driver was new. The regular driver, bus driver Stewart, who usually drove the #17 route on weekday afternoons, must be sick. Not an uncommon occurrence. But bus driver Stewart was a good egg. He'd give passengers a grin when they boarded the bus, never a full smile. Full smiles required reciprocal full smiles, and few passengers were in a full-smile mood by the end of a workday. Crystal wasn't, that's for sure.

Bus driver Stewart wore no wedding ring. Widower, Crystal had decided, not bachelor, although it rarely mattered. But Crystal had been pretty sure that bus driver Stewart was a widower, and on a Tuesday afternoon, months ago now, Crystal had matched bus driver Stewart with Penelope Paige Smith.

Penny had been a schoolteacher. Better yet, she'd taught kindergarten. Bless Penny's pitter-patting heart. For thirty years, Penny had taught in the same classroom: Room 105. She'd been born on a Minnesota farm, and unlike her younger brothers, Chester and Ira, Penny had enjoyed eating the head cheese her father made after every hog slaughter. This was not information Crystal had ever read in an obituary. There'd been a pickled herring reference once or twice, but never head cheese.

Penny's brothers had stayed on the farm to manage the hogs, but Penny had settled in town. When the elementary school opened, Penny had stepped right into Room 105. No husband had been mentioned; Crystal was quite sure that Penny had died an old maid. Perhaps she'd had a cat. Cats are good company.

The match had been made. Penny and Stewart. Stewart and Penny. Crystal had slept well that night; she'd hoped that Penny had finally rested well too, with bus driver Stewart's goodness to ease her along.

Enough reminiscing about past successes. Crystal turned her mind to the task at hand – finding a match for Rosalie. Today's driver's name was Everett. Everett was younger than bus driver Stewart which was a good thing, given how young Rosalie had been when she died.

When Crystal and Coralene had boarded the bus, Everett had flashed a full-toothed smile. *Rookie mistake*, Crystal thought. *He must be new. Perhaps he's a fill-in driver, hasn't been assigned his own route yet. By the time he has a route of his own, he'll learn his lesson about toothy smiles. Don't do it. It's too much at the end of the day.*

Everett's reddish-brown hair was cut short. Neatly trimmed at the base of his neck and above his ears. Not the shaggy style some men seemed to wear these days. Likewise, his tie was straight and his shirt was tucked. There was a John le Carré paperback tucked under his seat; Everett must use his spare time productively. Definitely another good egg. Just like bus driver Stewart. Who doesn't like a bus driver?

Crystal made her decision. The toothpick was clean; the cake was baked. Everett was the perfect match for Rosalie. Rosalie and Everett. Everett and Rosalie.

Satisfied, Crystal shifted her bottom back and forth a bit, the better to sit comfortably for the rest of the ride up Palisades Avenue. After Everett passed the stop before Crystal's, she gripped the bar of the seat in front and hauled herself up. Bus driver Stewart didn't require that passengers ring the bell when they wanted to get off; he just knew. But Everett might have a different way of doing things. Everett might scoot right past any stop that hadn't been requested via the tinkle of the bell. Crystal wouldn't risk it.

There was no one sitting next to her, which, as always, was a good thing. Crystal leaned toward the bell cord that ran above the bus windows and gave it a tug. She'd kept her coat on for the entire ride. On warmer spring days when she wore no overcoat, fellow riders who'd made the mistake of choosing the window seat might be whacked in the face by Crystal's arm fat as she reached for the cord – the same smack one would experience on the receiving end of a briskly-opened umbrella.

With nods to Coralene and Everett, Crystal lumbered down the steps onto Palisades Avenue. Turning south, she walked the half block to where Palisades intersected Northeast 14th Street and contentedly covered the two blocks to her apartment building. The sun had set for the day, but it was not yet fully dark.

Crystal's building housed nine units, on three floors. She felt that end-of-the-day, now-I'm-home satisfaction. Meager patches of snow attempted to conceal the beauty bark encircling the azaleas and a flowering plum tree in the front yard. Otherwise, the building was devoid of landscaping. Absolutely nothing caused it to stand out. Fine thing.

The Dexter, 1938, was noted in white masonry block letters above the otherwise brick façade. It was lovely. Understated and sophisticated, nothing like the newer apartment buildings on either side. Each of those had only two floors of apartment units; Crystal knew them to be cramped and cheaply constructed. They were laughable, posing as bookends to The Dexter.

Tiny balconies protruded like pimples from each unit on the new buildings so that residents could exit their living rooms and see what, exactly? Traffic on Northeast 14th Street? Contrasting the beautiful brick of The Dexter, the newer buildings were covered in stucco in a toothpastey shade of light green. Wooden letters in cursive script were affixed diagonally to the front of each, proclaiming them as *The Sunrise* and *The Sunset*. Swat that fly dead. Both buildings faced north.

Crystal entered The Dexter's small lobby. An overstuffed blue brocade chair was the only furniture; a round olive-green rug covered much of the hardwood floor. She rummaged in her purse for her keys and removed her lunch bag. Opening the tiny lock on her mailbox, she pulled out a few envelopes.

Holding her purse, lunch bag, and thin stack of mail,

Crystal unlocked unit #3. She inhaled deeply as she entered. Any smell? Any smell at all? Nope. It was safe to go to the kitchen first, before emptying the cat box which she kept behind the bathroom door.

Crystal felt a surge of pleasure at her evening's plans. She turned on the oven to 350 degrees and took the provisions she'd need down from her cupboards, arranging them on the counter. Fridays were not the nights for fumbling dinner preparation.

Next, she folded down the edges on her lunch bag to stiffen its opening. Stepping into the bathroom, she plopped Terry's poop into the lunch bag and rolled down the top. Knowing the oven would soon be hot, she went back outside. Garbage cans were arranged along the side of the building like a set of steel drums. Crystal dropped the poop bag into the can which boasted a precisely painted #3 on the lid, then returned to her apartment.

With an experienced stir, Crystal combined an egg and milk with a box of Jiffy cornbread mix, which she spread into a square buttered Pyrex. Once her cornbread was baking, Crystal opened a can of Van Camp's Pork and Beans and emptied its contents into a Revere Ware pan. Because it was Friday, and her evening of indulgence, Crystal lifted out the chunk of salt pork that sat like an island in the sea of beans. She sucked off the tomatoey sauce. Eat it now, or let it heat with the beans? Tough choice. With one more lick, she returned the piece of fat to the pan.

Opening a can of Wilderness Cherry Pie Filling, Crystal emptied it into a second Revere Ware, using a spatula to clean out every gooey, bright-red drop. She'd turn on the burner for her pie filling once her dinner was ready. Warm cherry pie filling on vanilla ice cream, now that was a peacock feather on a velvet hat. The perfect dessert.

Her cornbread baking and beans warming, Crystal opened a can of applesauce and poured half into a custard cup. She took the applesauce and a spoon into the living room, turned on the TV news, and settled into the La-Z-Boy. Terry appeared from under the sofa and jumped onto Crystal's ample lap, pawing at her as if plumping a pillow.

"You're only here for a few minutes," Crystal told the cat. "Dinner's not done. But once I'm back you can make yourself at home and we'll watch our shows."

Terry agreeably hopped down when Crystal returned to the kitchen. Leaving her custard cup in the sink, she filled her favorite bowl with the now-bubbling pork and beans and put the Pyrex of cornbread onto a folded dish towel. On a TV tray next to her La-Z-Boy, Crystal folded another dish towel, which she'd use as a napkin and positioned it tidily next to the butter dish and a tumbler of milk. Once her food was arrayed and the heat was on low under the pie filling, Crystal settled happily into her chair. Holding the bowl in both hands, she nodded at Terry, inviting the cat to return.

The chunk of salt pork sat atop the beans, shiny with tomato sauce and fat, as if offering Crystal a cheery hello. As if saying, "Welcome to Friday night."

CHAPTER TWO

Coralene

Friday, February 27, 1976

CORALENE WATCHED CRYSTAL plod up the aisle and turn to descend from the bus. Crystal's exit was always Coralene's cue to collect her things. Odd that Crystal did nothing on the ride home. She just sat. Never a crossword puzzle. No novel or grocery list. Nothing. What could she be thinking? Occasionally Crystal turned her legs into the aisle, as Coralene was also known to do, but other than that? Not a thing, for twenty solid minutes.

Coralene was willing to grant that Crystal was a people watcher, a pastime Coralene also enjoyed. On some days, Crystal appeared quite consumed with the fellow riders. Her eyes wandered across the mishmash of humans, as if taking stock of each one. But on other days? Crystal would deny it, but on other days Crystal slept, occasionally emitting a little snort, which usually roused her. Coralene always looked away when Crystal snorted. She had no desire to embarrass the woman.

For her part, Coralene liked to think that she made as good use of her time on the bus as she did every other minute of each day she was given. Glory be to the Lord. Each sunrise was a gift. Each evening, an opportunity for gratitude. Each bus ride, yes even each bus ride, was hallowed time to be put to good use.

Coralene's use of this particular afternoon had been to start the crossword that she and Jasper would complete together after dinner. Jasper was a peach when it came to crosswords. He always let her give it the once-over, meaning Jasper let Coralene answer the easy ones first. That way, each puzzle was partially completed in Coralene's hand.

A gift from God, was Jasper. As if God himself had lowered Jasper from heaven right onto Coralene's parents' front porch, twenty-five years ago. Jasper would say that he hadn't arrived via the God's-hand express, but had trekked across town for over an hour. But Coralene never thought of her husband as anything other than divinely delivered.

Tonight, their evening would start with dinner, which would be whatever Jasper had cooked up this afternoon. Coralene was hoping for macaroni and cheese, but Jasper likely had a hankering for sloppy Joes. Her man made a dandy sloppy Joe; he put in a bit of heat. There was coleslaw in the fridge, and some of that corn relish Jasper liked to make. Maybe they'd have some greens. Yes, macaroni and cheese would be her preference. But more than that, her preferred meal was any meal she and Jasper ate together. A peach, that man. Didn't hurt that he could cook.

Someone pulled the bell cord. One tug was sufficient for most people. Two came from folks who were running late, as if urgent dinging would rev the engine. Three dings were usually the work of people new to the world of bus riding, concerned that the driver hadn't heard the first two. Stewart, the usual bus driver, had been replaced today by a younger man, so perhaps the profusion of bells was meant to ensure that the new man didn't prolong anyone's ride on a Friday night. As riders began their exit at her stop, Coralene caught the eye of the new driver. She gave him a smile, that started and ended with only the slightest uplift of her lips. She hadn't caught his name.

Grasping the handrail just in case, she stepped down off the bus. Jasper was there. Jasper was always there. Each weekday, as Coralene's feet found solid ground, her mind would leave her world and return to theirs. Jasper didn't meet her at the corner, not even at the bus stop itself, but at the foot of the steps. Every day, every single working day, as far back as Coralene could remember.

"Hello, my Cory," Jasper whispered into her hair, with the gravelly voice of a Texas sheriff.

"Hello, baby." She reached for his hand – brown, warm, and as dependable as a saddle horn – and the two of them strolled home.

"So now, whatcha got there for me? Did you answer them all, or did you leave me a couple?" Jasper cleared the kitchen table as Coralene retrieved the newspaper from her bag on the counter and spread it out so they could examine her progress on the crossword puzzle.

"There's still plenty for you to do here, baby. I didn't want you feeling bad or nothin'. Didn't want you to think

I'd outsmarted you." Coralene laughed as she pulled her napkin off her lap to give her mouth one more wipe before putting the napkin and her empty milk glass into Jasper's outstretched hand.

"Good stuff?" Jasper asked. "Not that I'm fishing for compliments but…"

"Oh baby," Coralene cut him off. "That macaroni and cheese is only one of the things you do well. But it's one of my favorites. Not my most favorite, mind you. But high on the list."

"Anything for you, Cory," Jasper purred.

"Well, I need you to do something for me for sure on this one," Coralene said, taking a pencil out of her bag and tapping it on the crossword puzzle before extracting a pen for Jasper. "I was all-out confused on a few of these."

She snapped her handbag closed. "Can I wipe those?" she asked, getting up as Jasper filled the dish tub with soapy water and reached for a plate from the stack of dirty dishes on the counter.

"Sure enough. That'll get us to the puzzle sooner. Thanks, love. Besides, I want to talk to you about something. Let's do that before we finish the crossword."

Pulling a dish towel from the drawer under the silverware, Coralene stood beside her husband at the sink. No need to prod him. Jasper would speak his piece when he was ready.

Jasper slid the washed plates into the dish rack and rubbed the sponge around the rims of the glasses, eliciting a clean-glass squeak. "I talked to Tanner today," he said. "He's not in a good spot, Cory. I don't think the boy's in a good spot."

"Did he call you? He doesn't usually call. I'd be glad to hear he called."

"Nope, he didn't call. Just showed up. At the back door. About an hour after I got up. I was cooking and then there was Tanner, big as life. I was mighty surprised."

"Well, I suppose it's good he showed up, if he's got himself in a bind. What's the problem this time? Lost his job again?"

Jasper squeezed the last of the water out of the sponge and upturned the yellow tub, rinsing stray soap bubbles off its bottom. Coralene wiped the last few forks with the now-damp towel and put them in the silverware drawer, before putting the saucepan Jasper had used to cook the greens back on the stove. She turned on the burner and watched as water droplets sizzled and danced, and the pan began to dry.

Jasper beamed at his wife. "You always know. You're like some kind of savant. You read my mind every darn time."

"It's not that, baby, it's that our boy Tanner is a broken record when it comes to steady employment. And it's not like he ever saw that behavior in this house."

"No. No, he did not."

"But he saw it from his own daddy," Coralene continued. "And that matters more, don't you think? No matter how much we did for that boy, what his own daddy did or didn't do, that's what matters more." Coralene turned the burner off, leaving the saucepan to finish drying where it sat. She rubbed the back of her arm across her forehead, pushing stray hair out of her face.

"His daddy's dead," Jasper said. "Them's the facts. And if he not dead, then he might as well be. He's long gone. You know that. I know that. I think Tanner knows it too, even if he doesn't say so. But you and me? We can't be blaming Tanner's daddy for mistakes Tanner is making right now. And Tanner can't blame him either. The boy's gotta step up. And soon."

"You're right. I know you're right, but I promised my sister," Coralene said. "I promised DeCora I'd keep an eye out. But Lord above. That boy. And thing is, he's not a boy anymore. Not even close. He's twenty years old. He's gotta step up, like you say. I'm just not sure how to help him do it."

"We won't come up with an answer tonight," Jasper said. "Just wanted to let you know before we got started on the puzzle and I forgot all about it, then remembered when I got to work. I wouldn't want to call you then."

Coralene chuckled. "You always say that, baby, but I know you aren't going to call me in the middle of the night just because you've had a memory spark. I know you wouldn't do that. I need my beauty sleep."

Jasper laughed out loud. "Now you're the one fishing for compliments, Cory. You don't need any beauty sleep and you know it. You've got all the beauty one woman can hold, and you've got some you must've stolen from some other gal. Your beauty, and more beauty on top of that."

Coralene walked over to where Jasper stood against the counter. She put her hand on his neck and pulled him toward her. "Speaking of beauty," she said softly. "Speaking of beauty."

"Staring at these five little squares isn't getting me any closer to the answer." Coralene's pencil was poised over the crossword puzzle. Jasper leaned back in his chair.

"You know that one there." Jasper used his pen to point at one of the few remaining strings of empty squares. "You've got the X there, you just need the first four letters."

"I know what I need." Coralene tried not to sound annoyed. She frowned at Jasper. "Counting the squares isn't what's got me stumped."

"I know. You want another clue?"

"Well the clue here isn't nudging my brain in the right direction. '*Redone, in art, music, or literature.*' It's the X that's causing trouble. There aren't that many words that end in X."

"You're right. And I wouldn't say it's a common word, but it's not as obscure as some we've had. Remember that one a couple weeks ago? That one about the poem?"

"I remember. No idea how I knew that word. Took me back to high school, when we studied everything the Greeks had been up to over the centuries."

"Epyllion," Jasper said. "Epyllion. A short poem with a rhyme scheme from Greek or Latin."

"Gracious sakes, baby. I can't believe you remember the exact clue. You know what we need though? We need more references to African poems. African poets. Remember we read about that one? That Zulu poet? What's his name?"

"Kunene," Jasper said. "Whole book of Zulu poems, translated into English, few years back. We should find that book, Cory."

"Well, none of that is helping me with my five-letters-ends-with-X problem here."

"You know what I think this word sounds like?" Jasper asked. "Laundry detergent. Sounds like a brand of laundry detergent."

Coralene thought for a moment, before leaning back, a satisfied look on her face. "Ahh, yes it does. You're so right, baby." She pulled the newspaper closer and filled in the missing boxes. "Redux. I don't care about a redone piece of music. Tonight, I care about washing my clothes with Redux."

Jasper smiled as he pulled the paper toward him and refolded it. "Want to keep this one?" he asked. "Care to look back fondly at Redux?"

"Nah, I don't need it. That wasn't the best puzzle ever. But my puzzle partner? Now he's a keeper." Coralene pushed her chair away from the table. She walked behind Jasper and kissed the top of his head on her way into the kitchen. "I'll put your lunch together," she said, setting her hand on a cupboard knob and looking over her shoulder at her husband.

"Could confuse a man, having his lunch after his dinner," Jasper said from where he still sat at the table, "but I suppose that's the joy of the graveyard shift."

"Leave it to you to find joy even in a graveyard."

"Isn't really the graveyard I find joyful, but you know, some folks might be glad to be there. Think about it. It's the folks left behind who aren't so glad their loved ones are in the graveyard. Missing them and everything. But I believe there are some folks who are ready to go."

"Can we not talk about this now, baby? I'm not feeling the graveyard discussion. Let's take death off the table altogether for the night."

"I hear you Cory, I do. But you know I'm right. By the time they get there, some folks are perfectly fine with being in the graveyard."

"I need to head to bed soon, sugar," Coralene said,

waving a brown paper lunch sack between her thumb and middle finger. "I got an empty bag here that I'd be happy to load up with lunch so you can take it with you when you go. But tell me what you want in it. There's no tiger in my tank tonight. I'm ready for bed."

Jasper repositioned his chair at the kitchen table to look straight on at Coralene. "I know you're tired by Friday night," he said gently. "Let me tell you what I want so you can load up that bag and head to bed. It's not that I can't pack my own lunch."

"No one's wondering about that. I always pack your lunch. I want to pack your lunch. It's just that I'm ready to pack your lunch now. Now. So I can go to bed."

"Put some of that macaroni and cheese in a Tupperware. That's good cold. And get some of those carrot sticks I've got sitting in ice water and put them in a baggie. Or stick in an apple. Maybe slather some mustard on one of those hamburger buns and add a slab of bologna? I'll use the rest of the buns for sloppy Joes next week. Have we got any Nilla Wafers left? Those don't stay around for long, huh? I love those Nilla Wafers, and so do you."

"We're almost down to crumbs, but I left a couple for you last time I ransacked the box," Coralene said.

"We're set then. That'll be fine. That and my thermos of coffee. And my napkin. Don't forget my napkin, Cory."

"Racy little note on your napkin? Isn't that what you mean?" Coralene said slyly. "I won't forget that. You need something to spice up the night when you're sorting all those letters. Just don't let your napkin get tossed in a bin full of U.S. mail. The mailman who delivers that might be in for a shock."

"No return address though," Jasper said. "I don't want the mailman to know where to find the sexy woman who wrote the note on that napkin." He watched as Coralene packed his lunch items into the sack.

"Now, pass me that." Coralene pointed to Jasper's crossword puzzle pen on the table. She opened one of the kitchen drawers and extracted a dinner-sized white paper napkin. "No peeking," she said as she took the pen from Jasper's hand.

Her note complete, Coralene smiled at her husband, put the napkin on top of the other items in the lunch sack, folded down the top, and placed the sack in the refrigerator. "Bedtime for me," she announced as she came around to Jasper's chair, wrapping her arms around his shoulders and nuzzling his neck. "You've still got a couple hours before you've got to go. *Rockford Files* is on."

CHAPTER THREE

Sheila

Friday, February 27, 1976

IT HAD BEEN Sheila's decision to survey high school students on their menu preferences. It was a great idea, until it wasn't. Now, late on Friday afternoon facing the drudgery she'd taken on, she regretted it.

Crystal and Coralene had gone home the minute the clock struck 5:00. Like they did every freaking day.

Gordon had left at 5:15. Must have thought it made him a big man to leave later than those two. Sheila had watched as Gordon wriggled out of his office, turning sideways before he could clear the door.

You couldn't call Gordon's office an office, unless your tongue was tucked securely in your cheek. It had started life as a supply closet, but when Gordon had been brought in to create the Nutrition Services Department, he'd insisted he must sit apart.

Some higher-up, some muckety-muck or other, had

informed Gordon that if he wanted an office, he could repurpose the supply closet at the back of the room. Whoever had made that wisecrack had to have been joking. But moving into the supply closet? That's exactly what Gordon had done.

Sheila had a pretty good idea why it was that Gordon had been put in charge, but there was no way to confirm her suspicions. Besides, speculating on who Gordon knew, or was related to, was a king-sized waste of Sheila's valuable time. She was out of the Hanley High School cafeteria and working in an office; the arrangement suited her just fine.

It went without saying that Gordon's closet office had plenty of shelves, now that construction paper, crayons, staplers, and all manner of claptrap had been distributed to schools. Prominently displayed on a middle shelf was a photo of a black standard poodle. An engraved nameplate was affixed to the bottom of the ornate frame. *Napoleon*, it read.

Sheila needed a plan for dealing with several hundred half-slips of paper scattered across her desk like oversized confetti. The survey had sounded good in her head. She'd formulated the notion in the shower on a Monday morning, perfected it on her drive to work, and by the time Gordon had called their staff meeting to order, Sheila was ready to spew her idea like a misdirected sneeze in the general direction of her co-workers.

Letting the kids make decisions? This was going to go over big. Surveys were all the thing now. The fact was, Sheila didn't give a damn what the students might want to see in their school cafeteria. She didn't give a damn about much of anything. But the survey would provide a boast-worthy rationale for her menu choices, and perhaps a little recognition for the fact that her work was harder than anyone else's, and she worked harder to do it than the others ever did.

No one would argue with surveying high schoolers. Some of them were nearly old enough to vote. But the elementary kids? No reason to ask them. They'd want French fries. Cinnamon rolls. They'd want chocolate milk. Good God, they'd want candy. And Jell-O. No reason to ask them. Half of them couldn't read. And the other half couldn't write.

Gordon convened meetings every Monday morning at 9:15. But first he had to lug an arts-and-crafts table from under the windows and position it across the door of his office. Sheila, Crystal, and Coralene sat there, leaning over their respective stacks of papers, able to see down into their coffee cups. Gordon peered out from where he sat, pressed against the wall of his supply-closet office. They peered back, as if discovering a hidey-hole in the garden, which housed a gnome.

Sheila needn't have worried about the other women stealing her idea. Crystal had rolled her eyes. No way Crystal would have done the work to get the opinions of six-year-olds. Even if it did make sense, which it did not. As for Coralene, she'd stated immediately what Sheila knew to be true.

"One thing I learned early," Coralene had said. "Don't ask questions you don't want answers to. That's what I always told my daughter when she was growing up. My nephew too. No survey for the junior high kids. Not on my watch. That one's all yours, Sheila. God bless you."

Sheila had been pleased with Coralene's attitude if not with her incessant need to make it personal. Who cared what she'd told her daughter? As for her nephew? Sheila had heard that kid was a nogoodnik. And let's leave God out of it entirely.

Now, at the end of another long day that had included tracking down a new supplier for powdered eggs, Sheila gathered the survey slips and separated them into two piles, one for each high school: Norlin Hanley and Lake Sylvester. She left Gordon's Friday memo on her desk. She'd read it on Monday, when she knew there would be another one. The man loved a memo.

It was 6:15. She'd pay the price for having taken off her shoes the minute the others had left the office. Standing to her full five feet, nine inches, Sheila winced as she crammed her feet back into low-heeled pumps. She could barely discern where her ankles should be. Swollen flesh along the top of both feet seemed to meld, without the distinction of an appendage, into her lower legs.

Desk light turned off and coat retrieved from her coat stand, Sheila hobbled down the hall past the janitor's office and out the service door. Her car was the only one left in the lot. Of course it was.

Sheila pulled into the parking lot at the Denny's on Bullman Avenue and Northeast 51st Street. On Friday nights, she ate at Denny's. Denny's offered the Main Street equivalent of a school lunch, a compliment to Sheila's way of thinking. Balanced meals, but with an emphasis on the popular items. One rarely saw peas nudge French fries off a Denny's plate. But peas were available, or if not peas, then a nice side salad, with grated carrots, iceberg lettuce, and a dollop of French dressing. Check, check. Vegetables were covered.

As usual, the Friday hostess was leaning on her lectern, looking unprofessional. The girl's elbow was on the pile of oversized menus. Her chin was in her hand, which only made it more obvious that she was chewing the life out of an enormous wad of gum.

Sheila went directly to the farthest booth, along the window. This was where she sat on Friday nights. Here, and only here. She could look out the window and keep an eye on her Chrysler, nothing wrong there. More importantly, this was Lexie's section. Lexie's section was where Sheila belonged.

"There's my favorite Friday friend," Lexie said, approaching the table as Sheila settled onto the bench and once again removed her shoes. "How are you? Been looking forward to seeing you. It isn't a Friday without you. We're still on the Hamburger Hall of Fame, aren't we? You don't have many untried options, as I remember. What's it going to be? Patty melt? Brit Burger?"

~ ~ ~

Lexie had just graduated from high school when Sheila met her, years ago now.

"Aren't you our lunch lady?" Lexie had asked, the first time she saw Sheila at the restaurant. Lexie had been the new Friday hostess, waiting at the lectern with the menus. Lexie's hair was the color of beauty bark; she wore little combs above each ear which kept it pulled back. From her pretty face, Lexie offered a stunner of a smile to every customer, even grimy little kids.

"Well, I could be," Sheila had said, surprised to find that she was not at all peeved by Lexie's characterization or her casual way of engaging with an elder. "Norlin Hanley High School?"

"Yes!" Lexie had said. "I knew it was you. Just wait until I tell my friend Grace. We get hot lunch almost every day. I love hot lunch!"

Sheila had smiled at Lexie, another response that surprised her, and waited, knowing Lexie had more to say.

"Well, I guess I should say me and Grace *used* to get hot lunch. We just graduated."

"Just graduated high school?" Sheila had asked sharply. "Hanley High?

"Well, yes," Lexie had said, flustered by Sheila's tone.

"Then repeat after me, Miss Lexie who just graduated from high school: 'Grace and I.'"

"Pardon?" Lexie had paused, but only for a moment. "Oh man!" she'd said, "And I'm good in English. I took AP. So sorry. Grace and *I*." Lexie had stretched the word for emphasis. "Grace and *I* used to love hot lunch."

"There you go."

"And I know the trick," Lexie had continued. "If you can take one of the subjects away, the other one has to still make sense. So if I took away 'Grace' from what I said to you, you know, it wouldn't have made sense. It would've been me saying that 'Me loved hot lunch.' I love those tricks that help you remember things. Don't you?"

"I do. I used to teach high school English, many moons ago." Sheila had smiled. Again. Who was this girl?

"And then you became a lunch lady? Oh," Lexie'd said, stopping herself from saying more.

"Why?" Sheila had asked. "Is that what you're wondering?

Why would I switch from being an English teacher to being a lunch lady?"

"Well, yes. I don't mean to be rude, but that just seems a little weird."

"You're not wrong. But it was a good idea at the time. Now I'm not sure. But doubts about something I did years ago are neither welcome nor useful at my stage of life." Sheila had been startled to hear herself talking so openly with this teenage girl at Denny's. What the hell? She'd shrugged off her coat and draped it over one arm, letting Lexie lead her toward the booth by the window where Sheila sat every Friday night.

"I can hang that up for you," Lexie had offered. "We're always supposed to offer that to customers when they come in."

"No, thank you. I'll keep it with me." Sheila tried to shield her coat from the Denny's smell that permeated whatever she wore on Fridays. Knowing it was useless, she'd nonetheless roll it into a lumpy bundle, cover it with her napkin, and hold it on her lap as she ate.

"Well Ms. English-teacher-turned-lunch-lady, it's nice to meet you," Lexie had said warmly.

Sheila had grimaced at Lexie's use of "Ms." Some of the women's liberation business was over the top.

"I'm sorry," Lexie'd gone on, "even though I knew your face, I don't remember your name. Do you wear a name badge in the lunchroom?"

"I do. Miss Raymond. That's what my name badge says. My name is Sheila Raymond."

"I'm Lexie. Lexie Clark. Class of 1970."

"It's nice to meet you, Lexie," Sheila had said.

"It's nice to meet you too, Ms. Raymond."

"You may call me Sheila," Sheila had told her. "You're a high school graduate. You're a young woman with a job. I'm an old woman with a job. Two women with jobs can call each other by their first names."

"Thank you. Sheila." Lexie's reply had been stiff, but she was visibly pleased. "Your waitress will be right over. Shall I tell her you're ready to order?"

"I need another minute or two."

"Alrighty then, I'll bring you some water."

Once Lexie was promoted to waitress, she'd claimed Sheila as a Friday night customer; Sheila had claimed Lexie right back. No one could have been more surprised than Sheila to see how Lexie Clark – waitress, chatterbox, and seemingly friend to all – had wheedled into her affections and remained there, on firm footing. Lexie was an anomaly. A young woman content with her lot. No griping. No bitching. Gentle, without being sappy. Intelligent, without being a pain in the ass. So what the hell was she doing at Denny's all these years? This was one of two questions Sheila would never ask.

~ ~ ~

Sheila dipped her two remaining French fries into the ketchup puddle on the edge of her plate. The British Burger had been the right choice. Couldn't go wrong with bacon. She would never have thought to put it on a burger but saw the wisdom of the choice. Count on Denny's to get creative with a hamburger, something that was rarely pulled off in a school cafeteria. In schools, hamburgers were fine. Bacon could even be fine, accompanying a dollop of scrambled egg. But two meat proteins? Not on her watch. Too expensive. Besides, half the students would peek under the top of the bun, take that bacon off, and leave it on their trays. Or on the floor.

Sheila reached for her coffee cup as Lexie appeared. "Your timing is splendid," Sheila said. "As usual."

"Anything else? Pie? A scoop of ice cream?"

"Do you have apple? I lean toward apple. But you know that."

"Indeed, I do. Apple is your first choice. Cherry is a distant second. And you'll give a non-negotiable 'no' to a cream pie of any sort. I remember these things. You know I do."

"Yes. I do know that you do."

"There was only one piece of apple left when I checked a few minutes ago. Apple pie is selling like hotcakes tonight." Lexie giggled.

"Only one piece?"

"Yes, ma'am."

"And you put it aside for me, didn't you?"

"Of course I did. You taking that à la mode tonight?"

"Of course I am."

Sheila relaxed her body into the booth; it was a relief after sitting stiffly while she ate. Lexie had taken the empty pie plate and refilled Sheila's coffee cup; she wouldn't return until Sheila gathered her things to leave.

Sitting at Denny's on a Friday night, Sheila resigned herself to familiar thoughts. She propped a fist under her chin, tapping at the fleshy pouch that hung below her jaw. *Get on with feeling bad*, she told herself. *Just get on with it.*

She filled her lungs with the stale Denny's air – all the

breakfast-y grease of it – and let the place buzz in her ears, like an airplane in the distance. The bubble-shaped chandeliers warmed the space behind her eyes as she closed them.

The weight in Sheila's chest pushed against her lungs and down on her stomach. She'd named this weight. It was the loneliness one, made heavier by layers of regret. It showed up on Friday nights. She didn't think about it while she was eating; she had Lexie. But after dinner, Sheila was trapped. Heading out to her car and driving home would only make it worse. The cold, dark car. The enveloping solitude. No, she rode it out here. Tears made their way slowly down Sheila's cheeks. She let them be. They didn't mean any harm. Just doing their job.

How did other people manage their heavy stomachs of loneliness? Did everyone carry these around? Only a few? All that Sheila knew to do was to look to the past, or to not look at all. The past was the perennial victor in any emotional tug of war. Had she been asked, Sheila couldn't have said when she'd quit looking forward. But who would ask?

Pulled into the space behind her closed eyes, Sheila's mind wandered back, decade after decade after decade. Back to another life: high school and college. College was pretty much where Sheila's good memories left off.

She'd been in love once. In high school, Sheila had fallen for a likeable, intelligent boy. By college, that boy was an enchanting, clever young man.

He'd come at life with contagious eagerness. His mind delved into every textbook; his athletic body braved every race. Walking together along the river or exploring the vast abundance of the fields outside of Hanley, the two of them had shared a quiet contentment. In his arms, Sheila was safe and cherished. In his eyes, she could see their future. They'd been two sides of the same coin. Their path forward as smooth as a sandy beach.

Then he was gone. Just like that. As sudden as a door slammed shut by a gust of wind. Sheila hadn't watched the train pull away, but she'd heard its whistle all the same. She heard it still. All these decades later, Sheila no longer knew what else might've been true. For solitary women, the only truth that matters is the one that finds them when they're alone.

He'd moved to Minneapolis, then Chicago, then New York, as if it mattered. What mattered was that she still missed him. Every day. An absurdity she tried to keep from herself, and from the rest of the world. As if the rest of the world gave a damn that a sixty-something woman took her decades-old heartbreak out for dinner every Friday night.

All these years later, he still frequented a spare room in Sheila's mind. He'd arrive unexpectedly, overstay his welcome, and leave a mess. In his wake, Sheila would tiptoe her emotions about, setting aright the detritus of her life that only he could disrupt, and she'd brace her heart for the next time he appeared. She would never be free of him.

Sheila gripped her coffee cup like the handrail on a steep set of stairs. The weight in her chest was so heavy now that she doubted she'd be able to stand. *I could've had a real life,* she thought. *If things had gone differently, I would never have ended up in a booth at Denny's.*

Once, when Sheila was still an English teacher, she'd met the math teacher across the hall. They'd talked awkwardly, between classes. *That's how blind I was then*, she'd chided herself a thousand times. What had she been? Thirty-two? Thirty-four? The school hallways had been awash in seventeen-year-olds. How could she have imagined that they wouldn't get caught in that undertow?

Sure enough, the principal had pulled them aside. "The students are talking," he'd said. "Propriety is at stake. It's a high school. The two of you must be above reproach."

After that, the door across the hall rarely opened and Sheila had retreated deeper into the cloistered space within her own mind. She'd avoided interactions with others that she no longer understood how to navigate. What should she say? Who should she be?

She'd arrived at school early. She'd left late. She'd eaten lunch at her desk. The classes she'd loved to teach lost their spark: the Comedies of Shakespeare; Advanced Composition; the 19th Century through Dickens, Twain, and Alcott; American Poetry. Increasingly, as she'd looked in the mirror in the morning, Sheila hadn't known who she was seeing. Perhaps because she no longer had any idea who she was looking for.

The moments Sheila knew others took for granted were out of her reach. She'd had no reason to pack a picnic, or to buy a new sweater. Her life had backfilled with the futility of hope: that someone else would clean up the kitchen, take out the garbage, or bring her a second cup of coffee. That just once she could frame in her mind, and speak to the world, a sentence that began with "We."

When Sheila saw the announcement about Hildy Sherman's retirement as lunch lady, she'd taken the job and moved out of the classroom for good. Soon it was flour under her nails instead of chalk dust. She got lost in being a lunch lady, layering anonymity and necessity atop the person she'd once believed she'd be, until that person was gone for good. Until the old Sheila quit showing up to pester the new one about all she didn't have. All she was not. When the promotion to Nutrition Services had come along, she'd taken it, giving it absolutely no thought. What possible difference did it make one way or the other?

Sheila looked out the window toward the parking lot, watching as an old man left the restaurant and walked in the rain toward his car. He had a cane in one hand and moved as slowly as a dripping faucet. She wondered how many days he'd used that cane. Had he needed it for years, or had he just started with it the other day? And the day before that, did he know that he would never again walk without it? Probably not, poor bugger. But there's no going back.

Removing her coat from her lap, she prepared to leave. Any second now, Lexie would swing by to tell her to "have a good weekend." To "have a good week." To "take care." Sheila looked across the restaurant toward the counter where a few men always sat on Friday nights. Some alone. Some in pairs. Predictable as the cheeseburgers most seemed to order, or the last cup of coffee they likely didn't finish. Sheila saw the same ones every week. Butts on swivel stools.

Tonight there was a new butt in the lineup. It looked the slightest bit familiar.

MEMO

TO: Nutrition Services Employees
FROM: Gordon Hund, Nutrition Services Manager
DATE: Friday, February 27, 1976
RE: Bicentennial Celebration and other topics
           of interest

Ladies: It is time to start the planning for Hanley School District's participation in the bicentennial parade that will grace downtown Hanley, Minnesota on Sunday, July 4, 1976. How fortunate we are that this important day in the history of our city, county, state, and nation falls on a Sunday, facilitating full participation and enjoyment of the festivities for all who choose to attend.

The commencement of the parade will be at a time intended to accommodate local residents' Sunday morning worship schedules. The final decision will be announced by the mayor in a press conference next week. My presumption is that start time will be at noon.

I have determined that food will be produced by school kitchens across the district for consumption by parade participants and citizens in attendance. I intend that Miss Carmichael, Miss Raymond, and Mrs. Johnson will be responsible for coordinating the output of the school kitchens for which they are responsible, and for ensuring the timely and exemplary preparation and distribution of appropriate food items.

All Nutrition Services employees are required to participate in parade planning, which will begin in earnest next Monday, March 1, 1976, when we convene for our weekly meeting. The meeting will begin, as usual, promptly at 9:15. Please be on time.

Tomorrow, Saturday, February 28, 1976, Napoleon will be participating for the first time in the Wescott County Dogstravaganza at the Wescott County Community Center on the corner of Northeast Seventh Street and Palisades Avenue at 10:00. Tickets are still available.

CHAPTER FOUR

DARCY

SATURDAY, FEBRUARY 28, 1976

THE HOUSE ON Vermilion Avenue was painted a mossy green, with a shiny black door and white gutters. A white picket fence encircled it in a way that made Darcy smile, when it didn't make her cringe. It was all a tad too-too, made worse by her grandmother saying that because she had a green house on a red street, she was always ready for Christmas. Darcy wondered what stupid things she'd say when she herself got old.

The gravel ground noisily under her tires. Well-kept postwar boxes lined both sides of the paved street, but parking areas in front of the homes were graveled. Darcy liked to kick up a little dust in front of the Andersens' house and the Kahns' before coming to a stop in front of the prim green house where she had grown up, and where her grandmother still lived.

First thing out of her grandmother's mouth would be,

"Must you do that? Really, Darcy? It's annoying as all hell and some people are still in bed."

The scolding could wait. Darcy turned off the car and looked down at her new corduroy pants. They were a delightful shade of orange. Maybe more of a coral. Pockets, and pleats down the front. Currently they were covered in crumbs, which she brushed onto the black carpet of her still kinda new Pinto hatchback.

The crumbs were from the toast she'd declined to eat at breakfast. Once she was out of the Pancake House parking lot, she'd unwrapped what she'd saved in a paper napkin and finished it. Eating in front of her cousin was a fraught proposition. Darcy tried to make accommodations where she could, which included eating her toast in the car.

Looking up the front walk to the house, Darcy could picture her grandmother in it. She loved her grandmother. A lot. But there were so, so, so many things Darcy would rather be doing on a Saturday than helping Grandma and Grandma's old-lady friends plan for the float they'd ride in the Hanley Bicentennial Parade.

"It's a bit nuts, don't you think?" Darcy's cousin had asked over breakfast, two hours earlier. Saturday mornings often found Darcy and Crystal at the Pancake House. It wasn't an every week thing. It wasn't a "don't move or you're dead" thing as Crystal liked to say, but unless Darcy had an exceptionally late night on Friday — and she wished she had more — chances were the two of them would meet up at the Pancake House on Palisades and Northeast 7th Street at 8:45.

The 8:45 time had been Crystal's idea. Not 8:30. Not 9:00. 8:45. Fine. Who cares?

An event at the community center next door had brought new faces into the Pancake House to join the regulars for breakfast, which meant they'd had to wait. Darcy had amused herself watching the bustle of activity in the community center parking lot. At least a dozen station wagons had their back gates open as dogs of every shape and size leaped, or were lifted, onto the pavement. A seemingly endless procession of cars continued to pull in.

"Look at this," Darcy had said, elbowing Crystal. "Must be a dog show, don't you think?"

Crystal looked away, as if determined to ignore the dogs and dog people assembling outside.

"Is Grandma going to want you to ride on the float too?" Crystal asked, once they were seated. "That's taking it a bit far. I know you want to help and all, but if she wants you to ride on it, I'd say no. Swat that fly dead."

"No, she doesn't want me to ride on it, thank God. She and her friends will do that. I'm worried though. Grandma's shaky these days. I got called in because they don't have any idea how to pull this off. They don't have a theme or anything. Grandma just said the guild thought it would be fun; frankly, I think Grandma couldn't care less. But here we are, a float of old ladies from the hospital guild, what could go wrong?" Darcy had let loose a chuckle she didn't feel. "We'll figure it out."

"If anyone can, it's you. Rather hilarious that Grandma considers your job in Community Relations at Hanley Electric as evidence of your float management expertise. Glad it's not me."

"Why don't you come along? It's a couple hours. I know she'd love to see you. How long since you've visited?"

"Love to see me? Who are we kidding here? If I walked in with you this morning, she'd pretend I wasn't even there. She doesn't know quite what to do with me; you know that. Besides, I can't." Crystal was talking around the forkful of pancake she'd just put in her mouth. It wasn't pretty.

"Can't why? What's on your schedule today?" Darcy didn't usually press, but this morning she couldn't resist. Particularly since she was fairly sure she knew the answer.

"I have to go to a memorial." The pancake bite had been chewed and swallowed, but another full fork was poised, with huge drops of syrup dripping onto the plate below, where a triple stack was swiftly disappearing.

"Oh geez, Crystal. Really? I know you didn't ask, but this whole funeral thing of yours is a bit creepy. What's this one's name?"

"Roger Squirrel." Crystal opened her mouth wide enough to capture the forkful of pancake, pausing long enough to chew and swallow. "I haven't found a match for him yet, and it's already Saturday." Crystal wiped the syrup off her chin with the paper napkin. "And it's not a funeral. It's a memorial."

"For your purposes, is there a difference? No, forget I asked. I don't think I want to know."

"I need to go," Crystal said. "See what I can find out. I make a commitment to these people."

"I know Grandma will ask if we had breakfast today," Darcy said. "And when I talked to her the other night, she kind of hinted that she wanted you to come help too."

"Grandma doesn't 'kind of hint'," Crystal said. "You're making that up. You can tell her whatever you like. If it comes up, tell her I was busy. But it won't. Come up, I mean. Anyway," she said firmly, "I am busy. The memorial and all. Besides, I think we're going to have to pull off some big whoop-ta-do for the bicentennial parade at work. That's enough for me. I'll steer clear of Grandma's float." Crystal grimaced, revealing a small piece of pancake adhered to her lower teeth.

"But you'll go by soon?" Darcy was whining now. Not something she wanted to do. Crystal was eleven years older. Still, they were both grown women. The whine that might've worked on Crystal years ago was unlikely to do anything now but piss her off. And make Darcy look like what, exactly? A grandma's girl? Well, she was. At least a little.

"It's okay, spoonbread," Crystal said. "I'll go see her after work next week, if you'll come too. We can bring burgers and fries. Then you can drop me at home afterwards." Crystal put an elbow on the table and turned a forkful of pancakes in Darcy's direction. She bobbed the fork in front of Darcy, using it to make her point. "Dinner? Next week? Burgers? Will that do it for you?"

"Yes, that'll do it. Tuesday? And any time you'd like to come up with a new nickname for me, I'll be happy to hear it."

"Nah." Crystal's mouth was full again. "Spoonbread is a great nickname for a soft-on-the-inside girl like you."

Pulling herself out of the bucket seat took effort, but soon Darcy was standing on the gravel, flicking the remaining crumbs off her pants. She wriggled one arm and then the other into her corduroy jacket. This was one cute jacket. It hit right at the waist. Zipper up the front. Darcy pulled her blouse collar out to lay it flat over the jacket's fur-lined collar.

"Yep, that jacket's cute," Crystal had said at breakfast, rubbing the collar between her thumb and forefinger. "Just wanted to be sure that's not real fur. But I don't think the blouse works. It looks like you took it out of the charity bin at the old folks' home. Too flowery for someone your age."

"What? I'm thirty-one years old."

"So? Call in the cavalry. I'm forty-two. Still looks like something you swiped out of Grandma's closet."

Darcy had kept mum on the source of the blouse. Who cares? Thing was, Crystal's clothing critiques usually hit the mark.

"Grandma?" Darcy let herself in her grandmother's front door. She could hear voices in the kitchen. Increasingly, each time she walked in the house, Darcy found herself looking for signs: of what, she wasn't sure. Darcy suspected an illness of some kind. All was not well; she knew it in her bones. Now who was sounding like an old lady?

Grandma's pace had slowed, as had her appetite. Murky expressions of pain or fatigue appeared on her face with increasing frequency. Darcy had wanted to talk to Crystal about this over pancakes, but Crystal had dismissed her with a wave of her hand that was freakishly similar to their grandmother's.

"Leonora?" Darcy heard an old voice asking, "Should I put these cookies on a tray?"

No response on the cookies. Instead she heard her grandmother call out, "We're in here, Darcy. Loading up on snacks and waiting for you before we tackle our big project."

The front room flowed into a small dining room and on into an even smaller kitchen where five stooped ladies, and her own stooped grandmother, were watching the coffee pot as if it was the source of the second coming. Darcy saw the last surge of coffee bubble into the glass knob at the top of the percolator. Several of the women emitted happy chirps.

"Ahh, there we go," one of them said. She was short. They were all short. And old. Short and old. This particular short old woman had tight curls covering her head like a shower cap. They were dyed a peculiar shade of orange, similar to Darcy's pants.

Leonora held out an arm and Darcy wriggled past the gathered women to sidle up to her grandmother.

"Stop doing that with the car," Leonora growled under her breath, as she wrapped an arm around Darcy's middle.

Darcy leaned against Leonora and rested her chin on her grandmother's head. "No," she whispered. Stepping away, Darcy addressed the women queued for coffee. "So, do any of you have ideas on how you'd like to tackle this float project? Themes of any sort? Or are we starting from scratch?"

"Oh, we're starting from scratch, love." This from Cora, Grandma's best friend, whose daughter, Coralene, worked with Crystal. Cora frowned as if Darcy had asked a spectacularly stupid question. "Your grandmother says you're the expert on such things," Cora said.

Leonora was directing the women toward the front room, shooing them ahead as if they were small children, or perhaps a flock of geese. "Off we go. Into the front room. Scoot, scoot." Leonora looked straight ahead as she brought up the rear, avoiding Darcy's glare.

The women took their seats in the living room. Olive was the new one, a recent recruit who, Darcy learned, attended Cora's church. Olive landed with a thump into the rocking chair Darcy's grandfather had made. Darcy suspected Olive had chosen that spot so she could put down her coffee cup on the nearby hearth. Darcy slid in a coaster before Olive's cup could leave a ring on the brick. *Oh, Olive. Are you sure you want to be here? There are rules.* But Olive seemed content, enjoying the creaking she could muster as she rocked the chair on Leonora's brown shag carpet.

On the other side of the room, Cora sat in one of the two wingback chairs, facing the fireplace. The wingbacks were upholstered in a burgundy and brown vertical stripe, which Darcy loathed. No stains were visible on the dark fabric. Didn't mean they weren't there. There was ketchup on that chair, and grease, from the day Crystal had consumed a jumbo-sized bag of French fries while reading *A Tree Grows in Brooklyn*, and wiped her fingers on the seat cushion. There was also a tiny smear of cat poop that a young Darcy had once discovered clinging to her fingertip after she'd carried Crystal's cat to the back porch. Sitting back down, cat-free, Darcy had wiped her dirty finger on the chair's underside.

Cora shared an already be-coastered side table with Leonora, who sat in the matching chair, facing the fireplace and closer to the window. None of the old ladies would've been reckless enough to choose Leonora's chair. Darcy took comfort knowing that the cat poop was on the other chair, not the one where her grandmother perched several times a day.

The sisters – Hyacinth, Lobelia, and Gladiola – sat on the sofa. Even in their advanced years, they bore an amazing resemblance to each other. Their facial features seemed to run together like dripping paint on the side of a house. They rarely used their full names, preferring instead the nicknames they'd been given as girls.

Of the sisters, only Hyacinth had married. She'd fallen in love with a young soldier and married him when she was nineteen. A year later, her husband was just one more casualty of the Great War. Lobelia and Gladiola, only eighteen and seventeen, had moved in with their widowed sister and set up a home that had likely changed little since 1918.

Hy, Lo, and Glad had lived lives as intertwined as a tangled ball of string, from which no one could extract a beginning or an end. When her husband didn't return from the war, Hy had stepped into the shoes everyone had expected that her handsome young private would eventually fill. Instead of minding the stove in the family bungalow and tending to the flock of children she'd longed to have, Hy had taken over Larsen's Corner Grocery in downtown Hanley, which had been in her husband's family for two generations. With the help of her shattered mother-in-law, Hy installed Lo at the till. Lo, who was a whiz at numbers, meted out credit as frequently as she denied it. Glad, the biggest eater in the family, was put in charge of adding a delicatessen to the store's offerings, bargaining for the sausages and cheese that were the pride of local farmers. As for Hy, she had expanded the store's inventory beyond foodstuffs, to encourage the wives of Hanley to spend more of their money in one place by adding sundries, notions, and craft supplies. Following the sisters' retirement, younger generations had taken over

Larsen's, but even so, none of the guild members would've dreamed of buying their essentials anywhere else.

Gazing around the living room at the gray-haired guild members, Darcy struggled to picture them when they were young. Was girlhood even invented back then, or had all these little old ladies been spawned as middle-aged women? She decided against calculating the gathering's cumulative age. Math was not her forte. Besides, regardless of how daunting the number, her task was to keep the guild's attention on the float, rather than letting conversation wander in the direction it often did among Grandma and her friends: to the timing and method of their own deaths.

CHAPTER FIVE

CRYSTAL

SATURDAY, FEBRUARY 28, 1976

CRYSTAL SAT ON the aisle in the back row. The chairs were the type that hooked together, with the padded black vinyl seats. They wouldn't slide apart and were adequate for guests of all sizes. Good thing. There must be ten rows, split by a middle aisle, with maybe twelve chairs in each. Most were filled. Not a bad showing of mourners for Roger Squirrel.

Going to memorials was not something Crystal liked to do. Fortunately Roger's final roundup was at Woodlawn Cemetery, in their lovely Blessed Rest Chapel. Crystal preferred mortuary gatherings to formal services in a church. Easier to slip in and out. She needed information; as soon as she got it, she was out the door. Job done.

Only rarely did Crystal's matches require in-person attention at a memorial. It hadn't been necessary for Virginia Karsten

Knudsen or for Anton Becker. Hadn't been necessary for Declan Sean O'Grady either, whom Crystal had taken care of a couple months back.

Mr. O'Grady had been honored on the obituary page of the *Hanley Herald* on December 21st . Sad. So close to Christmas. His obituary had been brief:

Declan Sean O'Grady. Born March 7, 1902, died December 18, 1975. Da to Joseph, Sean, Maeve, and Gerald. Granda to Rory, Brendan, Joseph, Quinn, Mary, Patrick, Conor, Siohban, and Niamh. Retired from Milwaukee Road in 1971. Never to retire from our hearts. Until we meet again, may God hold you in the palm of his hand. Service on Tuesday, December 23, at St. Brigid's Catholic Church. 3:00 PM.

Declan O'Grady's match had been folding clothes at the laundromat.

The washers and dryers in the basement of The Dexter were slow and unreliable. And it smelled bad down there. So on Wednesdays after dinner, Crystal walked around the corner to Dunlap's Wash and Dry Depot. Stupid name. Good laundromat.

There'd been someone new at Dunlap's the Wednesday following Mr. O'Grady's obituary. Nice old gal, named Ada. Crystal would've known Ada was a widow, even without her announcing the fact within minutes of Crystal walking in the door.

Ada had been pulling a load out of a dryer, but abandoned

her task as Crystal shuffled in. "Let me get the door there, dear," Ada'd said, patting Crystal's arm as if this was merely an unremarkable reunion. "You'll freeze to the bone."

Crystal, steadying her laundry basket on one capable hip, had followed as Ada shuffled back toward the row of washers and dryers. "My name's Ada," Ada had said, as she dived back into clean laundry piled on the massive Formica-topped table. "Lost my husband a few months ago. Good man, my Joey. Miss him every day. I moved here a couple weeks back. Used to live in Fergus Falls. Me and Joey did. But all our kids are around here and now I live with my daughter, right down the street. But can't have her doing my laundry. Can you imagine? Your daughter washing your underthings? Absolutely not. I told my daughter, I said, Maura, I'll go to the laundromat. It's good exercise and it gets me out of the house. So Maura got me this little wheeled gizmo." Ada had pointed toward a contraption that looked to Crystal like a grocery cart for munchkins. "Clever, huh?" Ada said. "And here I am. What's your name, dear?"

By the time Ada stopped talking, Crystal had sorted her clothes and started a load of darks. "Crystal," she'd said. Her responses could be brusque, but this Ada woman seemed salt of the earth. Worthy of a friendly greeting. She was a chubby little gal, shaped like a cupcake. "Nice to meet you, and thanks for getting the door there. Sorry about your husband. Tell me about him."

Easy as that, Crystal had found a match for Declan Sean O'Grady, before her clothes hit the rinse cycle. Only time would tell if she'd also found a friend.

Waiting for Roger's memorial to start, Crystal surveyed the crowd. Two women, arm in arm, made their way up the middle and took seats in the front row. Must be Roger's mother and one of his sisters. But which one? Yvette or Annabelle? Surely both sisters would attend their brother's memorial. But no one joined the women who sat silent and motionless, like two leafless trees in winter.

Across from Roger's mother, a short, dignified-looking man sat solemnly, wearing a dark suit. He had a crisp white shirt and a dark tie, the pattern of which Crystal couldn't quite discern. Short-dignified man sat sideways in his chair. Even ten rows back, Crystal could nearly see her reflection in the shine of his shoes.

Short-dignified man wore misery like an overcoat. Crystal watched as he leaned into the aisle to speak to Roger's mother. But wait. What was that? Roger's mother seemed to rebuff short-dignified man. She remained as stiff as a fire poker, ignoring his gesture. Quickly, the sister – whichever of the two she was, Crystal decided it was Annabelle – stretched in front of the mother. Crystal watched as Annabelle reached for short-dignified man's hand, tenderly rubbing it with her thumb.

As the pianist began playing "Amazing Grace," stragglers filled the few remaining chairs and short-dignified man shifted back into his seat. There was another man – men being well-represented here – sitting beside short-dignified man. Sitting-beside man put his arm around short-dignified man's shoulders and pulled him into an embrace.

Crystal watched as short-dignified man put his elbows on his knees and held his face in his hands. His shoulders lurched, as if he was bobbing in a lifeboat in choppy water. He sobbed. Not noisily though. Not in a way that engendered anything but sympathy.

This man wasn't mourning a friend. He wasn't even mourning a brother, and besides, Roger hadn't had a brother. He'd had two sisters though, and Crystal was annoyed that Yvette wasn't here. Short-dignified man wept without ceasing as the service began. Sitting-beside man kept his arm tight around short-dignified man's shoulders.

Crystal had not removed her coat, so it took no time to exit through the same door she'd entered only minutes before. She wasn't needed here. Roger didn't need Crystal to find a match for him. He had one, who was grieving so deeply in the front row that his loss hovered like mist, over every person in the room.

Crystal decided to name short-dignified man Norman. Norman and Roger. Roger and Norman. She was glad there were so many men here; they would be ready to hold Norman's hand. And Norman, in his way, would accompany Roger, as Roger moved on.

CHAPTER SIX

CRYSTAL

SATURDAY, AUGUST 17, 1948

THE FOUR OF them must look like paper dolls, Crystal thought. The paper-chain kind her grandmother cut for Darcy. Running a perfectly manicured fingernail down each crease, Grandma would snip little triangles and trim around what became pairs of tiny feet. Then she'd pass the creation to Darcy to unfold, exposing two, then three, then four perfect little people holding hands, as if they'd been hiding in that paper for an eternity, waiting for Darcy to set them free.

Now, Grandma held Darcy's hand, and Darcy held Crystal's. Crystal had held Alfie's hand while the minister had been talking, but now Alfie had untwined his sweaty fingers and moved to stand above the two coffins lying side by side in the open grave, as if the two women inside them were stretched out beside each other in the sun, on an enormous brown beach towel.

Crystal scratched at the neck of the starched black dress

her grandmother had insisted she wear. The tag should have been cut off. Crystal hated this dress. She was too hot. On her feet, she wore a new pair of black patent-leather Mary Janes. She would not be caught dead in these shoes at school.

At the sound of the first thud of dirt, a jolt of pain shot through Crystal's body from her feet to her face. Without meaning to, she squeezed Darcy's hand; the little girl flinched. Another thud followed, as pronounced as the first. Crystal watched as Alfie took a step back from where he stood at the edge of the grass to look down at the shovelfuls of dirt on the coffins, as if he was an artist admiring his masterpiece.

Crystal looked away and tried to shake the image from her mind. Beside her, Darcy didn't say a word. Didn't move. Didn't cry. Crystal wanted to swoop the little girl into her arms, but that might cause a scene, which would earn Crystal a frown from her grandmother. Crystal ached to hold Darcy, to breathe in the smell of soap encasing Darcy's neck and hair. Perhaps that would ease the weight in her own chest. Instead, she stared into the big brown hole, which held her mother and her aunt.

There was still a gleam on the surface of the coffins, as if Alfie's attempt to sully them was insufficient, as if the two women were determined to go into the ground with as much glimmer and shine as their live bodies had held.

~ ~ ~

Crystal held her spoon above her cereal bowl. She ignored the dribble of milk making its way down her chin. Her father sat across from her at the small kitchen table. Its Formica top was cluttered with the cereal box, the bottles of milk and orange juice, the sugar bowl, and the blue plastic napkin holder with the white plastic flowers, where Crystal's mother had arranged paper napkins in a precise, perky stack.

"What do you mean, you're 'Going to head off for a while'?" Crystal knew her voice was harsh, but her father's words had stunned her, and tossing them back at him seemed the only way to eradicate them from the room.

"It won't be forever, Crissy," Alfie said. "It won't even be for that long. You'll be fine. You can help your grandmother take care of Darcy. In the meantime, I can find a new gig somewhere. Minneapolis maybe. Or even Chicago. Then, you know, start bringing in some real cash." He rubbed his fingers together to indicate his intent. "I'll be back."

Crystal watched her father casually rest his cigarette in the lumpy clay ashtray she had made for him the Christmas she was five. It was Pepto-Bismol pink, with two small humps between which Alfie could rest a lit cigarette. It appeared that Crystal had begun her creation hoping to craft a camel. Surrounding the burning cigarette were six or eight butts, gazing up like supplicants.

"I can't stay here, Crissy. What am I going to do here without your mom? She was the one who held us together. I can't do it without her. I just can't."

It seemed to Crystal that her father's words should be accompanied by some show of emotion. A tear. A crack in his voice. A sniffle. But they weren't. He stated his thoughts as if he were listing off items for Crystal to include on a grocery list: "Can't stay. *Buy eggs.* Can't do it without her. *Get some milk.* I just can't. *Don't forget my cigarettes.*"

Alfie kept talking. "Leonora's happy to have you. You like

it there; you know you do. You won't even need to ride the bus to school anymore. You'll be starting junior high. You'll be close enough to walk from your grandmother's house. It makes sense, Crissy. It just makes the most sense."

If she knew nothing else, Crystal knew that none of this made sense. She knew that from this day forward her life would never make sense again. Her mother had been everything Crystal needed. She had been the source of all sense. Its resting place.

Crystal put her spoon back in her bowl. A dozen limp Cheerios floated in the remaining milk like little life rings. Who would they save? They weren't going to save her today, any more than they'd saved her mother and her aunt.

Crystal's eyes filled at the image of Aunt Ruby and Mom, swimming in the same lake where they'd swum since they were girls. Rolling backwards out of the rowboat to land in the lake, playfully pushing each other under the water, splashing to the point of exhaustion before stretching out their beautiful lean legs and kicking as they pushed the rowboat back to the dock.

No one seemed to know what had gone wrong. The water hadn't been rough. The women hadn't been tired. Or drunk. Or stupid. Which one had struggled? Which one had tried to save?

When she'd finally gone looking for her girls, Crystal's grandmother had driven down to the lake and parked beside Ruby's car. At the sight of the listless rowboat, Leonora had screamed. At the disappearance of her daughters, she'd screamed. At the cruelty of solitude – twenty years after losing Badger, and now losing both her children – Leonora had screamed. Crystal hadn't been there. She hadn't heard. Still, her grandmother's screams echoed in Crystal's head.

Before the day was over, the bodies of Pearl Carmichael and Ruby Daniels had been pulled from the lake and laid out on its sandy shore.

~ ~ ~

Crystal knew the stories of her mother and her aunt. They'd permeated the walls of her grandmother's house like amorphous family lore. Their telling and retelling had lit a fire in her grandmother's eyes. But now? Now, Crystal knew, the fire would be gone. The stories would linger only as dust.

Pearl and Ruby. Beautiful daughters of Leonora and Badger. Pearl was their first. Poised Pearl. Tenacious Pearl. Loyal, loving Pearl. The apple of her father's eye; the dearest joy of her mother's heart.

For a long time, there were three: Badger, Leonora, Pearl. And then came Ruby. Tender Ruby. Unwavering Ruby. Magnificent, magical Ruby. How wonderful that Ruby came along, people had said. A sister for Pearl, at long last.

For six years, Leonora had her perfect family of four: Pearl, Ruby, and Badger – the man whose breath and heartbeat might as well have been Leonora's own. Then without warning, her world was split into pieces, like an axe through firewood. The accident that took Badger left Leonora to wonder whether her breath alone, her solo heartbeat, could possibly sustain her family. And yet, her girls grew.

Years later, Pearl and Alfie had their baby: sweet baby Crystal. Crystal who was never the apple of her father's eye, but was every bit the dearest joy of her mother's heart. Alfie doesn't deserve Pearl, everyone said. Doesn't deserve Crystal either. He's not the man Badger was. Not even close. What that family needs is another girl. Pearl had her Crystal, the only child she intended to have. And years later, Ruby had her Darcy.

Darcy had been a bit of surprise. But Leonora, who grieved the loss of her beloved Badger every day, was not about to turn her back on her unwed pregnant daughter. So together, Leonora, Ruby, and Darcy had thrived in every unexpected way, joined as they were by the spirit of Badger. Although she hadn't, Crystal felt as if she'd known Grandpa Badger, so pervasive was his presence in her grandmother's house. Crystal knew she would've loved him, and he, her. She also knew Grandpa Badger would never have left her in the way her father obviously intended to do.

CHAPTER SEVEN

Sheila

Saturday, February 28, 1976

IN THE YEAR since her mother died, the void in Sheila's life had mended. Not so much similar to the gradual healing of a wound, more like the efficient closing of a zipper. By the end, Mother had been primarily a time commitment that had reaped few rewards for either of them. A year had been plenty of time to shape a new routine, unencumbered.

On Fridays Sheila ate dinner at Denny's. Nothing new there. As certain as sunset. On Saturday mornings, she went to the grocery store. Once home, she made a peanut butter sandwich and sat at the kitchen table to call her niece, precisely at noon.

For reasons unknown, Sheila's brother often answered. He'd speak of nothing remotely interesting before handing the phone to sixteen-year-old Connie. Her brother, and his toothache of a wife, had moved with Connie to California around the time Sheila's mother's health began to decline. No big surprise; they wouldn't have been any help. But Connie? Connie was a keeper.

Connie played the clarinet. She was a Job's Daughter. She was on the honor roll, the volleyball team, and the junior prom committee. Sheila didn't try to relive girlhood through Connie's retelling of her own; there were too many years between them. But listening to the hum of Connie's voice, Sheila found herself back in her girlhood bedroom. Connie helped Sheila remember that she'd been happy once.

Sheila had never shared a dime with her brother, but what else would she possibly do with her money but save it for Connie? Had he been paying attention, her brother would've come knocking years ago. Sheila was a single woman with no mortgage and a pension. For God's sake, she was rolling in dough. Connie's parents might have been morons. But Connie? Connie was nothing but promise.

On Sundays, Sheila cooked. On Monday through Thursday nights, she ate the lasagna, or pot roast, or vegetable soup she'd made, followed by a scoop of Rocky Road. In a house that sheltered but did not embrace her, Sheila would sit in her recliner and steer her mind away from her now-dead mother, her feckless younger brother, the friends who had disappeared, and the years she knew she'd wasted. And she'd turn on the television, home as it was, to men who didn't disappoint: Barnaby Jones. Steve Majors. Starsky and Hutch. Hawkeye Pierce. And, of course, Marcus Welby, M.D.

She turned the heat up in winter; she could afford it after all. She opened the kitchen windows in the spring, but didn't notice traces of lilac and mock orange sneaking in from the backyard.

Infrequently, she'd retreat from the men on TV and reach for her sparsely filled diary. She would try to put words to her life, before either well ran dry. Maybe words could still save her. When she was young, they'd been sources of delight, emerging as unexpectedly as a crocus in spring. She'd woven them in and among each other as beautiful as a tapestry, before sharing them with the man she'd loved. What had been deepest in Sheila's soul flowed back and forth between the two of them, boundaries unclear.

Now paucity of beauty was what she expected. The words that came to mind were like schoolchildren, dashing around playgrounds with their shoes untied. Reckless and feral. They'd screech, and punch, and cheat, and when the bell rang, they'd scurry inside, leaving Sheila to stare at the blank page, that was all she had left.

~ ~ ~

Sheila was relieved, plain and simple, that she no longer spent her Saturday mornings tending to her mother. She'd resented the other people who'd made obligatory visits to the nursing home. It had been in and out for most of them; those people just crossed visits off their weekend to-do lists: clean the gutters, change the oil, pop a tuna casserole in the freezer, visit Grandma at the Golden Manor Nursing and Care Home. Those people had not been like Sheila, who had visited her mother three times a week.

There were several choices of where to put Mother after the last stroke had made staying in her own home impossible.

None were as nice as Golden Manor. None as clean. None where Sheila had as much confidence that Mother would be well cared for. But that wasn't saying much. There were good places. There were slightly better places; Golden Manor was one of those. There were no places that Sheila would describe as *best*. Not even close. So she'd chosen Golden Manor, paid the deposit, and moved her mother into a small private room.

For two years, Sheila had walked past formerly vibrant people, who were now veterans of confusion and regret. They'd drooled and napped in wheelchairs that lined the halls, the torpid air embalming them in odors of urine and soup. Occasionally an ancient hand would reach out as Sheila passed: its skin hanging like cobwebs, its bones as brittle as teacups. She'd felt like a voyeur, seeing things she shouldn't, like the afternoon she'd sat on her back porch watching an insect tear off its own wings.

Every time she'd walked into Golden Manor's sprawling building, and every time she'd walked out, Sheila had vowed that she'd jump in front of a bus, stick her head in the oven, or step off a chair with a rope around her neck before she'd agree to spend her last days at one of the Golden Manors of the world.

On that final Saturday visit, Teresa was at the nurses' station. Teresa had been good people. She'd known how to say what was what without infantilizing descriptors, without telling Sheila how "sweet" Mother was, or how "dear," or good God the worst one: how "cute."

Teresa had a ubiquitous nurse look: tall, on a lean frame, with brown curls scattered across her head as if still deciding how best to arrange themselves. That Saturday, she'd been wearing an orange polyester jumpsuit. Nursing garb to be sure, but garish. Standing up from her desk chair, she'd looked like a convict. Teresa reminded Sheila of Coralene, her co-worker in Nutrition Services. Coralene wore more colorful outfits than might be expected in an office, but she could pull them off.

"Good morning, Sheila," Teresa had said.

"Morning. What's the story today?"

"Copacetic. Not much change in our Evelyn since you were here on Thursday. I've been checking her undergarments every few hours. Night crew, same thing. But she's not putting much out. I tried to get a little broth in her before I left yesterday, but mostly it ran down her chin. I got a washcloth, warm one, you know, and wiped off her face and hands. Everyone feels better with clean face and hands, don't you think?"

"Indeed."

"I remember my mom washing my hands and face before I'd go to bed when I was a little girl," Teresa had mused. "She'd do it right before I headed out the door to school too. She'd be dragging that terrycloth washcloth across my face, slowing down to wipe the corners of my mouth and under my eyes, then across my forehead like it was a wide-open prairie." Teresa had let out a little hum. "I loved that," she'd said, closing her eyes for a moment.

"I'll wander on in now," Sheila had told her, turning away.

"Dr. Becker was by yesterday afternoon," Teresa called after. "He listened to her heart, you know. Gave her the once-over."

"And?"

"He told me that it wouldn't be much longer now. Doctor said she's wasting away. No food in days, and hardly no fluids neither. He listened to her heart, moved her arms and legs a bit. Said something about 'no muscle tone anymore' like we didn't already know that. He's one of the good ones though. I always like the older doctors, don't you?"

"Did he speculate on precisely on how much longer?" Sheila had asked.

"Nope. Didn't speculate. In fact he told me not to mention his visit to you. Funny how some of them want to pretend that we're all a bunch of dopes. That the doctors are geniuses of some sort, but the nurses and the families? We're just a bunch of dopes. Like we'll be completely shocked when the end comes. Like none of us has read the sign above the front door."

"I appreciate you being straight with me, and you're right. The fact that something's sad doesn't mean it's also a surprise."

"Now that's a good way to put it." Teresa had given Sheila an exaggerated affirming nod. "Go on in there now, and say hello to the old gal. Switch things around on the nightstand. I know you like to do that."

Occasionally glancing toward her mother's sleeping, seemingly peaceful face, Sheila had sat by the bed for half an hour, watching the birds outside the window. Cardinals had crowded out chickadees at one of the feeders; nuthatches had been busily dining at the other. So many of their compatriots left town at this time of year; Sheila had appreciated the hearty birds who stuck around to belt out songs in the middle of winter.

From the hallway, clangs, grumbles, and shrieks melded to become the ambient noise of Golden Manor. With little to do to fill the requisite time, Sheila went to stand at the sink where her mother's shabby toothbrush and a mangled tube of Colgate stood irrelevant in a plastic cup next to the faucet.

She'd gazed into the mirror in its cheap aluminum frame. Nothing to see here; absolutely nothing to see. Her hair had grayed beyond the shiny black it had been when a Sheila long since forgotten might have looked in the mirror with some contentment at the reflection she found. For a while, when youth was kind, and before she knew how fleeting satisfactory reflections could be, Sheila's hair had framed her face in waves that shined like obsidian. Now, she kept it tucked behind her ears; something resembling bangs swept across one side of her forehead.

Returning to her mother's bedside with a dampened hand towel, Sheila had lifted the lamp to wipe off the nightstand before tossing the magazines into the wastebasket. It made no sense to arrive at Golden Manor with outdated issues of *Good Housekeeping* and *Better Homes and Gardens*. But she'd brought them all the same; it was something to do. A week or two later, she'd replace them. That day, Sheila had pulled a *Ladies Home Journal* and another *Good Housekeeping* from her purse and stacked them neatly.

Sheila's mother had been a reader. Not a scholar by any stretch, but reasonably well-informed. She'd watched the evening news. She'd read the newspaper. She'd kept an orderly house, a full freezer, and a well-tended garden. After Sheila's father died, her mother had managed sensibly on his pension. She'd been a fine mother. Timid as a rabbit. Reliable as a redwood. But once she was old and infirm, all the accompanying fuss and bother had struck Sheila as pointless.

Sheila had become less likeable over time. Less patient. As her mother's questions became increasingly inane and her reasoning one-dimensional, Sheila had bared the true colors she'd kept under wrap for years. She'd quit shielding her mother from disregard now that Sheila herself was no longer young and couldn't envisage the world as anything better than she knew it to be. But rather than seeing the true Sheila, her mother had seen an opportunity to take Sheila's life in her hands, as she'd done when Sheila was a child.

"Everything in its own time," her mother would say.

"What does that mean? Truly, Mother, what does that mean?"

At other times, her mother would pause to consider losses, real and imagined, and comfort herself with words that might as well have been enshrined in needlepoint: "Love conquers all, Sheila."

"No," Sheila would reply. "No, it does not."

"All will be well," her mother had said over the years, but Sheila could no longer abide the sentiment. Additional gruesome platitudes eventually saturated her mother's once-clear mind. "God has a plan," Mother would say, but her resolve grew increasingly tepid, as if she knew the inevitable was overtaking her, writhing at her feet as if she was standing in a bucket of snakes.

Sleep had been hard to come by that Monday night. Sheila had mulled Gordon's memo which had carried on at length over procurement of office furniture. A few weeks before, he'd expressed concern that employees had nowhere to hang their coats. In the latest memo, Gordon had detailed his success in securing not only coat racks but brass desk lamps with matching pencil cups. Sheila had been unmoved about the furniture but glad to hear that Gordon had gotten himself a dog.

She'd punched her pillow and came close to getting comfortable just as the nightstand phone rang.

"Sheila?" Sheila knew who it was, and she sat back up in bed. "Sheila? It's Teresa."

Yes, she'd been sad. But mostly relieved. It was requisite sentimentality, Sheila knew, that has people saying what in their hearts they know isn't true. Most hearts, in their default states, are very dark places. Sheila had loved her mother, but it had been time for her to go.

The liberation she felt had little to do with release from thrice-weekly visits to a purgatorial existence endured by people who deserved better. It was that now, Sheila could mull. She'd made a shaky peace with the course her life had taken. Was she happy? No. No, she was not. But she challenged anyone to define the word; it had lost its relevance so long ago as to be ludicrous. Would Sheila stick with it a while longer? Probably. She had another fifteen years, maybe twenty; the number was still palatable. She dreaded the day when the number stunned her, but knew it would come. And then? Well, who knows? What Sheila did know was that it was within her own control now which of life's winds merely taunted the shutters, and which blew off the roof. She was, finally, fully in charge of her own life.

CHAPTER EIGHT

Leonora

Saturday, February 28, 1976

LEONORA SAT ON the edge of the bed reviewing her day. She'd sleep well tonight. That wasn't always the case, but she'd made a good call with the bath. Problem was, getting in and out was increasingly difficult. Hitting her head on the edge of the tub was not how Leonora intended to go out.

She centered a glass of water on the coaster she kept on her nightstand. Next to it, pill bottles were arranged like churchgoers in a pew. Four green plastic bottles with their snap-off tops: the blood pressure pill, the diuretic, the antacid, the painkiller. Opening the lower nightstand drawer, Leonora confirmed that the other pills were there too. They were. The ever-present knot in her throat lessened, just a smidge.

One hand on the mattress, Leonora eased off her slippers and turned back the covers. She fluffed the pillow so it rested against the headboard before climbing into bed to lean against it. Closing her eyes, Leonora mused over the morning meeting with the guild.

Darcy had been a trooper this morning; Darcy usually was. Patiently, and with some real skill, she'd encouraged the gals to suggest ideas for the float theme; Darcy seemed to think they needed a theme.

"How could we connect the work of the hospital and the hospital guild with the bicentennial?" Darcy had asked once they'd settled in the front room. The gals had gaped at Darcy as if she was a goldfish in a bowl. Not unkindly. They all knew her. Well, Olive hadn't, but she did now. Still, there'd been little excitement in the room. Nothing terribly exciting about watching a goldfish.

It had been a logical question. Thing was, Leonora didn't want any more to do with the whole idea. Her motionless body in this moment represented the extent of effort she felt able to expend. It was how she felt about everything. Just let it happen. But that was not to be with this float project, so she'd tried to "attend to the conversation," as Darcy had once put it.

"Maybe some examples of medical care in America over the last two centuries?" Darcy had suggested. "Something that shows field hospitals during wartime and up to present day? You know, now that we have state-of-the-art facilities?"

"Did they have field hospitals during the Revolutionary War?" Cora had asked.

"I don't know. I would think so. Maybe that's something you could research at the library? Maybe that's the way to go. Compare medical care in 1776 to 1976? Show how far we've come? Or maybe do 1776, 1876, and now?"

Darcy had positioned herself on the ottoman which she'd wedged between Leonora's chair and the sofa where Hy, Lo, and Glad sat together like birds on a wire. Always in the same order. Somehow this hadn't crossed Leonora's mind until just now. *Well,* she thought, congratulating herself on this insight into seating arrangements. *I've still got some bubbles left in the soda pop.*

"That doesn't really sound very interesting," Hy had said in response to Darcy's suggestion. Hy had looked to Lo and Glad for affirmation; her sisters had solemnly shaken their heads. It was unlikely that the three ever made any particular effort to discern which of them had just spoken or what the nonspeaking sisters were agreeing to.

Cora had leaned forward in her chair, bumping Leonora as she stretched across to catch Darcy's eye. Freezing in place, Leonora had been mortified that Cora would lean too far and find herself on the rug. There would have been no getting her up. Old women on the floor rarely get up. That's part of the problem with being old.

But Cora hadn't fallen. Instead, she'd addressed Darcy in a voice oozing with maternal indulgence. "Problem with these ideas, love," Cora had said, "is that they don't really represent the guild. They're about the hospitals. Their doctors, and nurses, and who-the-hell ever. Guild gals like us? We're volunteers. We work behind the scenes, don't we?" Cora had turned toward the other women, encouraging their agreement. With that, the air in Leonora's front room had nearly mustered a breeze as the sisters and Olive enthusiastically nodded their heads.

"That's a good point," Darcy'd said graciously. "How

about you all give me some ideas of the types of things you do as guild members. Well, you and all the other guilds? I know there are lots of them. I'm guessing you do slightly different things? Tell me what you all do, and we can figure out how to feature that on the float."

At this, the women had bent forward and begun flicking ideas in Darcy's direction like spit wads from a third-grade boy.

"The craft sales, love. Those are our biggest thing," Cora had said. "All the items we make and sell. All that money goes to the hospital, you know. We don't get a dime. Not even for supplies."

"What do you make?" Darcy knew the answer to this; she'd been a spectator to Leonora's guild work since babyhood. "I know some of what you do," Darcy had added. "But I want to hear it from you."

Well now, that was the right approach. Leonora chided herself for any criticism of Darcy. Criticizing Darcy was something Leonora rarely did. Except for Darcy's insistence on driving too fast in the gravel. Criticizing Crystal? Now that was another story.

"Those darling little hot pads," Olive had suggested. "I'm the newest gal in the group, but those darling little hot pads, the embroidered ones? Well, I think they may be our biggest hit."

No need to rank them, Leonora had thought. *Just list them, that's all we need.* "You're right, Olive," Leonora had said. "Those embroidered hot pads are popular. And," she'd shifted in her chair to face Darcy, "there are the scrubbies. The nylon net scrubbies, for cleaning pots and pans? You know those, sweetie. You've helped make them. Every imaginable color. I think that's why women like them. They can get one that matches their kitchen."

"I have an orange one sitting right next to my sink," Olive had agreed proudly.

"And there are the turtles," Hy had picked up the narrative. "Everyone loves those stuffed turtles. Every new mother wants one. They're perfect. Same size as the doily on the back of our sofa." Hy had looked toward her sisters to find Lo and Glad nodding in agreement. "Babies like corduroy. The turtles have little tab ears that they can gum. And no buttons, nothing sharp, nothing for the babies to choke on. We make bibs too, out of dishtowels and rickrack. They're so easy to clean.

"All the supplies? Rickrack and thread?" Hy was on a roll now. "We buy them at the store we used to run. It's the best place for such things. Plus there's our discount. Twenty-percent. Not too shabby."

"I do love the turtles," Cora had said. "You can usually find a good piece of corduroy in the remnant pile. They're cheap to make. Cheap is good. And they last. My granddaughter, Velly? She slept with hers for years. Still has it, and she's in college!"

"Our favorites are the plant markers. Everyone loves the plant markers." As she spoke, Lo had leaned forward to rest her elbows on her knees. She had been holding an Oreo and now waved it about to draw attention. It had been Lo's turn to seek affirmation from her sisters; Hy and Glad had nodded supportively. Lo had looked quizzically at Darcy, confirming that Darcy was familiar with the revered plant markers.

"Those little glass test tubes?" Lo had said. "With the rubber stoppers? We put slips of paper in them where people write the name of their plants and then they just stick 'em in the dirt. Cute little test tubes, poking out of the dirt right next to plants!" Lo gave a giggle, that was echoed by her sisters.

"They're better than wood markers; they don't rot," Glad said derisively, revealing the nuisance posed by a rotting plant marker. "You wipe off the dirt on your gardening pants and read the name of your plants, or when you planted them, which is the thing people usually write."

"Yes. That is what people write," Hy said with certainty. "Most people know the names of their plants, but they don't remember when they planted them."

"Unless they're tomatoes," Olive said. "There are so many varieties of tomatoes. I use them to label my cherries. To tell them apart, you know, the cherry tomatoes from my full-sized ones. I want to know which ones I'll be popping in a salad and which ones will end up on my sandwich. Everyone wants to know that."

The women had all nodded, and Leonora had found herself joining them. It was indeed important to know which tomato was which.

Within an hour, Darcy'd made a long list of crafting triumphs. How such information would translate to a parade float remained to be seen. Fortunately, the float itself posed no concerns. Cora had volunteered her son-in-law to build it.

"Jasper's a gem," Cora'd said. "An absolute gem. He's made my Coralene happy every day of their married life. Just a gem. And he can get my grandson to help. Tanner needs to learn some responsibility. And how to work with tools. What good is a man if he don't know how to use tools?"

Leonora had nodded along with Cora's proclamation. Indeed. Knowing how to use tools, really knowing how to use them, was important for any man. It was unlikely that Tanner would be genuinely interested, doubtful too that Jasper was as skilled as Cora might believe. Green glass on the beach don't mean you've found an emerald.

Men who worked with tools were the salt of the earth. They were what made the world go around. They were saints. They were craftsmen. They were Badger.

Leonora knew there was no man out there who was as good with tools as Badger had been. He'd been able to build anything. Fix anything. Envision anything, and bring forth from his visions a bureau, a headboard, a coffee table, each more beautiful than the last. Sanded to the smoothness of glass and smelling of tung oil, Badger's creations had been worthy of a palace, which was what he had made of their home.

Leonora turned off the light on the nightstand and punched at her pillow until it comfortably cushioned her neck. She closed her eyes, feeling her breath fill, then leave, then fill her lungs again. She reached out to pat Badger's side of the bed. "Good night, Badger," she whispered.

"Night, night, dreamboat."

CHAPTER NINE

Leonora

May 7, 1928

LEONORA HAD YET to achieve her vision for the back-yard. She was close though; it was lovely indeed. Taking a rest from pulling weeds and tying back foliage left weary by daffodils, Leonora surveyed the yard from her canvas chair and drank iced tea.

She'd need more rhododendrons to complete her undulation of spring color. As of now, broad-leafed plants, in shades of white and red, claimed the eastern stretch of fence. They reminded Leonora of candy canes brought out for Christmas, much too late. The touch-me-nots that flourished at their feet, filled in as gifts under the tree. Her small-leafed rhodies faced south, where they could be seen from the kitchen window, filling the garden bed with as many shades of purple as one might find in a bruise. Next, she'd plant pink and then yellow.

Leonora was loyal to rhododendrons, not to azaleas. She'd

tease her friends at the garden club that azaleas and rhododendrons were so closely related that they had dinner together twice a week. But azaleas shed their leaves with the arrival of winter, as deciduous as the birch tree. Rhododendrons held on to their leaves, as if refusing to face a Minnesota winter underdressed; Leonora respected their tenacity.

Nine years ago, less than an hour after she and Badger had moved the last of their belongings across town, Leonora had wandered out the kitchen door to her heretofore unexplored backyard. Standing in the summer sun, in the yard of her very own home in Hanley, Minnesota, she'd wrapped her arms around herself and sobbed. Crying such as this was rare; Leonora was a practical woman. Unflappable. But occasionally the enormity of her good fortune would back up in her throat, with no other release than to weep in gratitude.

On that long-past afternoon, she'd taken in the disorder of her new yard. It had been dense in buckthorn, wild grape, and Virginia creeper, and armed with bull thistles and stinging nettles that were intent on repelling efforts to bring the land to heel. At first glance, the backyard offered little promise of becoming a testament to her horticultural prowess or a haven of outdoor family life. But this house, this land for which Badger had signed his name and turned over to the bank the ungodly down payment of $800, was as meant to be theirs, as they were meant to be each other's. So she'd set out not to conquer, but to establish authority and elicit a partnership of sorts with the yard, to bring forth something beautiful outside her home that did justice to the beauty within.

Oh, the lessons she'd learned. They had made her a better

gardener, a worthy steward of this land she'd been given. They'd made her a better mother, and a better wife. Much of Leonora's education came from the bulbs she'd planted that first fall in 1919, and which she'd supplemented every year thereafter.

The hardy bulbs were like her older daughter, Pearl. Pearl had been five when the family had moved into this house. She was an easy child, and, like a plucky daffodil or lily bulb, required minimal care once she was properly planted. There could be no better garden bed in which a child such as Pearl could grow. Ensuring sun, water, and abundant love, Leonora and Badger had planted their girl deep, so her roots would gain purchase to keep her strong in frozen ground. With such care, they could ensure a gorgeous display of color, year after year.

It was after Leonora had given up all hope, that Ruby was born. Ruby was delicate in features and feelings. She was not rugged like her sister; she needed a different kind of care. So Leonora extracted rocks, sticks, and roots; she mulched the ground letting it warm so that the tender bulbs – the begonias and dahlias that were the very essence of Ruby – would burst forth resplendent. And every fall, Leonora took those bulbs inside to the safe, cool darkness of the cellar, not to be returned to the garden until spring, after the earth had warmed.

Badger was neither a hardy bulb nor a tender one. He was not a rhododendron, and he was certainly not an azalea. Badger wasn't of the garden. Badger was the soil. He was water and sunlight. He was shelter from the wind. He was nourishment and encouragement. Badger was life itself.

He had filled their home with beautiful furniture: beds

for both girls, a rocking chair for Leonora, an armoire for their bedroom, and a sweet little writing desk where Pearl had once done her schoolwork and which Ruby now claimed as the perfect spot for drawing and paper dolls.

When Pearl had started high school last fall, Badger had presented her with a gleaming oak library table. Its center drawer could be drawn out as quietly as a waxed ski. Pearl was a tall girl, so the legs on her library table were longer than most, the crossbar slightly higher, ensuring that she could rest her feet comfortably as she tackled geometry, biology, composition, and Minnesota state history.

Finishing her iced tea, Leonora put her empty glass on the picnic table Badger had made so the family could eat out-doors once spring weather welcomed them. By summer, mosquitos and bees were too interested in what was on the Daniels' plates, so they ate on the screened porch Badger had constructed off the kitchen.

Rather than indulge further musing in the garden, it was time to think about dinner. She turned toward an invisible second chair, which held her invisible husband, and spoke to him out loud. "What would you like for dinner, my love? Fried ham with creamed peas and onions? Or how about salmon loaf and some of my canned green beans?"

Indeed, Badger might have been sitting on the patio with his wife, so intimately known was he that her words were undoubtedly his. "Let's have the ham, dreamboat, and some of that salad you make with the pineapple, raisins, and wal-nuts. Pearl loves that salad; that girl of ours will eat anything. Maybe biscuits for Ruby? For our choosy girl?"

A tendril of breeze kissed Leonora's eyelids as Badger vanished into the May afternoon.

Badger's days at the railyard were long; he arrived home dirty and tired. But by fall, the new bridge would be complete, carrying ever-longer and ever-faster trains across the river.

As Leonora pulled provisions from her new electric refrigerator, she imagined Badger's pleasure when he saw his meal on the table. If the girls were in their bedroom when their father came in the back door, Leonora would slip her hand inside the collar of Badger's shirt. Sweat would glaze his neck like varnish. She'd kiss it away, savoring the salt on her lips, breathing him in as if he were a bouquet of roses, so sweet was the smell and feel of him. Badger would rub his stubbled chin across Leonora's cheek, lifting her mouth to his and cupping her head in his hands, kissing her fully for as long as either of them could bear. "Off with you, now," Leonora would murmur, but her body ignored her words and she pulled him toward her.

"I'll take a bath after the girls go to bed. Perhaps you'd like to join me?" Badger might say.

"Perhaps I would."

Leonora shook away such thoughts. Too early for all that. Her girls would be home soon, gasping for a snack.

Pearl and her friends would wait outside Ruby's school until the giggling first grader was absorbed into their midst as they all made their way home like a human tumbleweed. One of the older girls would hold Ruby's hand. It needn't be Pearl. Eventually, Pearl's friends would peel off in ones and twos, leaving the sisters together. Ruby would reach for Pearl, as Pearl reached for Ruby, and in synchronized steps they would return home to Vermillion Avenue.

Leonora sliced a blueberry muffin and put a half on each plate, beside which she fanned apple slices. She filled two small glasses with milk and placed them in the refrigerator. After placing the plates on the table, Leonora began folding each girl a paper tulip. These were the only tulips allowed in the Daniels' home, given tulip bulbs' popularity with chipmunks and squirrels.

The rapping at the front door wasn't a sound typically made by the girls. Their habit was to race up the back stairs and fall into the kitchen like puppies. Pearl, who might otherwise be too sophisticated to clown about, would gladly join Ruby in whatever silliness the younger girl might choose. No, that rapping was not the girls.

Leonora remained at the table folding the flowers. Perhaps the sound had not come from the front door at all, but was simply the girls' newest mode of noisy arrival. An unfamiliar stillness settled before the rap came again.

Leonora rose and walked from the kitchen through the small dining room, to the front room, and toward the front door. Silence consumed her, as animated as candlelight. Her ears were filled with cotton, her head encased in crumpled muslin. Not a single bird trilled through the open back door. The dining room held its breath. The front room was as quiet as a tomb.

Two men stood on the front porch. The taller one was a stranger. He wore the clothes of a working man, but his hair had been recently combed and was still damp. He teetered as if he had pebbles in his shoes and stood with his hat in his hand.

The other man was Dougie Hart. Dougie was Badger's pal from the railyard. On occasional summer afternoons, Leonora and Ruby would join Dougie's wife Sylvia, and their daughters June and Elizabeth, to play at the park down by the river.

Leonora nodded at the stranger before holding out her hand out to Dougie. Later, she remembered thinking that if she offered the pleasantries these men would expect from a social call, then the purpose behind their visit would transform. They'd accept her offer to come in; they'd welcome a glass of iced tea. Dougie would introduce Leonora to the stranger, and the girls – who would be home any minute – would charm both men with stories of their days at school.

Dougie held the hand Leonora had extended. His own hand was calloused, but his grip was soft. Leonora wondered why Dougie didn't speak. Why were they standing in her doorway as Dougie held her hand? She looked at the stranger and thought perhaps she saw his lips moving. If the men were talking, it was too quietly for Leonora to hear. But no, that couldn't be. Not a single sound broached the stillness. Leonora remained suspended in the silence that had beset her since she first heard the rapping on the door.

She shook her head, going so far as to yawn in an effort to clear her ears. Without knowing how they got there, Leonora realized she and Dougie were sitting on the sofa in the front room. The stranger stood discomfited in front of them, leaning toward her, his hands on the knees of his filthy work pants. His nail beds were rimmed in dirt, and dirt filled the crevasses in his knuckles. Why, Leonora wondered, was he standing so close that she could see his knuckles? Badger never came in the house with dirty hands. Why was this man here, with his dirty knuckles, leaning toward her but not speaking loudly enough for her to hear?

The man stepped back. Dougie shifted on the sofa next to Leonora. He sat sideways, as if wanting to see her face. Now he was holding both of her hands in his.

"Leonora."

Was that what Dougie had said?

"Leonora, do you understand?"

Understand what? Had Dougie spoken? She thought again about the iced tea. She should go to the kitchen and pour them some. She was being rude.

Dougie seemed to shift uncomfortably and Leonora wished he'd leave, and take the stranger with him, since neither of them had anything to say. The girls would be home soon, and this visit was wasting time that Leonora needed to prepare dinner for Badger.

Someone else had entered the front room. It was Dougie's wife, Sylvia. Dougie let go of Leonora's hands and stood, leaving a space for Sylvia to sit down on the sofa.

"Leonora?" Was that Sylvia's voice? "Leonora? Love?" Sylvia paused before she too took hold of one of Leonora's hands. "Leonora?" Sylvia said again.

Slowly, Sylvia's voice slid into Leonora's ears, like a rain cloud slides in front of the sun. Leonora tried to focus on Sylvia's face. She should fetch iced tea for Sylvia too. Don't these people know that it's time to make dinner? The front room felt crowded. There were too many people here. It was no longer Leonora who was being rude by not serving them, but these three – Dougie, Sylvia, and the stranger – who didn't belong. Leonora found her voice.

"Sylvia," Leonora said. "Why are you all here?"

Sylvia's eyes filled and she reached for Leonora's other hand. But Leonora had had enough of hand holding. The suffocating silence lifted. Leonora's heartbeat threatened to drown out any other sound in the room. The others' noisy breathing, and their similarly loud beating hearts were deafening. The front room was not big enough for all this noise.

"Leonora?" This time Sylvia's voice registered as a shout. Leonora slapped her hands to her head, covering her ears. Sylvia eased onto the floor in front of the sofa, holding Leonora's knees as Leonora pulled her body tight into itself. She crammed her head sternly down on her neck and pushed her chin to her chest, holding her breath. Flinging her hands away from her ears, Leonora wrapped herself in her own arms, doing everything she could to smother the sounds she could now hear, hoping to die before any more words could penetrate.

~ ~ ~

The railroad paid for the service; railroad men and their families filled every pew. On the day of the funeral, whistles on every train up and down the river blew long and loud at 1:55 PM, the exact time Badger Daniels had been crushed when a winch chain snapped, as the men loaded a railcar with metal joists, destined for the bridge to Wisconsin.

Leonora held hands with her girls – Pearl on her left and Ruby on her right – as they stood beside Badger's closed casket in the crowded church. As they walked away, the stranger from the front porch gave Leonora papers from the bank, verifying that her house on Vermillion Avenue was now fully paid for. His hands were clean; he wore a suit.

That night, Leonora, Pearl, and Ruby ate ham sandwiches in the backyard. Leonora removed the quilt that had covered the bed she'd shared with Badger since the day they'd married. She spread it on the grass and the three of them – in a tangle of arms, legs, and broken hearts – looked skyward until the moon rose, waiting to see Badger's star.

PART TWO

"Families come in all shapes and sizes. Some families might be missing a person or have someone who isn't blood. Some families are dull. That's not bad though, dull people keep life calm. Having a child in a family, that's wonderful. I have a little girl. But for real family, you have to have a sister. Sisters are the best. Sisters are forever."

RUBY DANIELS

1922 - 1948

MEMO

TO: Nutrition Services Employees
FROM: Gordon Hund, Nutrition Services Manager
DATE: Friday, March 5, 1976
RE: Bicentennial Celebration assignments, high school survey, and other topics of interest

Ladies: I have been pleased to overhear discussions this past week regarding your initial considerations for Nutrition Services' participation in this summer's Bicentennial Parade. I am confident such interactions are the byproduct of our staff meeting this past Monday.

Any questions generated among you through these early deliberations may be communicated to me through a memo or introduced as a discussion item in a future staff meeting. Should any of you choose to raise questions via an intra-office memo, please ensure that all of your fellow employees receive a copy to ensure concise communication among colleagues.

At next Monday's meeting on March 8, 1976, Miss Raymond will present the results of her student survey and discuss the implications, if any, for menu changes this school year, and relevant considerations for school year 1976-1977.

Napoleon earned best in breed in the Wescott County Dogstravaganza held last Saturday at the Wescott County Community Center. This achievement has merited an invitation to the bi-county competition in April. Details will be forthcoming in future memos, including information on securing tickets, which are expected to sell out quickly.

CHAPTER TEN

Sheila

March 5, 1976

"HE'S A NICE man," Lexie said.

For a moment, Sheila wasn't sure of Lexie's reference.

"Tom?" Lexie said. "I saw you talking to Tom last week. He's a very nice man. He reminds me of you."

~ ~ ~

A demanding rain had thrashed at the windows as Sheila headed for the Denny's exit last Friday night. She'd seen more than she cared to; but it was too late. Horrified, she saw the man on the swivel stool hop down and bound toward her.

"Sheila Raymond! Well, good grief, chief. I haven't seen you in an age. You remember me, don't you? Come on now. Tom? Tom Downlane? You must remember me. The guy who lives down the lane?" He'd chuckled at the joke he must have told a thousand times.

Tom Downlane was out of place. Foreign matter. No

more appealing to Sheila than a hangnail. His head crested level with Sheila's nose, so in speaking he'd had to tip up his chin and peer out from under a tattered blue baseball cap. This made his otherwise doughy face appear slightly beaky. But his eyes were bright and enough strands of blondish hair poked out from under the cap to know the man was not bald. He wasn't young, but neither did he appear ready to be old.

Tom had removed the cap and dangled it on a pinky finger before using thumbs and forefingers to hike up the waistband of a sagging pair of khaki work pants. He'd shimmied, ensuring that the butt crack Sheila had observed was hidden from view, at least momentarily.

Sheila had resigned herself to the inevitable and paused. "Tom. Hello. Of course I remember you. Been a while though."

"That it has." He'd taken a couple steps back and making one more tug on his waistband, rested his hands on his hips, facing Sheila with a full grin. "You left us behind at Hanley High. What's it been? About a year now? I wandered into the kitchen one day to unplug the sink drain. You remember that drain, don't you? Always clogging up as a bunch of hungry high schoolers were lining up for lunch." Tom laughed. "Spent a lot of time crawling around on the floor with my head under those drains. There was always something going on with the plumbing over there. I spent more time at Hanley High than just about any other building in the district. Yep, one day I wandered in and you were nowhere to be found." Tom had paused, waiting for a response that didn't come. "The new gal told me you'd gotten a promotion. Congratulations then. Belated of course, but still, congratulations. You escaped, I suppose you could say. That how you see it? You made your escape?"

Sheila'd had no interest in all this. Tom had answered the call when the sink was clogged with potato peels or the dishwasher crapped out, but she'd been sufficiently grateful at the time. Must they revisit these dregs?

"I suppose you could say I escaped," Sheila had said, knowing her tone was sharp. "It was an opportunity, so I took it. Just took it. Nothing wrong with an office job at this stage."

"You thinking about retirement then? That's up next for me. I could move on at any time. Just haven't done it yet."

"Haven't really thought about it. Just keep going to work…" She'd started to say that she had nothing else to do, but stopped herself in time. This was not a road she cared to go down. Not a lane, either.

"Well, I think the idea of planning my next step is exciting," Tom had said. "Might buy a motor home. Drive around the country, you know. Visit a few national parks. See my kids and grandkids. They're scattered all over. Got a couple ex-wives scattered around too. Probably won't drop in on them. What can I say?" Tom's demeanor had shifted and he'd looked at Sheila sheepishly. "I seem to make people scatter."

"I didn't know you had children," Sheila had said. "But why would I?"

Tom had paused for an instant, as if needing to shake off Sheila's comment before plowing ahead. "Well, I can't blame you for not remembering. Hearing stories of other people's kids and grandkids isn't the most fascinating conversational fare, now is it? You were always polite about it though. You pretended to be interested even if you weren't. Always appreciated that."

Sheila remembered nothing of conversations with Tom Downlane about his family or anything else. Other than the image of Tom's backside as he crawled under the sink – one she'd tried to shake each time he'd exited the school kitchen – Sheila barely remembered the man.

"So this your haunt then?" Tom had asked. "It's a decent spot. Makes a decent burger. And their coffee? Can't beat it. Friday's not my usual night though," he'd continued, seemingly intent on holding Sheila captive in the bonds of a one-way conversation. "I'm a Saturday guy. My schedule got a little bit upside down this week. My grandson's coming to town tomorrow. So I figured I'd nip over for a burger tonight so me and the boy can make a different plan for tomorrow. Hardly ever see my grandkids, or my kids either. This grandson's finishing up dental school and decided he wanted to stop by and see me. How about that, huh? Not sure a dentist would appreciate all the hot fudge I like on my Denny's sundae, so I'll take him somewhere else." Tom had paused unnecessarily for Sheila to get a word in. "I'm mighty proud of that boy," Tom had continued, the catch in his voice impossible to ignore. "Mighty proud."

Sheila had been unnerved. Here was a man she barely knew about to blubber over his grandson the dentist. Others' emotions were to be avoided. Nothing good came from random interactions like this.

"Well, hey now." Tom regained his composure, perhaps

sensing Sheila's discomfort. He'd put his cap back on and once again hitched up his pants. "I won't keep you. Just had to say hi. Nice to see a friendly face in here."

A friendly face? What the hell? Whose friendly face was he talking about? Hers? Still, she'd nodded cordially and when Tom had extended his hand, Sheila gave him her coat, allowing him to hold it as she inserted first one arm and then the other. Tom had gestured toward the door and Sheila had stepped in front of him, walking through as he held it.

"Can I walk you to your car?"

Patience expended, Sheila hadn't even tried to stem her rudeness. "Heavens no," she'd said. "I know exactly where I parked. I'm quite capable of getting to my car on my own."

"Well then, good enough." Unfazed, Tom had pulled down the bill of his cap and stepped out into the rain. "You have a good night, then," he'd said, hopping puddles until he reached the door of a massive pickup truck.

How on earth did he climb into that thing? Did he have a step stool? This was a not-tall man, driving a very-tall truck. Sheila snapped her rain hat under her chin and fumbled in her purse, trying to extract her keys with gloved fingers.

"G'night now!" Tom had shouted through his truck's open window. It was one of those four-door numbers. He'd backed the monstrosity out of its spot in the time it had taken for Sheila to gather her coat over the back of her neck.

"I'm usually here on Saturday nights," he'd bellowed. "I like to sit by the window. Just like you were doing. Join me some time, huh? See ya soon!"

Ignoring the rain, but careful not to slip on the invisible patches of ice, Sheila'd made her way to the Chrysler, unlocked her door, and with a sigh of relief, slid onto the frigid seat.

~ ~ ~

"How on earth does he remind you of me?" Sheila's voice notched up toward shrill. She was riled. She hadn't directed a scornful word in Lexie's direction since correcting her grammar years ago, but this comment could not go unchallenged.

"Don't knot your knickers," Lexie said gently. "I only mean that he usually eats alone, like you always do. He's almost always here on the same day, same as you. It's Saturdays for him. And he sits in the same spot, right here. Your spot on Fridays. Tom's spot on Saturdays. Sometimes he orders the meatloaf, or he'll get a steak or a burger. Loves his potatoes: mashed, baked, or fried. Doesn't matter."

"He worked for the school district," Sheila said, bringing her tone back in check. She was indifferent to Tom's potato preferences, but couldn't abide disharmony with Lexie. "He still does. I used to see him at Hanley High before I changed jobs. He's a plumber. Saved my bacon on a clogged sink more than once. You might've seen him there too."

"Nah, I doubt it," Lexie said. "We were pretty self-centered in high school, remember? None of us paid much attention to anyone who didn't give us something we needed. You know, like the teachers or the nurse."

"Or the lunch lady," Sheila said.

"Or the lunch lady," Lexie agreed.

~ ~ ~

By April, dinner options moved on from the Hamburger Hall of Fame to Treasures of the Sea; Sheila hoped that Lexie had likewise moved on from any notions of dinner with Tom. It was not to be.

One Friday night, in an uncharacteristic move, Lexie slid in across the booth from Sheila with something on her mind. "You sit here all by yourself every week," Lexie said, diving courageously into the deep end of the conversational pool. "Nothing wrong there. After a long week at work, it's nice to take a breath on a Friday. I understand. But how about a little company on a Saturday?"

What was it with Lexie? How did she get away with this? Charm. That was how. Lexie wore charm like a cashmere coat. Not dime-store charm – buy it cheap and slap it on – but charm that emanates from deep inside, charm that isn't that far from affection, or love.

"How about stopping in next Saturday night?" Lexie persisted. "Well, not stopping in really, but coming for dinner. I could mention something to Tom when he's here tomorrow. It's not like he's forgotten or anything. He's asked about you. More than once. He's hopeful, you know? Not like it's a big deal, more that he'd like to have dinner every once in a while with someone he likes, and he seems to like you. Maybe it's the school connection, I don't know." Lexie had caught Sheila with a teasing look. "Or maybe it's your charisma? That could be it, don't you think?"

"Oh good lord, who knows? Maybe he wants someone to pick up the check."

Lexie laughed. "I don't think so. A few weeks ago he told me he'd put in his papers. You know, for retirement. He's going to work out the school year, then be done. Wants to travel around the country. See the sights. I get the impression he's got money in the bank to do whatever he wants. And what he seems to want is to drive around the country in a motor home. Wouldn't be my idea of fun, but he seems to think it's a winner."

"No one else I know is considering retirement," Sheila mused. "I am, but I haven't made my move. Certainly haven't talked to anyone about it."

"You haven't even told me. I had no idea." Lexie waited until she had Sheila's full attention. "Have dinner with him," she'd said. "Just have dinner with him."

CHAPTER ELEVEN

Coralene

Saturday, March 6, 1976

SEVERAL SETS OF diners would have finished their breakfasts by now and be off enjoying their Saturdays. Coralene would never be among them. She worked too hard all week to start early on a Saturday; 11:00 was a fine time to meet her mother at the Pancake House. Her mother didn't sleep much, so timing made no difference to her. And timing alone was not going to determine whether Tanner would show.

"Thanks for coming, Mama," Coralene said as Cora eased into the booth.

Cora sucked her teeth. "What's that supposed to mean? What could possibly be happening in the world that would keep me from having breakfast with my daughter and grandson? How you doing? How's work? How's my grand girl? I haven't talked to her in over a week." Cora kept up the pace of questioning as she twisted out of her coat. Pulling it out from under her, she piled it beside her in the booth and rested her purse on top. "That's better," she said. "Speaking of grands, where's Tanner? I thought he was the reason we're here." Cora reached across the table to pat Coralene's hand, shifting as she did to scan the restaurant. "Not that you aren't reason enough," she said, trying to catch the attention of the waitress holding the coffee pot.

"I talked to Tanner on the phone last night," Coralene said. "Just for a minute. Pretty sure he'll come. Had to track him down at his friend Craig's. Told him to come at 11:15. Not that he's going to make a big distinction between 11:00 and 11:15. But I wanted a few minutes to talk with you. Talk through what's going on, you know? Although I don't really know much."

"Slow down there," Cora said. "Tell me where Tanner's living and what he's doing. You said he dropped in on Jasper? Couple weeks back?"

"Just showed up. And that's good; I want him to feel he can arrive any time. Any reason. He told Jasper that he's been living in Craig's basement. Remember his friend Craig from high school? He's a good kid. His mother works for the school district too. Craig frittered away some time after graduation, like Tanner did. But I hear that now he's taking classes at the technical school in Minneapolis. Wants to learn a trade. Maybe become an electrician. First though, he needs to pump up his math skills. Craig never did very well in math. Just didn't focus. Not like Tanner. Tanner could manage the math, no problem."

"Enough about Craig," Cora said kindly. "Tell me what Tanner's doing. Living in a basement? What's that about?"

"He'd been living in an old house with five other boys

for a few months. I didn't think much of that setup, or those boys, and I told him so. But Tanner, he gets these part-time jobs, you know. Had one at the gas station for a while. I thought that might stick, but it didn't. Last one I knew was at Burger Bill's. Part-time unskilled work? He'll never afford an apartment doing that."

"Think you can get him to move home?"

"I don't know. I wish Lola, she's Craig's mother? I wish she'd charge Tanner some rent, but she won't. She's a softy. Good woman, but no disciplinarian."

"What does Jasper think?" Cora asked.

"Jasper thinks we should keep the door open, like we've been doing, but not push. You know Jasper, his heart is soft as pudding, but he's a big believer in bootstraps."

"Too bad Tanner's daddy didn't believe in the pull-your-self-up-by-your-own-bootstraps theory," Cora said.

"Tanner's daddy's been gone for years. He can't be an excuse for Tanner not taking responsibility. Particularly when he's got us rooting for him."

"So what do you want to do? What do you suggest? I know we're not sitting here just for the pancakes. I know you've got a plan."

These were the times Coralene most treasured her mother. Cora was a lioness. The best person in the world when you needed someone in your corner, someone to lean on. And that was what Coralene needed now.

"I know you told Leonora that Jasper could build the parade float," Coralene said. "I think you even told all those ladies that Tanner could help. Wishful thinking, huh? Well, we need to make sure that's exactly what happens." Coralene's voice was firm. "We need to get Tanner moved back home, have him work with Jasper on the float to earn his keep, and make it clear he needs to step up. Find a trade and sign up as an apprentice, or get his behind back in school. Doesn't matter which far as I'm concerned. I want him to know I'm keeping an eye on him, but also that I'm keeping an eye out." It was Coralene's turn to reach across the table. She squeezed Cora's hand and took a deep breath. "I promised," Coralene said, her voice quavering. "I promised DeCora, Mama. I can't let her boy get lost. I can't."

Tanner's not lost," Cora said. "He's wandering around a bit, he isn't looking at the map, but he's not lost. Not really. You've done right by your sister, Coralene. You've done right by DeCora. And it's not for me to say, but from where I sit, you've done right by your God too. I'm proud of you Big Miss. And I know Little Miss would be proud too, if she was still with us."

Had Tanner not approached, Coralene would have given in to tears, but seeing his aunt and grandmother blubbering at the Pancake House was not going to entice Tanner into conversation. As it was, she barely got the paper napkin to her eyes in time.

"What's the matter there, Auntie C? You sad to see me?"

"Nah, I got something in my eye. A crumb or something."

Tanner grinned. He didn't believe her, and she knew it, but they both let it be.

"Morning, Grammy," Tanner said, smiling at Cora. He tried to slide in next to her but found himself straddling the edge of the bench.

"Give me your coat, Mama. I'll put it over here." Coralene

lifted Cora's coat and purse above her head, to avoid whatever was greasy or sticky on their breakfast table.

"I'm starving," Tanner said dramatically, sidling up to his grandmother. "I'll take one of everything on the menu." He beamed at Coralene. "Please."

"You order whatever you want. That's alright by me. I'm going with the pancakes. No one does them quite like this place, except maybe your uncle. Speaking of, I told him I'd bring home a cinnamon roll; don't let me forget when we leave."

Cora raised her coffee cup toward the waitress who arrived with the pot and an empty cup for Tanner. "Some for you too?" she asked him.

"Yes, please," he said. "And would you bring some cream?"

"There's a pitcher of it in with those." The waitress pointed toward a collection of syrup dispensers at the far end of the booth.

"I see that," Tanner told her, flashing his most charming grin. "But if it isn't about to overflow right now, then I'll need some more."

The waitress' name tag read Anita. She was young and pretty, and seemingly quite happy to supply Tanner with extra cream. "I'll be right back," she said.

"And some more sugar cubes too, please," Tanner called after her. "I go through a lot of them."

Tanner was clearly in a good mood. Thing was, he was always in a good mood. The young man was neither sullen nor disrespectful. He was amiable. Consistently kind. Coralene ached to see him settled, not bouncing from one dead-end choice to another.

When Anita returned with the cream and sugar, Cora put in her order for two pieces of wheat toast with butter and jam, and a side of bacon.

"That all you going to eat?" Coralene asked. "You'll waste away."

Cora laughed. "Unlikely," she said. "I already had an English muffin and peanut butter this morning. I'm not like you, Big Miss, I need to eat when I get up, and I get up much earlier than you!"

"Fair enough," Coralene said. "What are you going to get?" She looked toward Tanner.

"If it's okay, I really do want a big breakfast." He raised his eyebrows at Coralene, who nodded. "Then I'll have the pancake triple stack," he said, turning toward Anita. "And two fried eggs, and two slices of bacon, and some hash browns. Oh, and a side order of ham."

Coralene knew he wasn't finished.

"I'd better get some toast to soak up the egg. And some orange juice too. Please."

"You're going to have to run around the block six times to work off that breakfast," Cora said. "But you're still a growing boy. Or at least, I still like to say you are."

"We both know I'm not, Grammy, but I like that you think of me like that."

Tanner leaned over to put his head on Cora's shoulder. Coralene watched her mother kiss the top of Tanner's head. For the second time this morning, she thought she just might sob. Enough of this. Jasper would endorse whatever Coralene worked out with Tanner. Having Tanner help with the float would compound the work for Jasper, but it's time to get this young man's train on the track. Time to get him home. Time to get him working.

"Auntie C?"

Coralene had been too lost in her thoughts to notice Anita waiting, pencil poised above her order pad.

"You done ordering?" Coralene asked Tanner.

"Yep. It's your turn now."

"I'll have the Denver omelet," Coralene said. "I'd like a pancake on the side, no toast."

"Anything else?" Anita asked, addressing her words to Coralene but focusing her attention on Tanner.

"No, that's it. Thank you."

"It'll be out in a couple minutes. I'll bring the coffee pot back when I come. And more cream."

Coralene's omelet had been fluffy and filled to overflowing with green peppers and ham. Cora had eaten her toast contentedly. As for Tanner, he'd barely looked up from the multiple plates arrayed in front of him like oversized chips at a poker game.

"You done?" Coralene asked, after Tanner had wiped each plate clean with his last piece of toast.

"Done," he said. "Thank you, Auntie C."

"So," Coralene said quietly. "It's Saturday. What? About noonish now? 12:30?"

"Umm, it's 12:30," Tanner said hesitantly, looking at his watch.

"You have plans for today?" Coralene asked.

"No ma'am, thought I'd hang out with Craig. He doesn't have school today."

"Well then," Coralene said. "Maybe Craig can help you."

"With what?"

"With packing up your things and moving them home. You don't belong in Craig's basement." Coralene's tone was neither judgmental nor stern. "You don't belong at Burger Bill's either. Not without some longer-term plan. I have an idea what that plan should be. I want to hear what you think. Your uncle and I both want to hear what you think. Grammy wants to hear what you think. But bottom line is, it's time you make some changes. Would you agree?"

Tanner reached for the wad of napkin in his lap. He wiped at his mouth, perhaps finding crumbs that were invisible to Coralene.

"Would you agree, sweetheart?" Coralene asked again.

"Yes, Auntie C. I agree. I do."

"You want to talk through things now, or you want to bring your stuff over this afternoon and we can talk over dinner? I'm assuming Craig can borrow his mom's car to help you move?"

"He can borrow it. She doesn't go out much on the weekends. She likes to put her feet up and read."

"My kind of woman," Coralene said. She caught Tanner's gaze and held it, trying to telegraph the depth of the love she felt for him and for his mother, who couldn't finish raising him. "We good?" Coralene asked.

"We good." Tanner's expression relaxed. But Coralene sensed more coming. "I do have one question," Tanner said. "Is that okay?"

"Of course. What?"

"Is Grammy coming for dinner?"

"Yes."

"What we having?"

Cora's burst of laughter came out as a snort. She put her arm around Tanner and pulled him in.

"What do you want?" Coralene asked, smiling.

"Sloppy Joe's?"

"We'll see. You be at the house by 6:00. Now, go find your friend Anita there, order a cinnamon roll for Uncle J, and ask her to bring me the check. I'll see you at home."

Tanner eased his way off the bench and stood at the end of the booth. Such a beautiful young man. Coralene's throat tightened just looking at him.

"I'll see you tonight," Tanner said, his hands resting on the table. Leaning down, he brushed his cheek against hers. "Thank you, Auntie," he said, his voice as soft as a kiss from God.

Coralene watched him leave. *Now*, she thought. *Now I can have a good cry.*

Cora reached for her daughter's hand and squeezed. "You done good, Big Miss," Cora said. "You done real good."

CHAPTER TWELVE

Coralene
March 16, 1968

"I NEED YOUR promise, Coralene. Your pledge." DeCora's voice was as faint as falling leaves. She stared up from the bed with as much intensity as her deteriorating body could muster. "I need it," she mumbled.

Coralene tried to keep her expression even, as she took in what was left of her baby sister.

The daylight in DeCora's bedroom lingered tentatively. The lamp on her bedside table was doing its best to brighten the room. Lace curtains that usually covered the window facing the front yard had been opened wide to invite in every available ray of sun. But the room remained gray and hushed, as if showcasing the sunlight of early spring was inappropriate, or forbidden.

"You comfy there?" Coralene asked. "Can I prop up that pillow somehow? Get you a smidge of juice?"

"Nah. Nothing really settles." DeCora turned her head

toward the jumble of glasses cluttering her bedside table. "I'm not caring about juice right now. I'm caring about you promising me you'll take care of Tanner." DeCora's breathing was labored. "I need you to take him in, Cory. I need you to finish raising him. You and Jasper. Now that I can't do it no more. I need you to do it. Promise me. Please." DeCora leaned back against the pillow, spent.

"I promise, Little Miss. With my whole heart. With God as my witness. I promise I'll take care of your boy."

"He's gonna need you," DeCora went on in an unfamiliar voice, constricted by panic and pain. "You and Jasper. He's gonna need you bad. This is a terrible time to leave a boy. He's only twelve. He's still got so much growing up to do." DeCora closed her eyes. A few tears rolled down her face, replacing others that had been there moments before. "A terrible time," she said again.

Coralene sat on a kitchen chair. It was rickety, with a pronounced squeak, as if the wood that had borne the weight of so many bodies at so many family meals was objecting to being called away from the dinner table to sit at DeCora Deveraux's death bed.

DeCora was not so much propped by pillows as she was immersed in them. Many had fallen to the floor. A patchwork quilt, worn thin by age and use, rested lightly atop her as DeCora diminished and disappeared. Coralene was powerless to bring her sister back. From somewhere deep in the pillow pile, DeCora emitted a small snore, as quiet as a whisper.

"What are you doing still sitting in that miserable chair?" Jasper stood in the doorway of his sister-in-law's room. His flannel work shirt had come untucked from his trousers, and Coralene saw a streak of oil or dirt or some such, across the front of his neck. Disheveled was not a typical look for Jasper, which meant that Jasper and Tanner had been down in the basement.

"That's not enough chair for you," Jasper was saying. "Let me get one from the front room. I'll get the blue one, next to the sofa."

"It's alright, baby, you don't need to be hefting furniture around this house. I'm fine."

"You're not fine, Cory. Nothing about this is fine. And more than that, you're not comfortable either. I can't do much else to help, but what I can do is get you a comfortable chair." Jasper nodded toward the bed. "Looks like she's sleeping a bit. That's good. I've got Tanner downstairs, organizing all the tools his daddy left down there."

"DeCora made me promise," Coralene said, catching her husband's gaze and holding it. "Made me promise we'd take care of him."

"Did you tell her that was our plan all along?"

"Nah. I think she needed to say the words. Make the request, you know? So she'd feel like she was still in charge of what happened with Tanner. I went ahead and promised her. Wasn't a long, drawn-out conversation. I just made the promise, then she went back to sleep. That's about all she's doing now. Sleeping, I mean."

"Seems to me that's a good thing," Jasper said. "When sleep's all you got left, it's good if you can do it. There's no changing that, Cory. You know that. This is what's going to be. Nothing to be done."

Jasper entered the room and walked around the end of DeCora's bed to where Coralene sat on the wooden chair. Her wide hips extended beyond the seat on both sides, like thick icing making its way down the side of a cake. Jasper offered a hand, and Coralene let herself be pulled up from the chair and into his arms.

~ ~ ~

"I was thinking I'd go live with my dad," Tanner said. "I appreciate you letting me stay here the last few days, and I don't mean no disrespect, but I just thought I'd go find my dad. Live with him, you know?"

"Nobody's sure where your dad is these days, son." Jasper folded the newspaper that held the Sunday crossword. It had gone untouched since DeCora's funeral. He stood up to put it on the kitchen counter. Reaching for the coffee pot, he raised an eyebrow to Coralene. "Another cup?" he asked.

"No, baby, I'm good. But thank you."

"Tanner, you ready to take up some coffee drinking yet? I could get you a cup."

The surprise on Tanner's face made Coralene smile. "Load up that boy's cup with cream and sugar," she said. "We'll turn him into a coffee drinker."

"I took some of that sweet potato pie out of the freezer. I could slice it up. Sound good?"

"Sounds good," Coralene said. "Thank you, baby."

"Thank you, Uncle Jasper." Tanner's body relaxed into the chair. "I like that pie."

"There's lot of good eating in this house," Coralene said. "You'll be well fed here. You know you will."

"I know, Auntie, it's just that, like I said, I kind of want to stay with my dad."

"Here's the deal, son." Jasper put slices of sweet potato pie in front of his wife and his nephew before leaning against the kitchen counter, gazing at them both. "If your dad shows up, if things could work out with that, we can talk about it then. But we sent a letter to the last address your mom had for your dad, and we didn't hear back." Jasper paused, and Tanner started to speak before Jasper cut him off. "Now, before you go objecting, I know. I know it hasn't been much time. He might show up. He might call. And if he does, we can see what's what then. Cross that bridge when we get to it, so to speak. But for now, your Aunt Coralene has set up the extra room for you. And you're not a guest, son. You're family. There's lots that's good about that, sure enough. And there's responsibility too. You'll go to school, regular. Every day. On time. You'll have chores, just like Coravelle does. And speaking of, you and your cousin will get along. Your aunt and me? We won't tolerate quarreling in our home. No bickering. We settle problems like reasonable people. Understand? That's a lot of talking, I know. But do you understand?"

Coralene's eyes had filled as she listened to her husband. She loved that man. Loved him so much it hurt. A wonderful, profound, life-affirming kind of hurt.

Tanner leaned back in his chair. He crossed his arms, as if considering whether to be sullen, but he didn't have it in him. It wasn't who he was. He uncrossed his arms, put his elbows on the table, and rested his chin in his hands. "Okay. I understand." He paused, but Coralene knew he wasn't done. "But if he shows up? My dad? We can see what happens?"

"Yes, son. If he shows up we can see what happens. Now, do you want more pie? I'll get you another slice," Jasper said. "Not that I'm going to be waiting on you. Don't go getting the wrong idea."

"I know that. I get it. But yeah. I mean, yes, please. I'd like another piece."

"And then you go get your stuff put away in your room. We can go back to the house and bring over anything else you want. We'll do that tomorrow, after church. Coravelle's at the library now, studying with her friends, but she'll be home in a bit. Dinner's at 6:00. You be at the table with your hands washed. Hear me?"

Coralene didn't wait for Tanner's answer. She got up and pushed in her chair. "No more pie for me, baby. I've got to get some laundry done." Coralene stood behind Tanner and rested her hands on his shoulders. "We love you. You know that, right? You're family. You belong here." She leaned down to kiss his neck. "Now, when you're done with that plate, you wash it up. Do your uncle's plate too. And mine. Don't go leaving dishes in the sink for someone else to do."

PART THREE

"Don't rock the boat. If you play it safe, life will be easier. There will be fewer chances that you'll make a mistake or ruffle feathers. Those are things you don't want to do."

Evelyn Raymond
1891-1975

MEMO

TO: Nutrition Services Employees
FROM: Gordon Hund, Nutrition Services Manager
DATE: Monday, May 3, 1976
RE: Bicentennial Celebration: plan presenta-
             tions, and other topics of interest

Ladies: Per my Friday memo, in this morning's meeting we will discuss the plans you were directed to develop regarding participation of the elementary schools, junior high schools, and high schools in the parade festivities on Sunday, July 4,¹1976. Each plan must identify ordering requirements, delivery and distribution parameters, and plans for student participation, if any.

In the interest of a logical sequence, Miss Carmichael will present first and describe what will be produced by the Nutrition Services employees at Alicia Park, Hastings, and Prescott Elementary Schools to further the celebration of this important holiday.

Following Miss Carmichael's proposal, Mrs. Johnson will describe her plan for the food to be produced by F. Scott Fitzgerald and Sinclair Lewis Junior High Schools, and presented on Independence Day.

Upon completion of Mrs. Johnson's presentation, Miss Raymond will explain how Nutrition Services employees at the school district's two high schools,

Norlin Hanley and Lake Sylvester, will contribute to the upcoming bicentennial celebration.

On the heels of his exemplary performance in the bi-county competition in April, Napoleon has been invited to compete for best in breed at the upcoming regional Dogstravaganza, which comprises four counties and which will be held, once again, at the Wescott County Community Center this coming Saturday, May 8, 1976 at 1:00 PM. Tickets are still available.

CHAPTER THIRTEEN

Crystal

Monday, May 3, 1976

CRYSTAL SAT ALONE on the park bench eating her lunch. Today, solitude did not equate with silence. Teenage boys who should be in school had ditched classes to play touch football in the midday sun. Their shouts accompanied the whistle of a freight train as it crossed the railroad bridge into Wisconsin.

Hanley was in full bloom. Battalions of daffodils lined the path above the river, and young green leaves on the maples were mirrored in the expanse of new spring grass.

Crystal had left her coat on the rack by her desk and braved the breezes of spring with only her gray wool sweater, which spread comfortably across her broad shoulders and hung long to cover her similarly broad backside. The absence of other people on her bench was an unexpected pleasure. Crystal preferred solitude as a matter of course, but particularly when she needed a good think, which was the case today. She had this morning's staff meeting to chew over, and she needed to ponder a match for Patricia (Patsy) Louise (nee Tolofson) Davies.

Crystal's suggestion for the elementary schools' contribution to the big whoop-ta-do had been well received, all in all. As it should be. It was a good idea. The credit went to Ada, but there'd been no reason to mention that this morning. Those people don't know Ada. Why add to the cast list?

Gordon had proclaimed via memo that he wanted to start the discussion with the elementary schools, so Crystal had presented first. Coralene and Sheila had listened as if they were genuinely interested, which perhaps they were. They were good eggs, for the most part. But Gordon was a mosquito. Crystal would be as happy as a dry-diapered baby when July 5th came around and Gordon found something else to buzz about.

~ ~ ~

Crystal had been sure Ada would enjoy a snootful of Fourth of July festivities, seeing as how she was new to the neighborhood and all. No doubt she'd love that type of thing, perky little gal that she was. So Crystal had posed her question last Wednesday at the laundromat.

"Have to make my boss happy. Have to be a good egg with my co-workers. Any ideas on how to include elementary school kitchens in the big whoop-ta-do Fourth of July parade?"

Ada's face had balled up like a fist in a mitten.

"This is what I do all day, you know," Crystal had

reminded her. "Make sure the trains are on the tracks for the elementary school kitchens. Choo, choo! Got three elementary schools altogether. I was a cook at one of them for years, then I got a promotion. What a surprise that was. Now I'm out of the school and looking down on those kitchens from on high. Someday someone in a big office is going to figure out they made a mistake putting me in charge, but until then, I like my office job." Crystal intertwined her fingers at the back of her neck and spread her elbows as if leaning back in a desk chair. "It's because of the bicentennial. That's the only reason we're taking school food out to the masses."

Typically, Crystal was on the listening end of conversations with Ada, across any number of Ada's favorite topics: her grandchildren, her late husband, Joey, all the friends she'd left behind in Fergus Falls. Ada had even told Crystal about Baxter, the beagle that had lived until all Ada's children were old enough to take the school bus. Ada had loved that dog; she had no similar affinity for cats. Crystal had expected that Ada would be off to the races with ideas for the parade. She wasn't disappointed.

"It's simple," Ada'd said. "Cookies. Have your lunch ladies make cookies. Lots of 'em. More cookies than they've ever made before."

"All the same?"

"Nah, people like variety. Maybe one kind from each school. How many schools are there again?"

"Three."

"Perfect." Ada had flashed a grin, showing the gap where one of her top back teeth was missing. "That's just perfect." She'd paused before making her pronouncement: "Chocolate chip cookies. Sugar cookies. Oatmeal cookies. Maybe throw some raisins into the oatmeal ones. Kids like raisins."

"That could work. I could have those maintenance guys set up a table. Maybe at the beginning of the parade route. Stack the cookies on the table. Easy enough. I wouldn't have to do a thing."

"Nah," Ada had said again. "That's no fun."

"Huh?"

"That's no fun," Ada repeated. "It's a parade. It should be fun." Her eyes had sparkled from the pure joy of discussing cookies. "You don't want to stack them on a table. Then you'd have a big crowd, all wanting cookies. Getting in the way of the floats and such. Nah, don't do that. Let the kids pass them out."

"Huh?"

"Let the kids pass them out," Ada had said loudly, as if Crystal's hearing was causing trouble. "Maybe one kid from each grade at each school? Or maybe two? Or, wait. I know!" Ada's enthusiasm had bubbled over like an untended pot. "Let the kids walk alongside the floats and marching bands and stuff. Then they can go up to the folks on the parade route. Hand them a cookie. You know, like sometimes people throw candy at parades? But your kids? They'd be passing out cookies. Folks would love it. It's a sweet idea. All those cute little kids with their bags of cookies."

Crystal could picture those very kids proudly handing out cookies. They were Crystal's kids, after all. Making them happy was more important to her than she cared to admit. "Well, there we go," she'd said to Ada. "You want to help? On parade day? Be my cookie lieutenant? You're good at this."

Ada beamed. "Well, sure! I can help. Sure thing. I have to be good at this stuff. I have six kids. Fourteen grandkids. And one more on the way. Did I tell you? We'll have another one showing up pretty soon. Probably in time for Halloween. Another little pumpkin." Ada had laughed at her own joke.

~ ~ ~

"Costs will be low," Crystal told the others this morning. "Butter, flour, and sugar. Eggs, milk, and oatmeal. Raisins and chocolate chips." Swiping her hands against each other, Crystal accentuated the simplicity of her plan and the completion of her presentation.

Coralene had asked how Crystal would choose which children would hand out the cookies. "They'll all want to do that, wouldn't you think? You wouldn't want arguments, but then again, you wouldn't need every student to participate."

Ada had had a suggestion for this too, which Crystal explained as if that idea had also been hers. "We'll do a contest," Crystal had said. "The kids will come up with a project. Something that's about the Fourth of July. They can do it in June. Before school gets out. Youngest kids can draw pictures. The older ones? Fifth- and sixth-graders maybe? They can write something. A story maybe, or a poem. Then the lunch lady at each school will pick the best ones from each grade, and those'll be the kids who get to walk in the parade and hand out the cookies. They'll think that's pretty swell," Crystal had said with authority. "They'll be doing a school job, after school gets out. And on a Sunday, no less."

Crystal had brushed her hands against each other for a second time and reached for her coffee cup. As an afterthought, she'd peered in at Gordon in his cramped closet office. He was hard to see in there.

"You've put some real thought into this, Crystal." Coralene had offered a lips-only smile. "I think you've got us off to a good start. A very good start."

Sheila had mustered what Crystal took as an approving expression. "Good," Sheila'd said before the discussion moved on to Coralene's idea. Something about a garage and some relish. Gordon had offered no comments. *There's just no horn on his tugboat*, Crystal thought.

The onset of spring had inspired Crystal to make a change to her daily lunch. A tuna sandwich and an orange would be just the ticket through the end of the school year. When she finished eating, she wrapped the orange peel in the waxed paper with the crusts from her sandwich and put them back into her lunch bag before jamming the bag into her purse. Closing her eyes and raising her face to the sun, it was time to turn her attention to Patsy Davies, from yesterday's obituary page:

Patricia (Patsy) Louise (nee Tolofson) Davies. Beloved wife of Eugene Davies. Mother to Jeffrey Davies (Angela), Bruce Davies (Priscilla), Lester Davies (Anne Marie), Doreen Wolfson (Arthur), and Carol Davies. Grandmother to Bruce, Mark, Steven, and Keith Davies, and Benjamin and Erica Wolfson. Great-grandmother to Greta Davies and Patricia Wolfson. Patsy was born in Minneapolis on June 11, 1901. Patsy and Eugene met in high school and were married on April 22, 1919. Patsy loved her friends, her family, and her church. Her favorite holidays were Christmas and the Fourth of July. Every Christmas Eve, Patsy gathered her family for lefse, ham and Christmas cookies. Patsy's krumkake were a showstopper. We wish she was going to be with us for the bicentennial parade. We love you, Mom. We love you, Grandma. We love you, Great-Granny. A graveside service will be held on Saturday, May 9th followed by a reception at Gethsemane Lutheran Church. All are welcome.

There were only five minutes left on her lunch break, and no one in the park looked like a match for Patsy. This would have to wait. Patsy needed a family man. An older family man. Or a nice, old, retired gal. A friend-type gal whom Patsy might have known from some guild or other. Crystal's grandmother belonged to a guild. There were tons of them, ten or twenty at the hospital alone. Guilds were not for Crystal. Too many old ladies sitting around talking. Swat that fly dead.

CHAPTER FOURTEEN

CORALENE
MONDAY, MAY 3, 1976

"WHAT DID THE other gals think of our idea?" Jasper pressed a kiss against Coralene's cheek. It was a beautiful day; Jasper had walked to the bus stop in his shirtsleeves. This morning, Coralene had inaugurated the spring pantsuit Jasper had given her for Christmas. It had a long five-button vest that hit at her knees, under which she wore a white blouse, its big bow cradling her chin like a beloved aunt. The pants were flared and fit like a modest second skin. The suit was an attention-grabber, in a shade of green that was a dead ringer for lime sherbet.

"Seemed to think it was a fine idea," Coralene said, as they turned toward home. "Those two can be tough to read, but yes, I think they'd say it's a fine idea."

"You're lucky," Jasper said, "that your old junior high's right there on Cedar Avenue and Center. Right at the end of the parade route. It'll be easy as pie for folks to wander over for a hot dog. And easy as pie to keep churning those dogs out from the school kitchen."

"My cooks? Jan and Peg? Don't know them very well, but I'm sure they'll be okay. They agreed to tend the hot dog pot for as long as I need them."

"And the pièce de résistance?" Jasper asked. "Was that a home run?"

"Of course, baby," Coralene said, squeezing his hand as they rounded the final corner to home. "No doubt about it. That's what'll draw the crowds to the junior high school's hot dog stand."

~ ~ ~

"Good chili, Daddy," Coravelle had said at the dinner table.

Two Saturdays prior, Coralene had insisted that the family eat together to discuss the Fourth of July parade. Gordon had been fretting for months, memo after memo emerging from the supply closet. With help from Jasper, Coravelle, and Tanner, Coralene intended to pull the junior high school's menu together in under an hour. Enough food fussing. But there was still the float to think about.

"Yeah, it is, Uncle J." Tanner had tapped his spoon against his empty chili bowl. "Your chili is outta sight. Your cornbread too."

"Too bad I can't get cooking like this figured out for the parade," Coralene had said. She'd taken the last piece of cornbread and held it over her bowl as she drizzled honey. "But I don't see how we'd be passing out chili to hundreds of people. Don't see how we'd do hot food at all. Any of y'all have ideas for me? I want something simple. No need to make this as complicated as my boss seems to think it is. But I don't want to disappoint folks either. I need a good plan."

"Right on." Tanner had looked with disappointment at the empty cornbread plate. "You need something folks will scarf down. Same way we do with Uncle J's food."

"Cut some more, son," Jasper had said, catching Tanner's expression. "Bring some more over to the table."

Tanner returned to the table with the refilled cornbread plate. "All your food is outta sight," he'd repeated. "Like Auntie C says, we don't want folks to be disappointed."

Coralene caught Jasper's eye; both were enjoying Tanner's slang. Coralene tried to keep a lid on her unease about Tanner. After all, he'd started as an apprentice carpenter last week, working for someone Jasper had heard about at the post office. Tanner was good with his hands. He could learn to be an excellent carpenter, if he paid attention.

"What we should do is figure out some way to let Daddy cook something here." Coravelle had interrupted Coralene's thoughts. "Then we could drive the food over that morning."

"Hold on a minute, now." Jasper had leaned back in his chair, arms folded over his flat stomach. "I'm not running a catering service. No way on that." He'd looked across the table at Coralene. "Sorry, Cory. But…"

"No, baby. That you are not. That's not your responsibility. I think your daughter just wants to figure out a way to share your culinary talents with the good people of Hanley. Isn't that right?"

Coravelle beamed at Jasper. "That's right, Daddy. I'm not trying to put you to work, it's just that what you make tastes soooo good!"

Jasper clasped Coravelle's hand. "I'll take that compliment, Velly," he said. "I'll take it. But I won't be cooking for a bunch of parade-goers."

Tanner put his forearms on the table and leaned in; he'd eaten two more pieces of cornbread but had yet to wipe the crumbs from his mouth. Jasper reached for the last of the squares, leaving the plate empty again.

"I know you don't want to cook, Uncle J," Tanner said, wiping away crumbs with the back of his hand. "But what about some of that food you've already got? There are lots of jars on the shelves in the garage. A ton of 'em. Anything there parade folks could eat? Get a little taste of Jasper Johnson, without him having to cook?"

Jasper had weighed Tanner's idea before saying, "Come on out to the garage with me, son. Let's see what we've got out there. Lots of green beans. Some canned cherries. But nothing I can think of that would feed a crowd. But I appreciate you putting some thought to it. Let's go look."

Coralene and Coravelle were clearing the table when Jasper and Tanner returned. "Tanner's got an idea," Jasper had said, his eyes showing as much pride as if the idea had been his own. "Tell 'em, son."

Tanner had puffed up and grinned. "Well, I was thinking that since the school kitchen is close by, like you said, that maybe y'all could serve hot dogs. Just plain ones, you know, in buns. But plain. Then people could put what they want on 'em. You know, mustard and ketchup and stuff."

Coravelle had continued at the table, but Coralene had stopped to give Tanner her full attention, confused as to what this had to do with stockpiled food in the garage.

"Tell them what could go on those dogs," Jasper had prodded. "Tell them what you thought of."

"So. I was thinking in addition to the ketchup and mustard, maybe you could put out some of Uncle J's corn relish. That's real good, that relish. Real good. Especially on a hot dog." Tanner had assumed an officious pose. "A tasty addition to any hot dog," he'd said with a grandiose gesture.

Jasper let loose with a guffaw. "You're crazy, son," he'd said. "You're right, but you're crazy." Jasper turned toward Coravelle. "Velly, what do you think? Could be a good way to use up some of that relish. There's no end of jars out there. I overdid it on the corn relish last summer. Whatcha say? Not that everyone would put it on their hot dogs – fools that they might be – but it'd be there and the folks who tried it would be glad they did."

Coravelle had taken a swipe at the cornbread crumbs still on the table, catching them in her palm. "Alright. I'll admit it," she'd said, as she stood up straight to look at her parents and cousin. "It is a good idea, even if it came from him." She'd kicked Tanner's shoe.

"It a great idea, sweetheart," Coralene told Tanner. "I'll go with that. We'll call it good. Now we can be done thinking about the food." Coralene leaned against the counter, watching as Coravelle finished cleaning up. "We have another project, you know. We don't have to talk about it right this minute, but you two have to figure it out soon. Remember? Grammy volunteered you and Uncle Jasper to build the float for her hospital guild. It's going to have to accommodate the six ladies who want to ride on it. I hear they'll be waving their craft projects in the air for all to see. I talked to Mr. Berry, the janitor at Fitzgerald. He said you could borrow the school district's riding mower. The one they use to cut the grass in the ball fields. Now you two gotta figure out how that mower can pull a bunch of old ladies down Center Street."

~ ~ ~

Coralene suspected that Gordon was disappointed in the simplicity of it all: Crystal's cookies, Coralene's hot dogs, and even Sheila's idea – which would take more work, but could certainly be done. Gordon seemed to have a grander vision for how Nutrition Services would contribute to Hanley's Fourth of July celebration, as if someone, somewhere, was nudging him along. Coralene had no idea who that was, or what the vision might be.

She'd presented her hot dog plan without fanfare; fanfare wasn't Coralene's cup of tea. The head cooks from Sinclair and Fitzgerald would use the Fitzgerald Junior High kitchen to turn out boiled hot dogs by the hundreds and slip them inside buns. Student volunteers would be runners, bringing platters of dogs in buns out to a table in the school parking lot at the intersection with Cedar Avenue, where the parade would end. Coralene's family and a few students would wrap hot dogs in napkins, garnish with the requested condiments, and distribute to parade-goers with a smile.

"Nothing to it," Coralene had told the others at their staff meeting. "Hot dogs and buns. Ketchup and mustard. Napkins." These would be the only expenses. There would be no fee, she'd explained, for Jasper's corn relish.

CHAPTER FIFTEEN

SHEILA

MONDAY, MAY 3, 1976

ONCE GORDON RETURNED the craft table to its spot under the windows, Sheila had given no more thought to the staff meeting. Because truly, what was there to discuss? It was one event, two months away, in the hands of three capable women.

"Lettuce," Sheila had told the group, after Coralene explained her hot dog plan. "Lettuce, hamburger meat, cheddar cheese, and packets of taco seasoning. And some Fritos. That's it."

~ ~ ~

Sheila had held out for weeks before agreeing to have dinner with Tom Downlane; it was an asinine idea. But by mid-April, she'd given in.

Tom's enthusiasm had been immediately off-putting. He'd erupted with a cheery "Hooray!" when Sheila arrived and slid like an otter out of the booth, reaching for her coat as she took it off.

"I've got it," she said, rolling the coat into a ball and sliding in across from Tom.

"Can't I hang that up for ya?"

"No. It's fine." Sheila slid into the booth, shoving the coat onto her lap, and wrapping her arms around the bundle as if embracing a lap dog. "It's fine," she said again, intent on leaving no questions unanswered as to the disposition of her coat.

"This is grand!" Tom, still standing, extended both hands dramatically toward Sheila, then pivoting, splayed his hands toward his own seat. "How about this? Having dinner together. It's just dandy." He'd worn a blue collared shirt and darker blue cardigan, and, Sheilia had noticed when he'd greeted her, a belt. Sitting back down, Tom shifted cheerfully, as if finding himself with a front-row view of the first-base line. "Nice to see you again. Have dinner together and such. But I hope you don't want to share my French fries. I draw the line there," he chuckled. "Some things are just wrong."

What? French fries? What?

Picking up the menu, Tom flipped it front and back, then put it back down. "Not a lot of deliberating this evening," he said. "I'm going with your basic cheeseburger. Can't go wrong there. You ever tried their cheeseburger? It's a dandy. One of those big ones, couple of patties on a big bun, you know? Big slab of a tomato. No wimpy burger like you'd find at a drive-in. What say you? Join me in a burger?"

He was noisy. Too, too noisy. When he stopped speaking, a comforting Denny's buzz hovered, but each time he opened his mouth, Sheila felt cornered into a conversation in which she wanted no part.

"I've tried nearly every burger they've got, at one time or another," Tom said, "except the patty melt. Never took a shine to rye bread. It's the little seeds. Always getting stuck in my teeth. I avoid Reubens too, but no great loss there. Can't say that corned beef's a favorite. Something my mother used to cook. Didn't like it then, don't like it now. Although if you like a patty melt or a Reuben, I won't hold it against you." Tom grinned and took a drink from his water glass, leaving an opening for Sheila to speak. She didn't. "So, Ms. Raymond," Tom said bravely, putting his glass down, "whatcha gonna have for dinner?"

Oh no. He didn't really say Ms. did he? Should she chastise him for using a term that had become such a fad? *Miss* or *Mrs.* Both do the job. No one needs a third choice. But opening that discussion didn't interest her. If she was going to make it through this meal, she needed to keep to the basics. Small talk. Order dinner. More small talk. Eat. Wrap up small talk. Go home.

"I like patty melts," Sheila said. "That's what I'm going to order. I trust you won't mind sitting across the table from rye bread? And I'll skip the French fries and have a salad." These last words came as a surprise, but once uttered, Sheila was stuck.

"Good grief, no!" Tom exclaimed, relieved that Sheila had finally spoken. "Happy to share my table with rye bread, just not my plate. But no fries? I question the wisdom of that decision. You sure? Who passes up Denny's French fries on a Saturday night?"

"Clearly, I do."

"Well, suit yourself," Tom said good-naturedly. "It's a free country." He gave Sheila a grin, which she didn't return.

"What'll it be, friends?" Lexie returned to their table as Sheila laid down her menu.

How could Lexie act as if this made sense? Sitting here with Tom? This was a concession she'd made for one reason, and one reason alone: Lexie. Gratitude should be evident, perhaps even admiration that Sheila hadn't already made a dash to the door.

"You first," Lexie said, her attention on Sheila. "You going to keep going with Treasures of the Sea or take your dinner in a whole new direction?"

Sheila cringed. Tom needn't be privy to her dining habits. Let's not share details that aren't relevant.

"Patty melt, please," Sheila had said. "With a side salad."

"Sounds good. A little extra cheese on that?"

Had Lexie winked? Since when did she do that? "Yes, please," Sheila said. She couldn't be expected to resist every good thing, not if she was skipping the fries.

"Dressing?"

"French. On the side."

"I'll be getting that right out." Lexie had turned to Tom with a giggle. "And you, sir?"

Tom hefted the conversational load, nattering on about the varied and sundry plumbing issues at the schools. He queried about colleagues or acquaintances he and Sheila might share before giving that up as a conversational dead-end. It was when he started talking about retirement that Sheila's interest piqued, just as Lexie arrived with their meals.

Tom's cheeseburger was taller than any Sheila had ever been served. Too tall to comfortably bite. Huge. Not one, but two tomato slices teetered atop not one, but two hamburger patties. Goopy American cheese oozed from under the top bun like rubbery orange lava. No lettuce was visible, but Sheila saw several pickle chips peeking out. Two pickle spears, still damp with juice, were nestled among the French fries which struggled for space on Tom's burger-laden plate.

The sight of Tom's burger gave Sheila pause. Was he receiving special treatment? Jealousy twinged her upper lip, until she looked down at her own plate. Her rye bread was crisp, but still soft enough to wrap around the ample burger. The mouthwatering smell of grilled onions wafted off the plate; a few dangled over the edge of the bread, but most were secured under two thick slices of Swiss cheese. There were no pickle spears. Of course there weren't, Sheila didn't like pickle spears. They made French fries soggy. Instead, Sheila counted six crisp fries tucked under the protective warmth of her toasted rye.

"Anything else I can get you two?" Lexie set down the salad plate and surveyed the scene, as if Sheila, Tom, and every burger and condiment were a personal achievement.

"No, my dear," Tom said. "You've done it again. I'm a happy man right now, a happy man."

Sheila's gaze went to her rogue fries before she looked up at Lexie. "Thank you," she said. "This is perfect."

"Remarkable young woman," Tom mused after Lexie left the table. "One in a million, wouldn't you say?"

"I would." Sheila wanted to endorse all that was exemplary about Lexie but was loath to share her with Tom.

Tom beheld his dinner plate gleefully and tucked a paper napkin under his chin. "Pickle juice," he said. "I love pickle juice. I like the way the hot fries soak it up. Then I add some salt, a splash or two of ketchup, and it's the perfect side dish." Tom paused before erupting with a foghorn of a laugh. "I shouldn't say such things to a cook! Now I'm embarrassed. A side dish? Should've kept that one to myself, given the company I'm in."

"You like what you like," Sheila heard herself say. "We all do. Nothing wrong with that. We've earned the right."

"So I'm guessing I'd be off base if I offered you one of my pickle spears, seeing as you don't have any and I have two."

"You would be off base."

"Means my French fries are safe too, doesn't it?"

"It does." Sheila stealthily rotated her plate so that her own six fries were hidden from view.

A few bites into her salad, Sheila put down her fork. "Retirement," she said. "How much paperwork is involved? Much lead time? Good information available from the school district?"

Sheila suspected Tom's conversational engine would rev at the subject. Her opening questions would allow her to eat in peace, avoiding additional tête-à-tête. She cupped a fry in her hand before reaching for her patty melt.

"It's a pretty slick process." Tom pounced on the topic. "You just talk to one of the gals in the Personnel Department. I'm fond of Mary Ann; she's worked in Personnel since Hector was a pup. We had dinner a few times, me and Mary Ann. Or Ruth, she's the other gal there. One of 'em will stick some papers in the mail for ya. No muss, no fuss. I filled out everything at home in less than an hour, dropped my papers back in person a few days later. Sure enough, Personnel was having a retirement party themselves that day. Mary Ann's leaving. I stuck around for a piece of sheet cake and a cup of punch. They like to do parties for folks who've worked for the schools for a long time. You'd be in that camp, for sure. So would I, and I say, bring on the cake!" Tom looked knowingly at Sheila, revealing an awareness for which she'd yet to give him credit. "Something tells me you would say 'no thank you' to a party. Am I right?"

"You are right."

"To each his own. That's what I always say. To each his own."

Taking slow bites off her patty melt, Sheila watched Tom wedge the mile-high burger into his mouth. He'd had some experience with this.

"You were looking forward to dinner with your grandson last time I saw you." Once again, Sheila was startled by a statement that seemed to leave her mouth before it had been fully formed in her mind. "He's a dentist, as I remember."

Tom raised his eyebrows playfully and put down the juice-laden French fry he'd been about to pop into his mouth. "Good memory," he said. "Yep, I had a nice dinner with my grandson. We went to the new Mexican place over on Ramsey Avenue, just off Center. Had a real good time. Good dinner too, which was a bit of a surprise."

Tom left Sheila an opening, which she had no desire to pursue. Her patty melt was nearly gone, along with her six fries, and all the salad she intended to eat. Tom could carry the water on this one. If she said nothing, Sheila knew he'd keep talking. It was his grandson, for God's sake. Reliable conversation fodder.

Sure enough, Tom dived right in. "I'm proud of that boy," he said. "He's headed down to Central America, going to do some volunteer dentistry. I didn't know there was such a thing, but evidently, there is."

"Has he left already?" Sheila asked, surprising herself yet again.

"Nope. He wants to stick around Hanley for the bicentennial. He has friends here. But then I have no idea when I'll see him again." Tom had eaten his last fry and talked around it in a way Sheila found distasteful. "This bicentennial is going to be quite the celebration. The whole darn country. Big doings everywhere. Philadelphia for sure. DC. New York'll probably do it up big. Everywhere!"

Sheila was relieved that Tom didn't prattle on about celebration sites in all fifty states.

"We'll even be doing it up in Hanley," Tom continued. "When I was over in Personnel, like I was telling you, well, Mary Ann told me that there'll be a big parade, right down Center Street. Fireworks too. Well, and…" Tom stopped talking so suddenly it made Sheila's ears ring. "Now wait a minute," he said. Leaning back, he put his hands dramatically on his hips. "You know all this! Mary Ann said the schools are going to participate. Said there'll be food tables. Not sure what that's all about, but I just now put two and two together. Is she right? Mary Ann can go off a bit half-cocked." Leaning his forearms on the table, Tom focused intently on Sheila. "It's your turn. Do tell, Ms. Raymond, what's the story? You going to be cooking for the whole town?"

Sheila felt as if she'd been slapped senseless. Such an assault. Taking a deep breath and putting aside the whole "Ms." thing, yet again, she tried to shape an answer that would satisfy Tom's curiosity without tedium, and without revealing that she had no idea what the high school cafeterias would do on parade day. She needed to figure this out soon, or she'd end up annoying Crystal and disappointing Coralene. Worse, she'd look the fool, which was something Sheila Raymond did not do.

"Soooo?" Tom stretched the question. "What are the high schools going to put out that day?" He was as fixated as a Labrador Retriever on a dead duck. "Seems a bit of a stretch, if you ask me, which I know you didn't, but trying to feed parade-goers? My guess is they'll want popcorn and peanuts. And all that candy that gets thrown around. Folks don't go to a parade for a meal, do they? Maybe I'm dense."

He'd hit the nail on the head. This school food at a parade idea was dumb. No better word for it.

"You got some good gals to help you though." Tom quickly stepped back into his role as cheerleader. "I know Ms. Green, the one who took your place? She's a gem." He tried again to engage Sheila with a smile, his elbows still on the table. "So, what'll it be? What will the high schools be offering the lovely citizens of Hanley on parade day?"

More than any moment since she'd first sat down, Sheila wanted to be gone. Into her coat. Out to her car. On her way home. The evening was already grueling. So who the hell cared if she told Tom Downlane that she had no plan? Who would he tell? Who was he in the scheme of things? Maybe she should just retire quickly and skip the whole silly mess.

"No idea," Sheila said. "But I'll figure it out.

"Want a suggestion?"

Oh good God, he hadn't really asked that, had he? No. No she did not want a suggestion. She wanted to go home. She wanted him to stop talking. She wanted his nose and everyone else's out of her business. "No. I'll figure it out. It's my job."

"Oh, I know. It's that, well, maybe I'm still a little too enthusiastic."

"About?"

"I started to tell you a bit ago, then got distracted. The Mexican place." Tom paused as if that answered all pending questions. "The Mexican place? Where my grandson and I went? His name's Brian. My grandson, that is. He's my daughter Susan's boy."

He could not possibly have seen encouragement in Sheila's face, but Tom continued, undaunted. "Brian had been there with his buddies. To the Mexican place. He's kind of a health nut. Likes granola, that type of thing. Grinds his own peanut butter. He puts on tennis shoes and runs down by the river. Doesn't walk, nope. Doesn't take in the sights, nope. He runs, as if someone's chasing him. It's the damnedest thing. Anyway, he said we could go to the Mexican place because they have healthy Mexican food. I had to be careful. Couldn't say 'Who wants healthy Mexican food?,' now could I?" Tom smirked. His banter seemed to be gaining speed. "I just went along, and you'll never guess what we ordered. It was a salad. At a Mexican place. An actual Mexican salad. Brian called it a taco salad; he says it's quite the craze. Lettuce on the bottom, then meat, and cheese. They sprinkled a few corn chips on top, and, like I said, I'll be damned. They called it dinner. Thing was, it was good. Real good.

"Sorry if I'm carrying on, but maybe you could do something like that? The folks in Hanley would be surprised. Who eats healthy around here? Well, except my grandson. The Mexican place might even help you out. They had some kind of spicy chopped tomatoes that they put on top. 'Salsa,' Brian called it. Don't know if you can buy something like that. Maybe they'd give you some. I could ask them. Once you dished out salads at the parade, folks would be dashing over to the Mexican place to have them again.

"I'm talking too much, aren't I? Silly to get excited about a salad, but if you have to eat lettuce – and Brian says I do – it was nice to have it with some meat and cheese. It might be a hit at the parade. Wish Denny's would put it on the menu, but I don't see that happening any time soon. Just had to tell you about it. It might be a hit."

Tom's Mexican salad ambush left Sheila reeling, as if he'd been tossing verbal pebbles against a window. Rock against glass, rock against glass, rock against glass, each less welcome than the one before.

Lexie delivered Sheila's pie and Tom's sundae so slyly that Sheila had thanked her and begun eating, before realizing that neither dessert had been ordered. Now she'd had enough. This little dessert trick was the capper. When Lexie returned with coffee, Sheila declined, slid out of the booth, and unrolled her coat.

Tom, a smidge of hot fudge on his chin, scooted off his bench. "Give me half a second and I'll walk you out," he said.

But Sheila was done. Fatigue with the whole mess had struck hard and fast.

"Thank you for dinner. It wasn't necessary for you to pay."

Tom tried to grin, but Sheila's abrupt departure was taking him by surprise. "Happy to do it," he said. "Glad you could make it. Let's do it again some time."

A slow-rising heat was reddening Sheila's neck and face. This was not where she wanted to be anymore. She hadn't wanted to be here at all, of course. But now, she needed to be gone. Dinners such as these? They were not what she did. They were not what she wanted to do. Certainly not a second time. It was impossible to avoid Tom helping her into her coat, but once done, she gripped her handbag and stuffed her other hand in her pocket.

"Good night," she said.

Tom stood next to the table with his sundae spoon still in his hand, dripping ice cream onto his pants. As Sheila reached the door, Tom called out, "I'll check on that salsa for ya." Shaking his head, he hiked up his pants and turned away as Lexie came to stand beside him.

"Her sad runs deep, don't it?" Tom said.

"Yes, it runs very deep."

"Know why?"

"Not really. Does it matter?"

"Nope. Nope, it doesn't. It's different for everyone, certainly by the time you get to our age. No one's immune."

"I think that might be the part she forgets."

Looking down at his pants, Tom let out a groan. Using

a crumpled napkin, he wiped off the ice cream and slid back into the booth.

"More coffee?" Lexie asked.

"Nah, I'm about to slosh over."

"How about another cup of hot fudge? You've got a little ice cream left."

"Now you're talking." As Lexie returned to the kitchen, Tom settled back against the booth, intertwining his fingers at the back of his neck, and closing his eyes.

~ ~ ~

He had been here before: left behind in a car, on a bench, or in some restaurant booth somewhere. Of all the rebuffs he'd accrued, Susan's still carried the most sting.

"You don't understand, Dad," Susan had said, more than half a lifetime ago. Her eyes had brimmed with tears poised to fall. "It's not like I can just stick around here. What's the point? There's no one here for me anymore. Now that Mom's moved and the other kids have gone with her, there's no one here for me."

"I'm here for you." Tom had released the words cautiously, as if gently turning on a tap to give the water time to warm. No deluge. No splash. Just the comfort of warm water. "I'm here for you," he'd said again.

"But you're not. You weren't." Susan had shot the words back at him, each with barbs that could've broken the skin. "You moved out. You left. You left the four of us with Mom. Didn't even ask if we wanted to go with you. Didn't ask anything. You just left."

Sitting at the diner on that long-gone afternoon, Tom

had been loath to walk his daughter back across this well-trod ground. It seemed that none of them had forgiven him. Neither did any have a clue about what had really happened.

He'd suggested to their mother that she be the one to leave. That he be the one to wrangle four children. That he stay in the home he'd worked for. The home he'd bought for them, courtesy of untold hours of rust and muck, and an inescapable damp chill that clung to him twenty-four hours a day.

"It wasn't what I wanted," he'd reminded Susan gently. "You know it wasn't what I wanted." But he would not drag her back through the brambles of her parents' divorce. Through the confusion and misery that had come from her mother's infidelity. He wouldn't do it. Not to his child.

"I was thirteen, Dad. I was thirteen years old. I might've been the oldest, but I was still young. And Mom? She was young too. With four kids! I know we've talked about this before. I know you're not going to take responsibility. But it was hard, Dad. It was fucking hard. If it hadn't been for Will marrying Mom, I don't know what we would've done."

That was the tune they'd all learned to sing: *Thank God Will Came Along.* Tom had known they needed to love their mother. Needed to respect her. So he'd never told them. Never told them exactly when wonderful Will had first appeared. Freshly home from the war, Will had snatched Tom's family. The beautiful mother. The four beautiful children. Will had seen them down by the river one spring day in 1946 and made it his mission to have them. To steal them. No need to make his own, just take a family that belonged to someone else. The family that had belonged to Tom.

"Susie, I can only tell you what's true," Tom had said.

"I did not want to leave. I tried to see you guys. All of you. Your mom made most of those choices. And I did my best to do right by you."

"My name is Susan," she'd spit out. "I'm eighteen years old. My name is Susan. And it seems to me you're doing alright. You've got a new wife now, maybe you'll have four more kids to replace the ones you left."

"Your mom had married Will long before I met Betty. The one has nothing to do with the other."

"I don't know what to believe from you, Dad. I still shake my head about it all. We had so much fun when we were little, and then you were just gone. Thank goodness Will came along."

That again. Tom had caught Susan's gaze and held it. "Where are you headed?" he'd asked.

"I have a friend from school who lives in Minneapolis." Susan paused, and her voice softened. "My friend, Carrie. She works at a restaurant up there. It's a busy place, right in downtown. Lots of people around. Businessmen. She got me a waitress job. Her roommate moved out a month ago, so I'll move in and we'll share the apartment."

"Maybe I could come up and visit you someday. I could order up a burger and fries. Would that be okay? To come see you, I mean? I know you've been angry with me. For years. But I'll always be here, Susie. Susan. I'll always be here if you need anything."

Tom had watched as his firstborn twisted a paper napkin around and around her forefinger. Finally, she'd let her tears flow. Her jaw was set so tight. How could she cry and still keep her jaw so tight? Minutes had passed as Tom said nothing. Not daring to reach for her hand, he nonetheless had leaned toward her and waited.

"I'm just still so mad about it all, Dad," Susan had said finally, no longer meeting his eyes.

"I know, love. Me too. I'm sorry that you're mad, that you've been hurt. Sorrier than you'll ever know, at least until you have kids of your own."

"I find that kind of hard to believe."

"It's true. If you believe nothing else from me, believe that. When your kids are hurting, you hurt worse. When they cry, you cry harder. It might not look the same, but it is. I'm here Susan Marie Downlane. I'm here for you; I always have been."

"I need to go."

"Can I drive you to the bus station? Or just drive you up to Minneapolis?"

"No. No thank you. I'll do it on my own."

Tom had handed Susan the cash he'd put in his wallet. He wouldn't tell Betty how he'd spent the $100 they'd planned to put toward a second car. He'd find a way to make it up to her.

PART FOUR

"Sometimes people want other people to be different than the people they really are. That rarely turns out well."

ROGER SQUIRREL

1915-1976

MEMO

TO: Nutrition Services Employees
FROM: Gordon Hund, Nutrition Services Manager
DATE: Friday, June 11, 1976
RE: Bicentennial Celebration implementation
          updates, inappropriate reference, and
          other topics of interest

Ladies: Once again, I have been pleased to overhear discussions indicating that details for implementation of Nutrition Services' three parade food tables are coalescing. At Monday's meeting, each of you will be asked to provide an update, including evidence that ordering is in process or has been completed.

Be prepared to discuss the participation of the cooks who currently have responsibilities at the building level. All cooks who you each supervise directly should attend and contribute to the Hanley Bicentennial Parade, on behalf of the Hanley School District.

Please note that the only appropriate moniker for this effort is "Hanley Bicentennial Parade." I request that all other references, whether made in derision or jest, cease immediately.

Following his successful showing in the May 8, 1976 regional Dogstravaganza, Napoleon is enjoying a much-deserved rest. We hope to receive news soon regarding his potential selection as a participant in the statewide competition that will be held in August in Minneapolis.

CHAPTER SIXTEEN

LEONORA

SATURDAY, JUNE 12, 1976

LEONORA OPENED THE hall closet and slid her brown vinyl blazer off its hanger. Cora had called the night before to confirm their plans, so even though it would be Jasper behind the wheel, Leonora could expect a punctual pickup.

She eased in each arm, steadying herself on the table before pawing through her purse for her compact and lipstick. Her lipstick color was Rose in Spring, but Leonora preferred to think her lips matched an even more aptly named rhododendron in her backyard: June Pink. Wincing at her reflection in the hall mirror, she patted away the shine on her nose. There was so much that could no longer be patted away; patting was a fool's errand.

Midmorning sun shone through the window, dazzling the air with dust motes. Keeping her grip on the table, Leonora closed her eyes and conjured Badger. She leaned toward him, resting her head on his chest and mumbling into the worn plaid flannel he'd been wearing for years. He smelled of sweat and sawdust and the home they'd built together. He smelled of her. "Give me a little time," she told him. "Just give me a little time."

"No rush, dreamboat," he murmured, his face in her hair. "It's different here. You spend your time where you need to spend it. I'll wait."

It was not Jasper's knock she answered, but Tanner's. Leonora knew Tanner, but not well. She knew about Tanner's mother, DeCora, the daughter her best friend Cora had lost to cancer eight years ago. She knew Tanner had lived with Cora's other daughter, Coralene, and Jasper, Coralene's husband. She knew Tanner had moved out of Coralene's house only to return a few months ago. Most importantly, Leonora knew that Tanner was top of mind every time Cora bowed her head in prayer. Leonora wasn't interested in God much. But Cora? Cora's religious convictions were as solid as fence posts in concrete. And to hear Cora tell it, so were Coralene's, Jasper's, and those of Cora's granddaughter, Coravelle. In such company, Leonora was certain Tanner would find his way. It was just that, as Cora had said many times, "It was taking the boy a while."

Tanner held back the screen while Leonora locked her front door. He looked a bit like Cora; he must also resemble his White father. Tanner's skin was the color of coffee with lots of cream, which was nothing like Cora's, and his nose was chiseled. But his deep-brown eyes could have been Cora's own, and his black hair, in a well-tended Afro, had the structure of one of the guild's nylon-net scrubbies.

Tanner offered Leonora his arm as the two of them descended the front steps. "Steady there, Mrs. Daniels," Tanner said as Leonora clutched his elbow. "My grammy would be furious with me if I let you take a tumble."

"Well then, let's be sure you don't." Sarcasm escaped that was not intended for Tanner, but Leonora was tired of needing assistance to navigate the world. She'd captained her own ship for all the years since she'd lost Badger. Almost five decades of solo seamanship. She'd dispatched one daughter into the world, rescued the other, and then buried them both. She'd raised one granddaughter alone, and partially raised another. She'd date-stamped, lent, and reshelved every book in the Hanley Public Library for more fine Hanley citizens than she cared to count. She'd made her way. Needing anyone's arm to traverse her own front porch was an affront that was hard to stomach.

A rundown Datsun pickup was parked in the graveled spot outside Leonora's front fence. The truck must originally have been black, but with scrapes on the side and stretches of rust below the driver's door, it now defied a single descriptor. Tanner led Leonora around the back and opened the passenger door. Cora was sitting in the center of the cab, as if eager for some off-road adventure.

"Good morning!" Cora chirped, as Tanner offered his arm and then a shoulder to steady Leonora as she climbed into the truck's cab. "What you think of Tanner's new ride?"

"Well, it's not as cushy as your Chevy, but I guess it'll do." Leonora tried to keep her voice light, not wanting to tamp down Cora's enthusiasm. But what the hell?

"Tanner's working as a carpenter's apprentice now," Cora

said with pride so pronounced, it took up its own space in the small cab. "I bought him this here used truck. Gives him a way to transport his tools and such. I'll keep making payments as long as he keeps that job. Doing his best. Showing up every day on time. No silly stuff." These last words were directed toward Tanner, who had buckled himself into the driver's seat and was turning the key. The truck's engine made a satisfying rumble as the tires crunched through gravel and Tanner pulled the truck away from the house.

Tanner turned toward his grandmother, including Leonora in his gaze. "I'm on it, Grammy," Tanner said with a smile that shone in his eyes. "I'm on it. Doing good. Really, I am." He paused as he turned off Vermillion onto Northeast 35th Street. "I love this truck," he said.

"So nice to see you again, Leonora." Coralene offered her hand as Leonora, Cora, and Tanner came through Coralene's front door.

"Very nice to see you too, Coralene." And it was. Coralene was a lovely woman. Good to her mother and in love with her husband. The thought gave Leonora a familiar pang. Coralene worked with Crystal. Yet somehow that particular crossed path never seemed to come up in conversations. Not with Cora anyway, and not with Crystal either.

~ ~ ~

Crystal. What to say about Crystal? Leonora found it difficult to explain the rift between her and her eldest granddaughter. She loved Crystal. She did. Perhaps she just didn't like her much. Perhaps she didn't really know her. She'd tried to explain her dilemma to Cora, years ago now. "She's as confounding as a fitted sheet," Leonora had said to her friend, pleased with her illustrative metaphor. "No matter how you try, you can't fold it neatly."

Leonora's understanding of what made Crystal tick was patchy, at best. They had little in common, now that Crystal was long since grown. Truth be told, the bond had always been tenuous. When Pearl and Ruby died, Leonora had pulled her granddaughters under her wing and sheltered them as best she could. Darcy had been so young and had always lived with Leonora, so although Darcy's mother was gone, Darcy's world had been rocked only slightly.

But Crystal? Her world had roiled. It had mercilessly churned. Her mother was dead in a way no one could make sense of. Then her spineless father left town, only days later. Thirteen-year-old Crystal had been dumped at Leonora's with no more ceremony or kindness than when the milkman left the week's supply of cream and eggs on the porch.

Leonora had done it before: raised two girls so far apart in age as to be boats in different harbors. But Leonora's daughters had never really been two separate people. It was more that they were two embodiments of one glorious person. What was that expression? "More than the sum of… something." Who remembered? And eventually, who cared?

Darcy grew to be like Ruby, filling the house with the reflected light of her mother. But Crystal? Crystal was no Pearl.

Crystal was a puzzle. She was a peculiar girl, prone to silences, which Leonora eventually quit trying to penetrate. She was a reader, living in a home overflowing with books, so

Leonora liked to believe that Crystal was a thinker. That she was interested in the world. That she wanted to contribute. Perhaps she did, but the girl did such profoundly ridiculous things.

In her junior year of high school, Crystal had bought a motor scooter using money she'd earned from her first job scooping ice cream at Baskin-Robbins. Leonora suspected there were boys Crystal had wanted to impress, or even girls. But the scooter had garnered Crystal no social standing. No cachet. Before long, Crystal had gotten so heavy that the scooter was no longer a transportation option. Crystal sold the scooter and bought a used Ford from the neighbor. Leonora had helped with the purchase and Crystal had responsibly repaid her debt, having taken a better paying job at the Piggly Wiggly after school.

It wasn't only the scooter that had baffled Leonora. It was that her granddaughters seemed to come from different planets. As Darcy grew, Leonora's home had been chock-full of the little girls Darcy dragged home after school or who arrived on Saturday afternoons. Not once had Crystal brought someone home. How many times had Leonora offered to make tuna melts or cheeseburgers for Crystal's friends? "Bring someone home after school. Make some friends." But Crystal had shrugged off her grandmother's words like one more oversized sweater.

For a while, Crystal had built birdhouses, filling Badger's basement workshop with the bittersweet smell of sawdust and the sound of hammering at every imaginable hour. They'd been adorable little houses; Crystal had painted them a lovely robin's egg blue. But why? There was but the one birch tree in the backyard, and it could only accommodate so many. But Crystal had been determined – of what, Leonora had no idea – and had set up a card table in front of the fence to sell birdhouses to passersby, of whom there were very few.

Spring of her senior year in high school, Crystal had secured a spot at Darcy's elementary school carnival in a first-grade classroom reinvented as a Marrakesh Bazaar. Overly ambitious mothers from the PTA had draped bedsheets over scaffolding of chairs and poles to create stalls which offered up goods to hordes of energized children and their indulgent parents. The school librarian – typically a reserved woman, reliably attired in sweater sets – supervised the doorway wearing a caftan and huaraches.

On carnival night, Crystal had arranged her birdhouses atop the first graders' reading table and proceeded to hawk her wares. By the end of the evening, she had sold most of her inventory, her take far exceeding that of the Grandmothers' Club selling costume jewelry, or the Boy Scout troop, with their roasted peanuts.

Next door to the bazaar, the second-grade room had hosted a cake walk. In the fourth-grade room across the hall, children had tossed beanbags into the gaping mouth of a wooden clown, in the hopes of winning a goldfish. Surrounded by these youngsters, and as far from peers as she had known Crystal to be, Leonora came to understand that it was in spaces such as these that Crystal was most at ease.

Kudos were due when Crystal landed her job as a lunch lady at Hastings Elementary. To celebrate, Leonora took Crystal and Darcy out for dinner at Buckley's Steak House. Crystal ordered a T-bone steak and loaded up a baked potato with so much butter, sour cream, and bacon bits that it was the size of a small sofa pillow.

As years passed, Leonora and Crystal weren't estranged so much as they were just strangers. Only Darcy had sufficient influence to bring Leonora and Crystal together, which, bless Darcy's heart, she was willing to do. But Darcy was as social as her mother had been, and Leonora knew that her younger grandchild's time was filled with friends: going to movies, ball games, and parties. There didn't seem to be a young man in the picture right now, but there had been in years past. Leonora had her fingers crossed that there would be again. Time was a-wastin'.

Everyone loved Darcy. Leonora did, with a robust fullness that made her catch her breath. She was cautious about asking too much. Not wanting to be the grandmother who became a burden, or a punchline, Leonora prioritized her time with Darcy for drinking iced tea in the backyard, or making lefse and rosettes at Christmas. She didn't expect Darcy to take responsibility for bringing Crystal into the fold. Instead, she kept the door open, should Crystal choose to enter. And on occasion Crystal did, but she always had Darcy in tow.

A few years back, Darcy had told Leonora about Crystal's obsession with Hanley's burgeoning population of feral cats. According to Darcy, Crystal spent her weekends in the woods and underbrush by the river, trapping cats and delivering them to the humane society where they'd be vaccinated and sterilized. How many of those cats now lived with Crystal? Several. Of this, Leonora was convinced.

Eventually, the cat obsession had waned; perhaps they'd all been caught. Darcy had implied that Crystal had a new preoccupation, but hadn't provided details. Leonora had been relieved. Whatever Crystal was up to now couldn't possibly be as strange as crawling through bushes snaring cats.

~ ~ ~

Jasper welcomed them as they entered the garage. "Mother Cora, Mrs. Daniels, I do believe we have the answer to transporting all you guild ladies in style, from the start of the parade route down to Fitzgerald Junior High. And once you get there? Well, y'all will have the golden opportunity to enjoy a delicious hot dog, with some superbly delectable corn relish." Jasper chuckled, waving his arm like a car salesman in the direction of the newly constructed parade float. "Tanner and me, we got this figured out. I'll let Tanner tell you all about how it's going to work. It'll be fine. Just fine."

Cora's face lit up as her son-in-law and grandson held court, explaining each feature of their creation, which extended several yards into their driveway. It was a beautiful float. Gone was any hint of a riding mower or salvaged pallets. When Cora had first described what she knew of the float's construction, Leonora had been dubious. Perhaps they should sink the whole float idea. Who the hell cared about a float full of old ladies who would be doing what, exactly? And why?

But seeing it, Leonora softened. The head end of the float was attached to the back of a fully festooned riding mower. The three visible sides of the pallets and the plywood that had become the float's deck were bordered by what Leonora could only describe as a red, white, and blue dust ruffle. That must have been Coralene's doing, leaving Tanner and Jasper to scavenge the float's requisite parts. She mustered a smile as Tanner described the float. The young man was proud. Fair enough.

"See here, how we've got four pallets? We arranged them side by side, see? And then we secured them to the chassis we made. That's this structure here." Tanner pointed down to three sturdy axles which extended beyond the pallets. He looked up at Cora and Leonora to be sure they were following along. "See, Grammy? Uncle J, he knows a guy named Oscar who works in the garage at the post office. Oscar helped us put it all together. We attached the tires to the axles, see? Six of them. And they all turn like we need them too, while the chassis supports the floor of the float. You know, the flat part you and the other ladies will be sitting on. Sometimes they call it a deck. See?" Tanner stopped talking, turning again toward Cora and Leonora, confirming that they understood.

"I've got a question, Tan," Cora said. "Are those all parts from old mail trucks?"

"Some of them are. Oscar helped us find them. But the pallets and the plywood, that's stuff me and Uncle J got. We found it, or we bought it. For cheap. Then Auntie C, she's going to borrow six office chairs from one of the schools so y'all will have a place to sit down. We're going to bolt them down to the plywood part, see?" Tanner pointed to where he and Jasper had used crisscrossed pieces of duct tape to mark off six spots for chairs.

With the energy of a woodpecker, he went on with his explanation. "And Uncle J and Oscar? They rigged up that harness thing, see? Between the front of the float and the back of the riding mower? We call it a harness, 'cause it's kind of like a harness on a horse that'd pull a wagon. But this is a harness on the riding mower that's pulling a float of little old ladies."

Tanner froze, his expression that of any young man anywhere who knows he's said the wrong thing. He slapped his hand over his mouth in the second before Jasper swatted him with a newspaper that had been lying on the workbench. "Oh Grammy, I'm sorry," Tanner stammered, offering full chagrin to his grandmother before casting an embarrassed look at Leonora. "I apologize, Mrs. Daniels. I didn't mean any disrespect."

Cora and Leonora laughed out loud. "You're alright, baby," Cora said. "We are a bunch of little old ladies, and we going to sit on this beautiful float and ride down the middle of Hanley on the Fourth of July. Isn't that something? We couldn't do that if it wasn't for you and your uncle doing such a good job. You go ahead and call it as it is. Little old ladies. That's what we are."

"Darcy coming over this afternoon?" Cora asked once she and Leonora were back in Tanner's truck.

"That's the plan," Leonora said. "She didn't want to come for lunch, but I told the gals to come at noon. Olive said she'd bring some sandwiches. I was too tired to figure out anything to feed everyone."

"I could've brought lunch," Cora said. Leonora heard the irritation.

"Oh, I know. I didn't mean to leave you out. You know I didn't. I'm just..."

"You're just tired," Cora finished Leonora's sentence,

annoyance gone from her voice. "I'm worried about you, Leonora. You haven't been yourself lately. You seen a doctor?" Cora patted Leonora's knee as Tanner pulled his truck cautiously onto the gravel in front of Leonora's house and turned off the engine. "Have you?"

"Yes," Leonora said. "I've done all that."

"And?" Cora asked.

"I've done all that," Leonora repeated. "Nothing to worry about. Some things just are what they are."

Cora frowned, returning her hand to Leonora's leg and giving it a soft squeeze. "You'll let me know if you need something, won't you?"

"You, my friend. You give me what I need, exactly what I need. You always do."

Tanner came around to the passenger door. Cora put a hand against Leonora's back and Tanner offered his shoulder; together they eased Leonora out of the truck's cab.

Cora wriggled across the bench seat to the truck's door and climbed out. She slapped away Tanner's hand before realizing Leonora was watching. "Thank you, baby," Cora said, exaggerating her need for steadying from Tanner. "Off the old ladies go."

Leonora squeezed Cora's arm as they proceeded up the front walk.

"What time you want me back, Grammy?" Tanner asked as he held the screen and Leonora unlocked her front door.

"Darcy can take you home," Leonora told Cora. "She'd be happy to. That'd give our carpenter's apprentice here the afternoon off. That okay by you?" Leonora directed her question to Tanner.

"That be nice, ma'am. I'd appreciate that. But I can come, Grammy." Tanner shifted attention back and forth between the women, knowing better than to speak for his grandmother.

Cora pondered a moment. "Yes, Tan. Come on back. Around 2:00. Then Darcy and her grandma can have a little time together after all the little old ladies go home." Cora beamed at her grandson, her love as visible as the moon on a clear night.

Olive's sandwiches would do in a pinch. But they would never be anyone's first choice. Leonora wished she had indeed asked Cora to take care of lunch. Like an enchantress, Cora would have conjured a warm casserole and a Jell-O salad. Perhaps a basket of rolls. Maybe a plate of brownies. Cora was that kind of person; she was that kind of friend.

As for Olive's lunch offerings? None of the guild ladies would let a sour word slip. But still. They clustered in Leonora's kitchen, eyes as always on the coffee pot, watching Olive lay out their meal. The back door was open and a congenial midday breeze blew through the screen. Leonora pulled out a chair and sat at the table. Hy, Lo, and Glad leaned against the counter, lined up in birth order as Leonora had finally realized they always did. Cora rested against the door jam in the dining room, seeing as how kitchen floor space was spoken for. Olive was at the sink washing her hands, taking in the view of the backyard. Leonora's rhododendrons were still in full bloom, boasting to all that it was June in Minnesota.

Olive arranged the sandwiches in precise little stacks on

a Corelle plate. She was offering three choices, each on perfectly quartered white bread with the crusts cut off. Lunch meat, masquerading as ham, was paired with squares of American cheese and a thick swath of mayonnaise. Tuna, resplendent with pickles and celery, boasted tiny green caps of iceberg lettuce. And Olive's favorite – the one she referred to as her signature sandwich – with chopped olives, mustard, and cream cheese, rounded out the display. Olive's masterpieces were skewered with toothpicks, their papered ends coordinating with the sandwiches. Orange for ham and cheese; green for tuna; and blue for chopped olive.

Hy, Lo, and Glad had arrived with lunch embellishments. Leonora pointed toward the cupboard where they'd find serving dishes, and the sisters presented their contributions next to Olive's sandwiches. Hy emptied a bag of ruffled potato chips into a wood salad bowl, while Lo arranged apple slices on a glass dessert plate. With much fanfare, Glad produced a package of Lorna Doones which she arranged on a silver tray as if they were the crown jewels.

Once they'd loaded their plates, the ladies would select their typical seats in the living room and, like a dog circling in front of a fire, settle in to eat, gossip, and bemoan their aches and pains. They'd curse the cramp in Lo's hip, which must be something worse than arthritis. They'd weigh the pros and cons of prunes versus Milk of Magnesia in battling constipation, a widely shared condition and one frequently discussed. And likely Olive would revisit the headaches she'd get in the morning before she had her coffee. Surely she had a brain tumor. Each woman knew her own affliction was more dire than those of the others. Not wanting to waste a moment, they'd verbally elbow each other to make sure that their respective bursitis, psoriasis, indigestion, and bunions were thoroughly discussed, before Darcy arrived.

CHAPTER SEVENTEEN

DARCY

SATURDAY, JUNE 12, 1976

DARCY SKIPPED THE tweak she usually gave her grandmother by spinning her tires in the gravel, opting instead to park in front of the Kahns', who didn't appear to be home. Turning off the engine, she sat for a few minutes, picking fuzz off the passenger seat. Here she was. Another Saturday at her grandmother's house. Darcy felt suspended between her earlier life and one she strained to see in the distance but couldn't yet grasp.

She didn't resent her grandmother, not in any direct way. It was the need she resented: the relentless aging, the advancing infirmity which seemed to have replaced who her grandmother had always been with a disheveled assortment of ailments and inconveniences.

Darcy longed to sit at the kitchen table like they used to do, to drink coffee, to be heard. Her date for the senior prom, her college ambitions, her career choices, all of her steps and missteps had been dissected at that table. Each had been analyzed with exquisite care before her grandmother dusted the pieces, glued together the parts, and put a buff and shine on the building blocks of Darcy's life.

Darcy had never claimed she'd done it all on her own. Why would she? Leonora Daniels, the ghost of Ruby Daniels, and the omnipresence of Badger Daniels had shaped Darcy into the woman she'd become. As for Crystal? Well, perhaps along the way Crystal had added what her grandmother would call "local color." So Darcy kept showing up. As her grandmother had always done. She tried not to think about it as some inevitable role reversal. Too trite.

Today was not a particularly important stop for the guild along the path toward what Crystal insisted on calling the "big whoop-ta-do." Grandma and Cora had been to Coralene's for a viewing of the float in its almost-ready-to-roll glory. It had been Darcy's suggestion that the two women represent the guild and report back, rather than having all six guild ladies tromp through Coralene's front room.

Darcy had begged off the invitation to join the guild ladies for lunch, knowing that the excruciatingly detailed discussion of the float's pros and cons would still be underway long after the women had made their way through Olive's sandwiches.

Darcy liked Olive, she was a charming little nitwit, but it was unlikely that Olive's lunch offerings would be anything Darcy would be sorry to have missed. Besides, she'd had breakfast with Crystal today.

Darcy's eggs, bacon, and toast would hold her until dinner. Crystal's pancakes were unlikely to hold Crystal until lunch. Popping her toast into her purse hadn't been necessary this morning. By the time they'd left the Pancake House, toast crusts and a smear of yolk from her over-easy eggs were all that remained on Darcy's plate; Crystal's was wiped clean.

~ ~ ~

Darcy had been dreading this breakfast. She and Crystal needed to have a difficult conversation. Crystal would bob and weave. Crystal didn't do difficult conversations; she'd managed to avoid them her entire life.

On the plus side, it had been a few weeks since they'd met for breakfast. Darcy had been pleased to beg off, both for a break from her cousin, and because she'd had an actual date last Friday, and something she liked to think of as a date the Friday before, meaning she'd slept in on the two previous Saturday mornings.

His name was Mark. He worked for the City of Hanley in the Office of Planning and Public Works, which, Darcy had been amused to discover, was pursuing a city-wide project to increase the inventory of sidewalks on residential streets.

"Would that mean no more gravel?" Darcy asked over her first glass of chardonnay, when she and Mark had struck up conversation at the Come On Over pub after work. Darcy had arrived with her best friends Carol, Ann, and Rebecca; they all knew the drill. When Darcy found herself chatting with Mark – whom she'd quite literally bumped into on her way out of the restroom – none of her friends had come looking. Soon Mark had ordered Darcy another glass of wine, had the waiter bring him a second beer, and together they'd worked their way through artichoke fritters and cheese curds. Beyond sewer systems, street lights, gravel, and golf, Mark's conversational repertoire was limited. Still, Darcy had agreed to an official date and on the following Friday the two of them had shared a pizza at Luigi's before going to see *Jaws*.

Mark's hand had been clammy when he gripped Darcy's leg during the movie. Perhaps the skirt had been a mistake. The hand arrived during one of the moments when some poor sucker on the screen was in danger of imminent bloody death. Cue ominous music. She'd shifted in her seat, which served to return the hand to its rightful owner. Later, it occurred to her that perhaps Mark had needed reassurance that he was sitting in a movie theater in Hanley, Minnesota, far from shark-infested waters off Long Island.

Alas, poor Mark. His kissing was not remotely shark-like. No going in for the kill from old Mark. Instead his lips were reminiscent of some other waterborne creature. A jellyfish maybe? Who cares? There was no potential there.

Darcy had feigned fatigue and mustered a cough, which successfully sent Mark on his way. There would be other Marks. This town was crawling with Marks. What Hanley needed was a few more men who were funny. And tanned. And rich. More men like Johnny Carson, with whom Darcy had spent the rest of the evening.

"You alright, spoonbread? You're a little distracted. Hot date last night?"

"Nah." They'd needed to get to the subject of Leonora, but first – if only for the entertainment value – Darcy had lobbed a question.

"Got a funeral to go to today? Or, excuse me, a memorial?"

She was getting bolder about bringing up Crystal's obituary obsession. At some point, the blinding light of day would have to illuminate for Crystal the absurdity of her little hobby.

"Nope. No need. I only took one, who I've been sitting on all week. Older guy, named Ralph Blatson. He grew up here, then moved away, after college, I think. Worked in advertising is my guess. Lived in New York. Met Eisenhower once. Not something you'd expect to see in an obituary, but there it was." Crystal had rubbed the back of her neck, as if the discussion was a serious one. Darcy had tried not to roll her eyes.

"It read like an obit he'd written for himself," Crystal said. "Not clear who else would've done it, so that would've been the way to go. Never married, no kids. Left New York and moved back. Recently, sounds like. I'm guessing he knew he was about to play his last card and wanted to do that back here. Made me a little sad. That's why I chose him. I think Ralph Blatson died a lonely guy."

Darcy wished she wasn't pulled in so easily. It was hard to be critical when she couldn't keep herself from asking, "So who did you match him with?" As if this was a logical question here on planet Earth.

"I haven't yet." Crystal held up her coffee cup as the waitress passed their table. "I'm slowing down. This one's taking longer, but there's someone I'd been wanting to use as a match for a while. It can be hard to find the right one, you know? Not that many to choose from. You'd be surprised. But this gal? She seems like she needs one. Not that I'd ever say that out loud. Not to her anyway; she's a tough nut. But matching her with Ralph feels right. No kids for her either, far as I know. Definitely no husband." Crystal had looked at Darcy, as if waiting for a reply. As if she'd answered the question.

Darcy glared. "Come on," she said, not trying to hide her irritation. "I didn't really want to ask about this, but I did. So just tell me."

Startled, Crystal puffed out her cheeks. "Not trying to be difficult. Like I said, it's a bit sad. More than a bit, actually. Maybe I'm getting tired." Crystal spoke haltingly, as if the words caused her pain. "Maybe I'm getting tired of doing this."

Darcy softened her body into the booth and waited for Crystal to say more.

"Gal I work with. Her name's Sheila. She's not a bad egg, not really. She does her job, no question about that, although she takes on projects that aren't really necessary. Sort of makes things harder for herself."

"Are the two of you friends?"

"No."

The answer startled Darcy, like an ice cube down her back. How does Crystal do this? Darcy's own friends were as essential to her as water or air. But Crystal? "Are you at least civil?" Darcy asked, with a heavy dusting of judgment.

Crystal's expression went cold. "What are you talking about?" she said. "Why would you ask that? Of course we are."

"I'm sorry, that did sound snotty. It's just that you don't usually talk about people at work."

"I know Coralene better than Sheila. You know Coralene. But Sheila has lots of sharp edges. I think she's just, I don't know. She's broken. Do you know what I mean? Do you know anyone like that?"

This was unlike any conversation Darcy could remember; perhaps it was a stall tactic. Did Crystal sense that Darcy had serious business to discuss? Crystal would veer far off the road to avoid talking about Leonora. She must be picking up on something.

Darcy watched Crystal swipe her last piece of pancake through syrup. "Ralph and Sheila," Crystal said, mostly to herself. "Sheila and Ralph." Putting down her fork, Crystal appeared to wait for whatever Darcy might say next.

Crystal had given her alive-meets-dead update as if there was nothing unusual about it. As if she'd been reading the *Hanley Herald* weather report. But blue skies were not in Leonora's forecast, Darcy thought. It was time for Crystal to understand that. It was time for her to help.

Realizing she was leaning heavily on the sticky table, Darcy pulled her arms back and put her hands in her lap. *Focus*, she thought as she gazed across the table at Crystal. *Focus*.

Darcy felt overwhelmed by responsibility. As if she needed to be the one watching out for Grandma all the goddamn time, while handling Crystal with kid gloves or something. Why was that? Crystal was a grownup too. Why tiptoe around her? Crystal could be as weird as she wanted. Make friends with dead people. Who cares? But must she abandon the woman who'd taken her in? And leave Grandma's care to Darcy, who only wanted to be the younger one? The protected one?

Darcy didn't believe for a second that Crystal was unaware of their grandmother's decline. But Crystal wasn't responding the way she should. Wasn't there a gap here? Shouldn't Crystal be filling a preordained spot in this little family drama? There'd been enough emptiness in their lives. Darcy didn't want to be wise; she didn't want to be responsible. She wanted help. She wanted to be understood.

She studied her cousin across the table: there was Crystal, squeezed into the booth and not saying another word. Darcy was surprised by how badly she wanted to slide out from her side and go over to Crystal's, lay her head against Crystal's shoulder, and say out loud what she'd never said: that she, Darcy, had lost her mother too. That Crystal didn't have exclusive rights to the grief that had shaped her into who she was: sarcastic, peculiar, and out of reach when Darcy needed her most.

Instead, she said, "You need to get over there more often. To Grandma's house. Watch her. She's always holding onto something, steadying herself, you know? Never just walks across the room anymore. She's tippy. And she's in pain; I know she is. She'll give a little start, like she's stuck her finger in an outlet. Or she'll screw up her face, wincing. But only when she doesn't see me watching."

"So in other words, she's getting old. Is that what you're telling me?" Crystal's tone was distant. Detached. The question hung in the air between them.

How was Darcy supposed to respond if this was going to be Crystal's approach? God dammit. She was always the one left to handle things. Always. "That's a bit harsh, don't you think?" Darcy said finally.

"It sounded harsher than I meant, spoonbread."
Darcy waited.
"I'm sorry," Crystal said after a moment. "But I'm not sure what you think I can do. Not sure what you're thinking

you'll do either. Has she asked for anything? Has she talked to a doctor or something? Help me out here."

How quickly the tables had turned. Help Crystal out? What the hell? "Can we keep the focus on Grandma?" Darcy said. "Please? Not me. Not you. Her."

"Sure enough. We can do that." Crystal sounded more indifferent than miffed.

Their conversation had sputtered like a sump pump. There was so much more she wanted to tell Crystal. But she wanted a different Crystal; she'd always wanted a different Crystal. Could she tell Crystal about the pills she'd found in the nightstand? Probably not. Despair over their grandmother's care settled into an aching stiffness at the back of Darcy's neck.

~ ~ ~

Darcy leaned against the Pinto's headrest. If she sat in her car much longer, she might fall asleep. It was midafternoon. It was sunny. It was Saturday. Sum those up and you've got the makings of the perfect nap. But not in her car, dear God, and not until she'd wrapped up this particular *Saturday with Grandma.* Her family was gobbling up entirely too much time today. Crystal had left her feeling vulnerable and bruised, but Darcy needed to perk the hell up. Be who her grandmother needed her to be. Get the flock of guild ladies to the parade finish line. Good God, she was tired of this project.

"I thought that went alright, didn't you?" Darcy asked. After sending the guild ladies on their way, Darcy and Leonora had settled at the kitchen table. Darcy rose to pour her grandmother a second cup of coffee.

"Grab a Lorna Doone if you want one," Leonora said. "And bring me one too."

"You're on your own there. Those cookies taste like buttery sawdust."

"What's wrong with sawdust, as long as it's buttery?"

Turning from the cupboard with the cookies in hand, Darcy stepped quickly back to the table. "Whoa there," she said. Leonora appeared to be sliding off the chair. "You okay?"

"I'm fine. Just tired. Sit down and drink your coffee. Let's be sure we're on the same page about the float." Darcy steadied the chair while Leonora planted her feet on the linoleum under the kitchen table and pushed her bottom back up on the seat.

It was nearly 3:00 PM. Any breeze that might have visited the kitchen through the screen door was long gone, but Darcy left the back door open anyway. The air was heavy and warm, heralding the onset of summer when discussion of whether to leave the back door wide open, or close it tight, wouldn't be worth the exertion required to have it. Without air conditioning, every room in the house sweltered from July through September.

"You don't think the whole thing's a bit too simple?" Leonora asked. "It's just that after all the planning we've done, as far as I can tell we'll be six little old ladies sitting on chairs, being pulled down Center Street by a riding mower."

"You forgot the part about waving your craft projects in the air. Just like a queen at a coronation. But no white gloves for you all; you'll have nylon net."

"This isn't funny. Don't you think we've landed in a peculiar place?"

"No. No, I don't." Darcy couldn't bear to revisit this again. "Each of you will be holding your favorite crafts. You can wave them toward the crowds or not. I'll find some wicker baskets that'll look cute and put red, white, and blue bows on them or something. Then you can have bibs, and turtles, and pot holders, and scrubbies all tumbling out of baskets. Put lots of turtles out. You've all said it yourselves, people love those. We'll bring some quilts too. There's a box in the basement and Glad said the sisters have a few at home. You can go wild; all that will fill the space on the float. Well, except for the plant markers, but it's not as if anyone is going to feel cheated that they don't see little glass markers up there."

Leonora sighed. "I guess you're right, but…"

Darcy interrupted, determined to put the whole thing to rest. "Attaching umbrellas to each chair, that was a good idea of Coralene's. The parade doesn't start until noon. You all could get very hot otherwise."

"Don't want little old ladies fainting dead away."

"No. No we don't. There's another perk too. There will be little kids handing out cookies. They'll be walking alongside all the floats, including yours. Crystal told me that's what the elementary schools are doing for the 'big whoop-ta-do'."

"The what?" Leonora asked.

"Never mind. Just Crystal being Crystal." Darcy put down the coffee cup she'd been cradling and reached across the table for her grandmother's hand. It was as soft as it had ever been, but in a different way now. When Darcy was young, there was a strength in her grandmother's softness. But now, the soft skin lay precariously across arthritic knuckles and protruding blue veins. As for strength? Physical or otherwise? It had seeped out of Leonora like a slowly drying dishrag, warm and damp when first draped across the faucet, but dry and stiff if left too long.

"You feeling okay? I know you don't like to talk about health stuff, but do you need to see a doctor? I could take an afternoon off and take you."

"Darcy, for heaven's sakes. When I need to go to the doctor, I go. I've been calling cabs for things like that for years."

"But what does the doctor say? About you being so tired and all? It's not that I don't notice; I'm worried."

"Sweetie, you're not the only one who notices that I'm tired. I notice too. That's all there is to it. Find something else to worry about; leave me out of it."

The two of them sat in silence. Even in the heat of the kitchen, Darcy's insides were cold. Leonora had closed her eyes. Darcy doubted that she was sleeping, more likely the busy day had brought her to this point: ready to be finished with tasks, and conversations, and speculations. As her breathing slowed, Leonora was once again sliding off the chair. *Must be sleeping after all. Or worse, losing the sense of her own body in space.* Darcy shuddered. More than fire, flood, or pestilence, Darcy knew her grandmother feared falling.

Darcy eased her body close to the table to prevent Leonora's continued descent. She put a hand on Leonora's shoulder. "You want to head into your room and take a nap? It's been a long day."

Leonora spoke without opening her eyes. "That's exactly what I'm going to do," she said. "For a minute or two, yes, I think I will. There are a few of Olive's sandwiches in the fridge. That was nice of her to leave them." Leonora opened her eyes, warming to her subject. "The sisters though? Those women? I love them, but they're hard to figure. They intended to take every crumb of their lunch contributions back home. But I stuck the Lorna Doones in the cupboard where they wouldn't find them. Told Glad we'd eaten them all. Olive left the sandwiches though. I'll have a tuna one for dinner. The tuna ones weren't that bad. Take one with you. Take two."

"No," Darcy said, too quickly. "But thank you."

Leonora put both hands on the lip of the table and managed to lever herself into a stand. She reached for the half-eaten Lorna Doone on the napkin next to her coffee cup, but reconsidered and left it where it was. "I used to love those cookies," she said. "They were great for dunking into just about anything. Coffee, milk, whatever. You girls used to dunk them in Kool-Aid so you could turn them orange or purple and see how long they'd stay in one piece before the dunked end fell off." Leonora gave a soft chuckle. "It didn't take much to amuse you two. Little girl you, and teenager Crystal, sitting at the table dunking cookies."

"I don't remember that at all," Darcy said.

"Crystal used to think up all sorts of things to entertain you," Leonora said. "You followed her around like a puppy dog."

"I did not." Darcy tried to sound indignant, but she was confused. "Didn't I have friends of my own? Didn't she?"

"Sweetie, you were only two when Crystal came to live with us, and…" Leonora paused to remember. "You were eight when she moved out. You didn't have a bunch of friends at two, that's for sure, except for Crystal. But you're right, by the time you were eight you had a whole passel coming in and out of this house."

"What about Crystal's friends?"

"What about them? There weren't any. Any more than there are now. I think it was hard for her when you went off to school and started making friends. Once she had less time with you, she spent even more time on her unusual pursuits. I remember coming home from the library one day not long after she graduated from high school. She was in the kitchen, making an ungodly mess. Told me she was teaching herself to cook. But within a year, she got the job with the school district, found herself an apartment, and moved out. You were so busy with your friends and activities that you barely noticed."

A chill spread through Darcy's insides. Her mouth was dry as she fought off tears. "Oh my God," she said. "I don't remember any of that. Not at all."

"I'm the grandmother," Leonora said gently, turning toward the dining room. "I remember everything."

"Can I help you settle in?" Darcy struggled to swallow the lump in her throat. "Throw a quilt over your head or something?"

Leonora moved haltingly through the living room toward her bedroom, with Darcy on her heels. "Calm down, sweetie," she said. "I can put myself down for a nap. I can even get myself back up again, if I choose to." Stopping in her doorway, she steadied herself on the frame. For a moment, an aggressive silence occupied the room before Leonora turned. Her expression had changed, the color in her face disappearing, like chalk drawings in the rain. "But Darcy…" The stern tone caught Darcy off guard.

"What?"

"Stay out of my nightstand. Leave my things alone. I mean it."

CHAPTER EIGHTEEN

SHEILA

SATURDAY, JUNE 12, 1976

NOT FOR AN instant had Sheila thought there'd be a second encounter with Tom Downlane. The first had done her in. The contrivance of it all. The nonsense. Leaving the restaurant that night in April, she hadn't needed to look back to know that Tom remained standing by the table, overwhelmed by having spent a meal with a lunatic.

So much of who Sheila knew herself to be had been subsumed that night by the necessity of engaging with someone she hadn't seen in over a year and didn't know in the least. Alone was what she knew. She had neither capacity nor will for anything else. Who she'd been, or could have been, was as gone as a child's lost balloon; once let loose its only purpose being to fly away, to simply be gone. Sheila was gone. She'd been gone for a long time. She knew gone.

She also knew that when Friday rolled back around, Lexie would not be gone. The week after the dinner with Tom, Sheila had been back in her booth, and Lexie had been beside it.

Salmon croquettes and sole almandine were her remaining choices in Treasures of the Sea. Sole was a bland fish. Sheila had ordered the croquettes, craving something worthy of a Friday night as she regained her footing at *her* restaurant, with *her* waitress. Lexie had chatted with the familiarity of any other Friday, and as usual, saved Sheila the last piece of apple pie.

After she ate, Sheila's thoughts went where they always went: consumed with who she'd wanted and what she'd missed. Surprising Lexie with an earlier than usual departure, Sheila had apologized, her voice tentative. "I didn't finish my pie. I just need to go home." She'd reached to pat Lexie's arm, but found herself grasping Lexie's hand instead. In that moment, Sheila's large, rough-skinned hand felt sheltered in Lexie's smaller but stronger one.

Tom Downlane's name never came up.

~ ~ ~

The next week, Lexie handed her an envelope. "I promised Tom I'd give it to you."

"What is it?"

"I don't know. He left it with me last Saturday. Didn't make a big deal of it or anything. Said he'd done 'some research' which he wanted to pass along. So, I'm passing it along."

"I'll read it later; right now I need to figure out what I want for dinner."

"Sounds like you have bigger fish to fry?"

"Have you been wanting to make that joke ever since I started Treasures of the Sea?"

"Nope. Although I'm surprised I didn't think of it earlier. You only have the one option left."

"Which I'm going to skip. I don't like sole. Makes no sense to spend good money on it. I'll order something random, like the other peasants here at Denny's."

"Burger? Spaghetti?" Lexie waited while Sheila scanned the menu. "You've tried just about everything on there, except the breakfast items."

"I'm not going to eat breakfast for dinner. Never liked the idea."

"So what'll it be?"

"I'll have the Monte Cristo. Haven't had one of those in a while."

"Good choice. Salad? Fries? Both?"

"Just fries. I'll read my correspondence while I wait for my dinner. I'll be happy to tell you what he says, if you're interested. There's nothing Tom Downlane could say that I wouldn't be happy to let you read."

Lexie pushed her hands into the front pockets of her uniform and turned back toward the kitchen. "Roger that. Let me get you some water."

Watching her walk away, Sheila was struck by how Lexie's hair suspended almost unperceptively off her neck, as if there was a newborn breeze in the oppressive Denny's air, which only had interest in Lexie. Wonderful girl. Lovely girl.

Slipping her thumb into the unsealed envelope, Sheila pulled out the note. Here came Tom Downlane again. Uninvited. Disrupting stasis.

Dear Ms. Raymond,

I spoke with the owners of Fiesta about that salsa topping for your Mexican salads. They offered a gallon of the stuff as their contribution to the bicentennial celebration. I could fetch it before the parade and help out with setup and serving at your salad table. Could be a hoot. If you'd like to join me for dinner again some Saturday, we could chat about it.

Sincerely,

Tom (Downlane)

When Lexie returned with Sheila's dinner, she picked up Tom's note and read it quickly. "You going to take him up on his offer?"

"Good lord. Why would I?"

"Because it'd be great to have the salsa, and because you're going to need some help that day," Lexie said. "Don't you think? I'm assuming your cooks will show up with all the other fixings; that'll be a lift just by itself. Having someone else around to fill the bowls and pass them to folks? Hand out forks and napkins? I'd say you can't have too many cooks in that particular kitchen. You could be swamped."

"But must it be Tom Downlane? The man's so cheerful. He gives me an ache right behind my eyes."

"Then close your eyes. I'll help too, if you want. I don't work on Sundays. Thank goodness. Sunday breakfast customers are a rowdy bunch. I'm glad it doesn't happen on my watch."

Sheila frowned, as if unable to process what she'd just been told. "What?"

"I said the Sunday breakfast shift is a pain. Noisy and hot."

"No. I don't mean that. *You'd* help at the parade? Why? Why would you do that?"

Lexie sat down on the corner of the booth, facing Sheila. She folded Tom's note and put it in the envelope before passing it back across the table. "What do you mean?" she said. "Why *wouldn't* I do that?"

Sheila felt as if someone had kicked up the heat, flushing her neck and face. She picked up her Monte Cristo, avoiding Lexie's gaze. When she looked up, Lexie's eyes were on her. Kind, but firm. "You're my friend, Sheila," Lexie said. "Aren't you? I mean really, aren't you? How many Fridays have we spent together? And Tom? He's my friend too. This is how friends act. This is what friends do. They lighten the load."

Taking a bite of the sandwich, Sheila chewed longer than necessary. Drumming the table with her fingertips, Lexie stood up. "I need to tend to the rest of my posse," she said. "I'll swing back by in a few."

"Are you truly suggesting that I take Tom up on his offer?" Sheila asked when Lexie returned.

"I am."

"And yours too? Take you up on it?"

"Yes."

"I think this parade food idea is nuts. The town knows there's a school district, and that we feed those rug rats five days a week. Never on a Sunday, though. Never outside. Not during the summer. Never when any human you please, from a babe in arms to a little old lady, is invited to come on over for lunch."

"I agree. But your boss, what's his name? Gerald?"

"Gordon."

"Well, Gordon seems to be full steam ahead. So let people help you, and get it over with. You're the most no-nonsense person I know. Seems to me that the no-nonsense approach is to just get it done."

Sheila sighed heavily. "You're right," she said.

"Will you have dinner with him again? Tom? Make a plan?"

"Hell, no. I am not having dinner with him again." Sheila sprinkled her two remaining fries with more salt before she put them in her mouth. "I'll stop in for pie tomorrow. Or maybe just coffee."

"I'll let him know."

"I need coffee and pie now too, please."

"I know you do."

~ ~ ~

"That's a relief!" Tom teased as Sheila approached the table the next night. "I finished my fries just in time. I didn't want any left when you arrived. You might steal them."

Sheila slid into the both across from him. Not the fries schtick again. It wasn't funny the first time.

As if reading her mind, Tom asked, "I should drop the fries joke, shouldn't I?"

"You should."

"And so I shall. Good to see you again. I'm glad you came."

"It seemed the least I could do to express my gratitude. It was thoughtful of you to talk to those restaurant folks about the sauce."

"Salsa."

"Right. Regardless. It wasn't necessary, but thank you."

"It'll be the cherry atop your taco salad sundae," Tom said, then shook his head. "That doesn't quite work. Let's just think of it as the perfect condiment for the high school cafeterias' contribution to the parade. Taco salads, with salsa. I'd been calling them Mexican salads, but the restaurant folks – Garcia is their name, Paolo and Elena – they told me to call them taco salads."

"And they offered a gallon? Is that enough?"

"Don't know. They upped it to two gallons. One of those bucket's worth. We'll have to keep an eye on it. We don't want to run out."

"About that," Sheila said. "It's not necessary that you fetch it. I can stop and get it that morning. Nor is it necessary for you to help with setting up, or serving."

Tom sighed. "There are many things in the world that aren't necessary, Ms. Raymond. Doesn't mean they aren't wise, or useful. Wouldn't you agree?" He looked at her, his eyes penetrating in a way she found unsettling. "I'd like to think I could be useful. I'd appreciate the opportunity. I worked for the schools too, but as of parade day, I'll be retired. Seems like a good way to make my exit. Helping out with one of the food tables. Doesn't mean I don't want my going-away cake though," he'd laughed. "I wouldn't want anybody to get the wrong idea about that. I'll have to be sure Mary Ann understands that."

"I expect that you'll still get your cake."

"So you'll let me help?"

Sheila shrugged in defeat. "I will. Lexie will help too. But I'll be glad to see the last float go down the street that day. And the last parade-goer."

"It's a celebration, though. A two-hundredth birthday celebration! We don't want that fact to get lost. But we should probably figure out the particulars."

"Pardon?"

"Figure out the particulars, you know. How to set up the table. Where to stack the bowls and such. We'll need napkins, of course. You won't need anything to be hot, although the hamburger would taste better warm. But you'll for sure want the lettuce and cheese to be chilly. That might be a challenge. Do an assembly line maybe?" Tom had caught Sheila's expression and paused. "Uh oh. I'm overstepping, aren't I?"

"You are. Don't. This is my job."

"I apologize. I'll keep mum on the whys and wherefores and focus on the celebratory aspects. It's our bicentennial, for the love of Pete. Got a pair of red suspenders that I'm thinking I'll wear with a white shirt and blue jeans. I'll call myself a patriot. Maybe I'll go as Nathan Hale. What do you think?"

"I can imagine you doing that very thing."

"You planning to dress for the occasion?"

"I am not."

"What about the fireworks that night? There's supposed to be quite a display."

"You mentioned that, last time I saw you."

"I love a good fireworks display. So much noise and excitement. Pretty too. Would you like to go with me?"

Sheila had been intent on forking up her last bite of pie, but her eyes shot up at Tom. "What did you say?"

"I asked if you might want to go to the fireworks show with me? On the Fourth. It'll be a doozy, I'm sure. Good fun."

"No thank you." Sheila urgently needed to leave. She took a final drink of coffee, wiped her mouth, and wadded the napkin on the pie plate. "I'll be going," she said.

"Oh." Tom looked as startled as if Sheila had kicked him under the table. "Oh," he said again. "Thought we might chat a bit. I know I'm not supposed to stick my big nose in, but I am curious how you're planning to pull off parade day. What time should I be there? Anything else you need me to pick up? I'm happy to do anything at all." His voice had taken on the panicked tone of one being abandoned. Sheila knew that tone, but in her case it played silently in her own head.

"I'll let Lexie know on timing," Sheila said. "I'll ask her to pass that on." She stood and unrolled her coat. The weather allowed for her spring one, which was lightweight, a practical navy number with buttons down the front. Tom slid out and stood beside her, cupping his fingers. Sheila passed him the coat before turning her back to him, allowing him to help her put it on. Turning, she'd adjusted her collar and buttoned the top button. "I'll see you in a few weeks," she said, and walked toward the door.

CHAPTER NINETEEN

Sheila

Friday, June 18, 1976

SHEILA DIDN'T SUBSCRIBE to the newspaper. She preferred to watch TV news, if she preferred anything at all. Should someone leave a newspaper lying about, she might read it, or she might not. On Monday, Crystal had left the last two weeks' Sunday papers on the table in the shared lunchroom. She was probably too lazy to put them in the trash.

Sheila laid one of the papers on her lap. As she ate her pot roast sandwich, she absentmindedly skimmed through news, weather, and the stock market before flipping to the obituary page. As the paper fell to the floor, Sheila struggled to take in what she'd just read. The sandwich stuck threateningly in her throat. She hadn't seen Ralph's name in print in over forty years.

~ ~ ~

Ralph Blatson, age 66. Proud son of Hanley, Minnesota. Proud man of the United States of America. Traveled the world and saw the sights. Sold the goods and met the players: Elvis, Marilyn, and Ike. LBJ and Neil Armstrong. Everything to tell, but little to speak of. Last known address: New York City, before returning from whence he'd come... He tried to live his life well, but found himself alone at the end of it. No surviving parents or siblings. No wife. No children. Two roads will always diverge, it's who we travel with that makes all the difference. There will be no service.

~ ~ ~

Sitting at her table by the window, Sheila pushed aside her water glass and laid the newspaper on the table in front of her. The creases had weakened over the past week as she'd read and reread each word. She could recite it from memory. But to whom? She should quit carrying it around in her purse. Better to put it in the nightstand before the ink smears over the words: "…Two roads will always diverge, it's who we travel with that makes all the difference."

For the last four days, Sheila had gone to the office as usual, pushing aside any thoughts other than those required for flawless execution of the taco salad plan. She pictured herself holding a dustpan, ready to sweep up any memories of Ralph that might creep in, disguised as specks of dirt.

It had been business as usual in Nutrition Services. Coralene was typically efficient; Gordon burrowed in his tiny office. Only Crystal had behaved oddly, scrutinizing Sheila as if she were a museum exhibit, or in line to be fitted for a new suit.

From Monday through Thursday evening, Sheila had confined her thoughts to the narrow alley in her mind between one day and the next, restrained in the stupor of her TV shows, relying on them to fill the hours before she went to bed.

She had no recall of what she'd eaten for breakfast or packed for lunch. No memory of what she'd worn to work. Had she showered? Gone to the bathroom? Had the house been too hot, or had it perhaps rained? Had she stopped for gas? Checked the mail?

As Lexie approached the table, Sheila fumbled to refold the newspaper and return it to her purse.

"Big news today?" Lexie asked, in the instant before she saw Sheila's face. She sat down, holding Sheila's gaze. "That's not a face I know," she said tenderly. "What are you reading? What happened?"

Sheila had no words for this. All week, the only conversation she'd considered was the one to which she'd eventually concede, in her own mind. Those words were still dammed; she didn't dare allow a breach. Not until she was ready. That she would speak of this to Lexie had simply not crossed her mind. So she didn't; she couldn't. Instead, she cried.

Lexie said nothing as tears drenched Sheila's cheeks. Huge and plodding, they fell off her chin as if off an icicle upon a sudden warming. Customers and cooks seemed to recede into the walls, and the clamor of dishes and voices dimmed until it was just the two of them, smothering under the immensity of Sheila's pain.

Sheila put her elbows on the table, holding her face in her hands. Pulling the newspaper toward her, Lexie read Ralph's obituary, running her finger along the words that Sheila had caressed a hundred times in the last week.

"He was the one?" Lexie asked.

"He was. The only one. A lifetime ago. My whole lifetime ago."

Silence settled back around them. Lexie refolded the newspaper as if wrapping a delicate Christmas gift and slid it back across the table. Sheila raised her face. A stack of paper napkins had appeared on the table. She used one to wipe her cheeks, then rested her head against the back of the booth, pulling absently on her upper lip.

"I'm going home," she said suddenly, disrupting the intimacy that had held them. Sliding out, she stood and unrolled her coat, a napkin still balled in her fist.

"Want to take something with you?" Lexie asked. "A piece of pie at least?"

"No. I have plenty to eat at home."

"I could stop by after I get off work. Just to check in? I could bring something then. Maybe you'll be hungry later? For something you don't have to cook yourself?"

"Stop by?"

"Yes, not to bug you or anything. Just to check in."

"No." Sheila put on her coat and adjusted the collar; reserve returned to her voice. "Nice of you to offer, though," she said. "I need to go now. I really need to go."

Lexie leaned against the table, ready to reach for Sheila's hand should the opportunity present itself. "If you need anything, you know…"

"I know. I don't, but I know. I'll see you next week." Sheila reached for the remaining paper napkins, folded them, and put them in her coat pocket.

In the Denny's parking lot, Sheila eased onto the front seat of the Chrysler, turned the key, and adjusted the radio. She wasn't much of a radio listener. Her passing familiarity with popular music came from having worked in high schools. The music of her own youth, her college music, her Ralph music, would no longer be found on an AM station in Hanley. Besides, that wasn't what she needed. Tonight she needed fierce, brave, soulful music that would saturate her, muffling the sounds she needed to make and the words she needed to say. She turned the dial until she found Motown. Martha and the Vandellas. The Supremes. They would cushion her as she drove too fast, and turned up the volume unspeakably loud.

Exiting the parking lot onto Bullman Avenue, she took a left to drive north, out of town, along the arrow-straight roads that defined where fields started and stopped, toward the miles of curves bordering Lake Sylvester and the countless other lakes that appeared across Minnesota like just so many molehills.

Rolling down her window, Sheila pulled the napkins out of her coat pocket, wedged them under her thigh, and accelerated. Sixty miles per hour, then seventy, then seventy-five. These roads had been here for her before, but she'd never needed them quite so much as she did tonight. Fields of corn and potatoes sped by. An anonymous bit of grit blew in the window, lodging in her eye. Driving with one eye closed, she wiped copious tears until whatever had flown in was washed away.

The needle swept past eighty; the fields were now behind her. Her vision was blurred, her face as wet as the beach under a wave. Using a napkin, she wiped the tears that ran along her jawline. And then she started to scream. Releasing her anguish in gasps and shrieks, she screamed out the window toward Ralph, toward wherever he might be huddled and hiding in these fields they both had loved. She screamed at him to show himself. The goddamn coward. Catching her reflection in the rearview mirror, she screamed at her own ragged, ruined face.

How had she let this happen? An incomprehensible mix of panic and hope settled in her chest. Could she renegotiate the course of her life? Had all this time really passed? Maybe she wasn't a woman in her sixties, with all that could have been precious visible only in a fun house mirror. Surely she and Ralph could go back to the edge of Hanley. They could start down these roads one more time. They could chase thunder clouds and race the moon. They could be young. Smart. Beautiful. Together. Must that be impossible?

With no chance that Ralph Blatson would ever again entwine his fingers with hers, without possibilities for anything at all, Sheila screamed into the perfect sky.

As the miles accumulated, tears curdled in the back of Sheila's throat. She was spent. She let up on the accelerator as she reached Holler Lake. There was no one around; it wasn't intended as a recreational spot. The lake was small, with no shore to speak of, no dock. But that hadn't stopped generations of teenagers and college students from wading in and squishing mud between their toes until the moment they broke into a swim.

Holler Lake wasn't its real name, but it was the name that had stuck between Sheila and Ralph. They had swum here many times, ignoring the signs that told them it wasn't allowed. Wading in, her hand in Ralph's, Sheila had loved how the invisible lake bed would claim her feet and ankles, loved the idea that there was another way of being in the murky, mud beneath them, and in the dark, cool water.

Ralph would set out first. Reaching the middle of the lake, he'd suspend himself effortlessly, extend his arms toward Sheila, and holler her name: "Sheee La! She, She, She, Sheee La." He'd slap the water, adding percussion to his chant, urging her out to him. "Sheee La." Slap, slap, slap. "She, She, She, Sheee La." Slap, slap, slap.

Sheila had never been a strong swimmer, but she hadn't needed to be. Ralph waited for her in the middle of Holler Lake. When she'd reached him, she'd known he would hold her forever.

In the spring, they'd brought the canoe, tied to the top of Ralph's father's station wagon. Paddling along the weed line, they'd poked clumps of grass to scatter crappie and bass, and scanned moss-covered logs for snapping turtles and sun-hungry bullfrogs. When they tired of exploring, they'd splayed their bodies over the seats in the canoe, talking, kissing, and eating the chicken sandwiches Sheila would bring, which somehow they'd managed to keep dry.

Sheila eased the car down the rutted road that took her as close to the lake as she'd be able to drive. She thought about getting out, removing her shoes, letting mud once again conquer her feet and ankles until she had no choice but to reach out her arms and force her body forward. But toward what? Toward whom? There was no one here for her. There was no one for her anywhere.

If Ralph had stayed, would her life have been any different? Perhaps she was too far gone to compare what was with what could have been. For decades, she'd told herself it was better to live alone. Maybe that was only true for women, or only for those who confront the lakes of youth with no way of turning back and no desire to continue forward in the lives they're living, which they know were never meant to be theirs.

Sheila felt another surge and shrieked out the window toward the apathetic lake. The napkins were gone, so she wiped her eyes on the sleeve of her coat. In the vacuous car, could she just stop breathing? Sob to the point of exhaustion? Maybe she'd evaporate here. Vaporize. Become a whisper on the wind, someone no one would remember or miss.

The weight of silence made it almost impossible to move. *Damn it to hell, Ralph. You shortsighted, selfish, pompous ass. "Two roads can diverge anywhere?" Now you decide to interpret poetry? What did you ever know about it? How dare you pilfer something beautiful? You were looking for something better. Did you find it? Hell no. But that choice kept you away from what life might have been, leaving me to think of nothing else. Go to hell.*

She remembered how she liked it. Neat. Wild Turkey was in the cupboard beside the sink, behind bags of flour and sugar and a box of baking soda, that were all past their pull dates. Who is going to bake? Really, who is going to do a goddamn thing?

Leaving the living room dark, Sheila let the recliner enfold her, containing all that she had left. The warm glass was in her hand; the bottle on the table beside her. This is not what she would have expected, had she looked ahead to this day. This wasn't grief. This was rage.

PART FIVE

"You got to get back up, even when life suggests you sit down. Everything is more comfortable for folks who just take a load off. Don't be one of them. The people passing by while you're sitting there aren't going to be the ones you want to walk behind."

DeCora Devereaux

1932-1968

MEMO

TO: Nutrition Services Employees
FROM: Gordon Hund, Nutrition Services Manager
DATE: Friday, July 2, 1976
RE: Bicentennial Celebration: Blast Off!, post-
          parade review, summer vacation, and
          other topics of interest

Ladies: I am certain there is no need to remind you that Sunday is a big day for Hanley, Minnesota, and for the United States of America: our nation's Independence Day celebration. On Sunday we commemorate the passage of the Declaration of Independence by the brave men of the Continental Congress.

Sunday is also a day of enormous import for the Nutrition Services Department as we contribute to the celebration by offering our food and labor. I am confident that implementation of your respective plans for the elementary, middle, and high schools will proceed smoothly.

Monday, July 5th is a full workday, which we will use to conduct an all-encompassing review of the implementation successes and failures of the district's food tables and Nutrition Services' participation in the Fourth of July parade. Your summer vacations will begin on Tuesday, July 6, 1976. You will be expected to return to work on Monday, August 16, 1976.

As the winner of the four-county regional competition for best in breed at the May 8, 1976 Dogstravaganza, Napoleon has earned a place in Sunday's parade alongside other regional winners in the standard poodle category. The statewide champion will be named following the August 7th competition, which will be held in Minneapolis.

CHAPTER TWENTY

Crystal

Sunday, July 4, 1976

CRYSTAL WAS CONTENT on many fronts this morning: picking up the effervescent Ada, appreciating the perfect parade weather, and the marshmallow on the cocoa? Imminent completion of the big Fourth of July whoop-ta-do.

Crystal would go to work tomorrow to discuss the parade and wrap up paperwork. Come August, after some top-notch time off, she'd return to the office, along with Coralene and Sheila, and do the whole thing again: feed the kids, ignore the boss. These were tasks Crystal was exceedingly well-qualified to do.

"Hope you don't think I overstepped here," Ada said, as she positioned her stubby body on Crystal's front seat. Ada's feet fell just short of the passenger-side floor, onto which she'd hoisted a cardboard box the size of a small ottoman. As Crystal pulled away from the curb, Ada extracted a stack of brown paper lunch bags from the box. She flapped them in Crystal's direction. "I had five of the grandkids yesterday. Thought this would be a good way to keep 'em busy."

"Hold on there," Crystal said, "or I'll run us into a telephone pole."

"I think these'll be good by you," Ada said, oblivious. "I had the grandkids do some coloring. Cute, huh?" She consolidated the bags she'd been waving about into a pile on her lap, tapping them on her chubby little legs as if they were an oversized deck of playing cards.

At the first red light, Crystal looked over. Sure enough, the bags were covered in childish drawings of stars, flags, fireworks, and no end of smiling suns – all appearing triumphant from what must have been several boxes of crayons. "Well go to the head of the class. Look at those!" Crystal said. "And if we run out of those artistic ones, I've got a box of plain ones in the trunk."

Crystal was pleased to be back behind the wheel; she had a spiffy car after all. She used The Dexter's garage for much of the fall and all of the winter, preferring not to drive in the rain and never driving in snow and ice. That's why God invented the bus.

Once temperatures warmed and a smidge of sunshine was likely, Crystal was delighted to drive around Hanley in her 1966 candy-apple-red Ford Fairlane. She'd had a motorbike once. Bad idea, and short-lived. Then for years, she'd driven the 1949 Ford she'd bought used from Mr. Kahn when she was still in high school. Good egg, Mr. Kahn. Perfectly adequate car. But in 1968, Crystal had purchased her dream car. It still looked good as new, protected as it always was from bad weather.

Her Fairlane earned the occasional admiring look when Crystal pulled into the parking lot at Doubles and Bubbles Hardware Store or the Piggly Wiggly. Admiration stopped when Crystal opened the door and heaved herself out. Oh go sit on a screwdriver, she'd fume, glaring at the backs of the men who turned away. You don't deserve a car like this anyway.

"Cookies going to be there when we arrive?" Ada asked. "Your cooks showing up with them?"

"That's the plan. I made sure they each had those plastic tubs with the lids. You know, the big ones with handles? So tubs of cookies should be waiting when we arrive."

"That's good of them to do all that," Ada said.

"It's their job." Crystal gave a little snort.

"Still good of them though, dear. Even ladies who are doing their jobs deserve a little appreciation. A little appreciation makes the world go round."

Crystal snorted again, but her heart wasn't in it.

Crystal had requested that two folding tables be set up end to end at the head of the parade route. The parade was scheduled to start at noon, which meant it would be underway some time south of 1:00. If the setup guys had paid attention to directions, there would also be two folding chairs. Crystal didn't want to consider the possibility that she'd have to stand for the duration of the parade. She could feel her feet swell at the very thought.

It made sense that the elementary schools' table came first. At the starting line. That way, elementary kids could walk the full seven blocks smack down the middle of Hanley with their cookie bags. Coralene, on the other hand, belonged at the end of the route, close to Fitzgerald Junior High and its boiling pots of hot dogs. This left the middle of the route for Sheila. Fine place for her.

Crystal found a spot for the Fairlane a block from where she expected to find her tables. Stroke of luck. The streets surrounding downtown were quickly being stripped of available parking. Walking toward the tables, she was tickled to see that they were exactly where she wanted them, and doubly pleased to see not two but four folding chairs. Hot diggity. So far, so good.

Lawn chairs, step stools, and even the odd pair of shoes dotted the curbs and parking strips of Center Street, like mushrooms emerging from the forest floor. A few early arrivers safeguarded stretches of curb which they'd shrouded in blankets and beach towels, as if that entitled them to valuable parade route real estate. These poor buggers must have drawn the short straws. Their friends and family were probably enjoying a second cup of coffee over at the Pancake House, or if they were lucky, a triple stack.

At what appeared to be the official launching spot, floats were being jostled into place, leaving gaps for the forthcoming invasion of marching bands, drill teams, and vintage cars. The whole crazy mess was quickly becoming congested. God help the dim-bulb driver who tried to get any closer to the parade route than Crystal just had.

A gaggle of parade lords and ladies were bustling among the floats, clipboards in hand. Boxes of popcorn, peanuts, noisemakers, and American flags occupied every inch of vacant ground. Eventually, a ragtag band of street vendors would shoulder their wares and slog through the crowds in pursuit of a buck, further complicating what Crystal knew would be goddamn hubbub, before the sun finally set on the big whoop-ta-do.

Betsy Becker, who had replaced Crystal at Hastings Elementary, was standing by the table as Crystal and Ada arrived. Betsy was a good egg, but one of those women who was always in motion. She and her husband took their children hiking, swimming, and God knows what else every summer. In the winter, to hear Betsy tell it, her family spent every weekend skiing and snowshoeing. Too much activity as far as Crystal was concerned. *Sit down, Betsy. Take a load off.* Crystal and Betsy had little in common, beyond their shared interest in the elementary school students of Hanley. Betsy's tubs of oatmeal-raisin cookies were on the ground by the chairs and appeared to be full to the gills. *Good job Betsy*, Crystal thought, but didn't say.

Betsy had taken it upon herself to wrap the table in butcher paper, painted with perfectly straight red and blue stripes. Stretches of unpainted paper stood in as white stripes, presenting the simple folding tables to the parade-goers of Hanley in a style worthy of a bicentennial celebration. *Hanley Elementary Schools* was painted across the banner in perfect ball and stick. In smaller letters, Betsy had added the names of each building: *Hastings*, *Prescott*, and *Alicia Park*. Crystal opened her mouth to give Betsy a well-deserved thank you, but Ada beat her to it.

"Well now, would you look at that?" Ada gushed, as if what she had feared was a mirage turned out to truly be a watering hole in the desert. "That's the most festive table I've ever seen.

It's downright perfect, I must say. You're Mrs. Becker, aren't you?" Ada asked. "Some of my grandkids go to Hastings and they talk about you all the time. Stephen? He's wily, that one. He's my son Bob's boy. Well, Stephen says that 'Mrs. Becker is the best cook ever.' That's a quote now, believe you me. Stephen tells me you always give the kids an extra pat of butter for their rolls and mashed potatoes. Tells me it's not just for the good kids, but for all the kids. That's exactly what Stephen says. 'Mrs. Becker takes care of all the kids.'"

Betsy busted out in a toothy grin. "Ahh, now you're sweet to say that," she told Ada. "Your Stephen is one of the good kids. But thing is," she leaned in as if to share a secret, "they all are. Good kids, I mean. If you tell them they are, if you treat them as if they are, then most of those kids will be good most of the time. Like grownups, I expect." Betsy turned toward Crystal. "Good morning. Beautiful day, no? This idea with the cookies? Brilliant. Just brilliant. Thanks for cooking it up." Betsy chuckled.

Before Crystal could comment, the two other cooks arrived, with two men trailing them: one tall, but otherwise nondescript, the other bald as an onion and exceedingly short. They were all lugging tubs. Lola Berg, the cook at Alicia Park, was chattering before she came to a full stop. Lola was the type who, as Crystal's grandmother would say, "filled a room." She wore her cook's uniform this morning, complete with black apron and name badge. Her gray top-knot was pulled so far forward on her head that it looked likely to slide down her nose and right off her face.

"Oh my, Betsy," Lola cooed. "That banner's perfect. Absolutely perfect." She paused long enough to speak to

Crystal. "Here are our tubs," she said, with a nod toward the short bald man behind her.

"We've got more chocolate-chip cookies here than the entire town could eat," Mr. Lola declared. "Have fun." He stood on tiptoe to deliver a peck on Lola's cheek. Before any of the women could respond, he escaped down the street, likely in search of a more desirable pre-parade landing spot than the cluster of women and bins of cookies.

The taller man remained, standing next to Midge Nygard, the cook at Prescott. It occurred to Crystal that Midge really should've paired up with Mr. Lola. Midge was a tiny woman. Tiny hands, a tiny waist, and a teeny tiny little head. Crystal found Midge's appearance troubling. It wasn't her fault that she was short. But if that was her lot, than perhaps she should beef up a bit, like Ada.

Midge's husband stood still as a scarecrow while Midge said hello to Betsy, Lola, and Crystal, and was introduced to Ada. Finally Midge turned toward him. "This is Lloyd. My husband."

Lloyd's graying hair sported a crew cut, freshly shorn this morning if his pink neck was any indication. "What we have here," he said, "are the best sugar cookies the city of Hanley has ever tasted. I've made sure of that. Tested more than a few." With that, he too escaped. Lloyd – like Lola's husband whose name Crystal never caught – was wearing jeans and a work shirt, the much-respected uniform of local farmers.

It was July. Farmers' wheat, corn, and soybeans, to say nothing of their hogs and cows, would be demanding every scrap of their time and energy. That Midge and Lola's husbands – and perhaps also Betsy's, who'd escaped before

Crystal arrived – supported the schools and their cookies pleased Crystal in a way she couldn't quite describe.

Crystal had known farm boys in high school. They were tanned and strong. They drove tractors and pickups. They sat in the back of class with mud on their boots and occasionally fell asleep. When Crystal had shown up at school on a motor scooter, most of the farm boys had laughed. Most, but not all. There'd been some good ones; they were the farm boys who drank coffee before anyone else their age even considered it. They worked hard, went to bed early, and never brought attention to themselves. Crystal's father had been born on a farm, but he hadn't stayed there. No one had ever thought Alfie Carmichael was farmer material.

Ada had dived right into conversations with Betsy, Lola, and Midge. Ada's grandkids were spread all over town. Soon Crystal heard that not only did Stephen attend Hastings and dearly love Mrs. Becker, Carol Ann was in the fourth grade at Alicia Park and thought the world of Mrs. Berg, and Stephanie, who'd just finished kindergarten at Prescott, thought Mrs. Nygard was "a nice lady and a real good cook."

Ada and the three cooks stood in a circle that, while not deliberately excluding her, left Crystal to the side. They yakked, engaging each other in a way that made Crystal feel peripheral. Unnecessary at her own event. Nothing in their words or demeanor was anything but kind; still, Crystal wondered whether they'd notice if she left. It hadn't occurred to her as she'd envisioned today's activities that the cooks would stay. Tubs of cookies would be delivered to the table one way or another, which was where the relevance and presence of Betsy, Midge, and Lola would begin and end. It would be

Crystal and Ada. Ada and Crystal. The two of them would round up the children, give them their bags of cookies, pull off cookie distribution, and bring the big whoop-ta-do to an end, at long last.

Ada was Crystal's friend, after all. Crystal couldn't avoid the next thought which logically followed: Ada was her *only* friend. Now Ada had stepped into the orbit of the cooks, who had a gravitational pull all their own. Crystal was out of her depth.

Flipping through a handful of lunch sacks as if perusing a magazine, Crystal felt a profound contradiction in her feelings for Ada. Having the grandkids decorate these bags? That had been so thoughtful. Such an Ada thing to do. But now, when women of more interest, or perhaps more relevance in Ada's life were in the picture, Crystal felt as she often did, that she'd do best to just disappear.

CHAPTER TWENTY-ONE

Coralene

Sunday, July 4, 1976

THE MORNING SUN invading her bedroom refused to allow Coralene even one more minute's sleep. The sheer curtains were no match for the light outside. Stretching under the covers, she pointed her toes up toward her nose and twisted her ankles to form the letters of the alphabet. "Keeps you from getting those leg cramps," Mama would say. Which was true, it did.

These were the days she craved, when the blessings of sun and heaven would nurture the people below. Keep them safe. Help them do their best. Yet beside these thoughts were Coralene's memories of another bright morning, which brought only heartache.

She pictured DeCora's withered face, her hands as motionless as shadows on top of the covers, as she'd teetered between sleep and somewhere better. Coralene had been sitting in the soft blue chair at the side of DeCora's bed, the one that Jasper had lugged from the living room. She'd held DeCora's nonresponsive hand and willed toward her baby sister all the love she'd held since the day DeCora was born.

~ ~ ~

Coralene, who was hardy and large, had marveled at DeCora, who'd been small, as delicate as a robin. Her nose in a book, her feet on solid ground, DeCora had tended to her studies, and side by side with Coralene, had tended as well to the mama and daddy they both adored.

When she started high school, DeCora announced that she planned to be a nurse. No one who knew her doubted that one day she would don the thick stockings, bobby pin the cap on her dainty head, and offer up care and devotion, the very legacy of goodness, which was all she and Coralene had ever known.

Coralene remembered the day DeCora graduated from nursing school. Her thick stockings, her sturdy shoes, her nurse's uniform were all as white as a cloud. DeCora's cap was so perfectly pinned that only a tornado could have sent it askew.

Early days at the hospital had been heady. DeCora had been one of the first Black nurses. Eventually, as DeCora had told Coralene, she was no longer "that Black nurse," but just a nurse. For most doctors anyway. For most patients. In most circumstances. DeCora didn't dawdle over the obstacles other people put in their own way. She didn't have time. She had a job to do.

When DeCora met Randy Deveraux, Coralene had hoped it was a passing fancy. She had no real issue with the man, he was just so unworthy of her sister. But he was handsome, Coralene had to give him that, with skin as pale as Minnesota snow, and eyes as blue as the Minnesota sky. He was a sturdy man, and in his height and strength he reminded Coralene of the paper birch trees that had stood in clusters as if talking among themselves in the fields behind the house where Coralene and DeCora had grown up.

From the day Randy Devereaux stepped down from the cab of his delivery truck, loaded up the hand truck with boxes of gauze, sponges, and bandages, and wheeled his bounty past the nurses' station, DeCora was captivated. Randy, who was so different from the men DeCora knew from church or the neighborhood. Randy's skies were wider than DeCora's had ever been. Randy wanted adventures. He had big ideas. He had big dreams. He made DeCora feel like a ballerina in a music box, cherished and free to spin.

The bloom faded quickly once Randy and DeCora were married. Even before Tanner was born, Randy cast his eye, and his ambitions, in a thousand different directions. But DeCora had taken vows. Tanner stayed with Mama and Daddy when DeCora was at work. Some evenings Randy would come home from making deliveries and the three Deverauxes – DeCora, Randy, and Tanner – would sit in their tiny house doing what families do. They'd eat dinner, they'd watch television, they'd read books together, and when night fell, DeCora would be in Randy's arms.

But eventually, Randy spent less time at the dinner table, in front of the TV, or holding his son to read a story. He spent less time, and then none, in DeCora's bed. By the time Tanner was seven, Randy was pretty much gone for good.

Occasionally he'd show up for a birthday or a meal. With each appearance, he told tales of his work as a carpenter "a couple counties over" where he would learn more, earn more, and be more worthy of his wife and his son than he could ever be driving a delivery truck.

Once, he'd scratched out a phone number telling DeCora it was a house in Minneapolis where he was staying "for a bit," still declaring that he'd return, and when he did he'd be riding high. What this high riding would look like, or how it would occur, was anybody's guess. Randy had left his warmest jacket on the hook by the back door and most of his tools in the basement, so for a long time DeCora thought he might show back up. When he didn't, DeCora asked around, sacrificing her self-respect in an effort to bring father and son back together. But Randy was gone. From their home and from their town. But never from Tanner's dearest hopes, and never from DeCora's heart.

Coralene had to search long and hard to find the hand of God as DeCora's life had ended. She found it in the speed of the cancer, in the lack of a protracted death. She found it in knowing that God had blessed her, Coralene, with the best sister He would ever create. And Coralene found God's hand in knowing that Tanner would be safe and loved in the home into which God had already granted such an abundance of blessings, in the form of Jasper and Coravelle.

~ ~ ~

Coralene looked at the clock radio - 9:00. She patted Jasper's side of the bed, knowing it had long gone cool. Jasper was an early riser on Sunday mornings, treasuring the one day each week when he needn't contort his activities into the upside down world of the graveyard shift. He would've been up at least three hours by now. Tanner was an early riser too. But Coralene and Coravelle? They'd rather pull the covers back over their heads. Coralene would've done exactly that had it been any other Sunday; the family didn't usually attend church until 11:30.

But it was not a typical Sunday; it was parade day. Coralene would make the most of it. Her family, her co-workers, the whole motley citizenry of Hanley would have her full attention. Hot dogs all around. One more day. Then she'd wrap up the school year tomorrow, and settle in for some summer time at home. Enough fussing with floats and hot dogs. Enough fussing with corn relish too, although she felt only gratitude to Jasper and Tanner for figuring that one out. Coralene felt gratitude for Jasper every day, something she'd mentioned to the Lord just this morning when she'd counted her blessings before finally getting out of bed.

Coralene zipped up her robe and stuffed her feet into the turquoise Dearfoam slippers Coravelle had given her last Christmas. Sweet Velly. After a stop at the bathroom, she shuffled down the hallway, past Coravelle's closed door and Tanner's open one. She shuffled past the gallery of family photos that lined both walls: baby pictures of Coravelle and Tanner, Coralene and Jasper's wedding photo, and the photo of DeCora, the day she graduated from nursing school with Mama, Daddy, and Coralene beside her.

Coralene shuffled into the kitchen where Jasper would be holding the pot above her favorite Sunday coffee mug. He wouldn't pour until he heard her coming down the hall.

Pouring the coffee too soon meant it would be cooled when she went to drink it. In twenty-three years of marriage, Jasper had never presented Coralene with a cold cup of coffee. There was nothing about Jasper Johnson that could be described as "cold."

Sure enough, Jasper was waiting by the counter holding the pot. He wore a pair of dark brown pants and a short-sleeved casual shirt with a half zipper. Coralene had bought him that shirt for Father's Day. Its orange background and yellow stripes played perfectly off Jasper's dark skin.

Coffee being the next order of business, Coralene sat at the kitchen table as Jasper handed her the mug. She smiled up at him, catching his eye for the first time since she'd entered the kitchen. Jasper's eyes did not smile back.

"What's up, baby? That's not the face of the handsome man who hands me my coffee on Sunday mornings."

"No, it's not, love. And you know I don't have a troubled face on your account."

"So what is it then?"

"Tanner," Jasper said, as if that was the extent of the answer required. "It's Tanner."

"Oh Lord." Coralene held her mug in both hands, taking a quick sip. "What did he do?"

"Well, I don't know that he did anything. Or if he did, I don't know what it is. I saw him first thing this morning when I was sitting here reading the paper. Told him you'd be up in a while, and then all four of us – him, you, me, and Velly – we'd be heading over to the parade route. He looked like he was going somewhere. Had the truck keys in his hand. I asked him where he was going, but he said it was a surprise. Said he was going to pick up his friend Craig. Said Craig was in on the surprise too. Something about Craig's mama having to be at the parade early today too. Handing out cookies or some such."

Coralene nodded. "Craig's mama is Lola Berg. She works over at Hastings. Works with Crystal. You've heard about Crystal. She's Leonora's granddaughter. Leonora? My mama's friend?"

"Oh, I know Leonora. Don't know anything about Crystal other than that you work with her, but no matter. Thing is I don't know where Tanner went off to. Lots of folks counting on him this morning. Thought he'd be back way before now. I'm both angry and worried. Know what I mean?"

"Oh, I know," Coralene said. "I'm feeling both those things myself. Maybe he decided to meet us at the parade?"

"No way to tell. Maybe we pull Velly out of bed and head over there now," Jasper said. "We can leave a note for Tanner. Whatcha think?"

"I think that's a good idea, baby," Coralene said, taking another gulp before pushing back her chair. "Sorry I'm not going to be sitting here having coffee with you, but you're right. Heading over there now is a good idea. I'll get dressed."

"I don't want to be dealing with another mess from that boy," Jasper said gruffly, as Coralene stepped away from the table. "Summer's coming. You have vacation coming up. I'm taking that week off end of the month. Don't want Tanner stirring the pot. Any pot. I don't want it."

"I'll get dressed," Coralene said again. "You wake up Velly."

CHAPTER TWENTY-TWO

Leonora

Sunday, July 4, 1976

LEONORA SAT AT her kitchen table in the quiet of the morning. The back door was open. The screen held the bugs at bay while inviting in the early July breeze. She'd always been an early riser. Over decades of raising girls in this house, Leonora had needed this time to herself. A cup of coffee, a piece of toast, and the calm that came from hearing no one's breathing but her own.

Yet in her morning solitude, Leonora had never been truly alone. For the fifteen years they'd been married, and the forty-eight since he died, Badger Daniels had sat with his wife as she started her day.

They had bought this house in 1919, when the war was over, and the prospect of a home for their beloved Pearl had brought Leonora and Badger joy that could not be contained, any more than they could have held back the steady flow of the Mississippi.

Leonora had savored every day they'd spent together here: the smell of him, the way he'd brushed her hair aside to kiss her neck, the constancy of his love for her. All had surpassed the riches held by any other woman in the world.

When Ruby was born, Leonora had nestled her into the crib Badger had built, next to Pearl's hand-crafted sleigh bed. Their "two perfect gems" was how Badger and Leonora referred to their daughters as they'd stood together in the doorway of the girls' bedroom late at night. Leonora would tuck herself under Badger's arm and he'd pull her to him, resting his chin on her hair. Nowhere, Leonora had thought then, nowhere on God's green Earth, was there another family as blessed as this one.

Thousands and thousands of mornings had been spent by this window, watching as rain, or snow, or magnificent sun showed itself in the side yard, doing what it would to the plants cultivated there. Of late, Leonora had planted foxglove – in every imaginable shade of pink. Cone-shaped blossoms on tall stems camouflaged the fence Leonora shared with the Kahns next door.

Grasping her coffee cup, her feet firmly on the floor lest she slip out of her chair, Leonora closed her eyes as the sun warmed her back. How many more mornings? She didn't know. What she did know is that she'd stewarded her life, nurtured her home and family – in all the forms it had taken over the years – and she was ready to go when the time was right.

There are days when people know they have been less than they should be. In those lesser moments, we are people we don't recognize. And then there are days – and Leonora understood that there were more of these now – when the only thing we recognize is what we look back on, who we used to be. We have lost ourselves, and going forward we will never truly know ourselves again.

Leonora had been contemplative over these months, telling herself she was peeking behind the curtain to compare the view from audience or stage. Her time was limited; her options were diminishing. But of course, whose weren't? She intended to own her own passing, as she'd owned her own life. She'd lived so much of that life alone, with no one to ask for help, and no one to whom she must account. She would account to no one about her death. There was nothing left that she must do. She would leave no commitments unmet once she and the ladies had ridden down Center Street behind a riding mower: their comical contribution to Independence Day.

Olive's son-in-law, Donald, owned a rug cleaning business. When Darcy had guided the guild through the discussion of how they'd arrive at the parade, Olive had gleefully volunteered Donald to drive them right up to their float in his new *Donald's Divine Rug Cleaning* Econoline van.

Leonora was lukewarm on the idea of riding in a rug cleaning van, as was Cora, an opinion the two women exchanged in a glance. So it had been decided that Hy, Lo, Glad, and Olive would go with Donald. Cora and Leonora would go with Darcy.

The float itself would be transported to the parade starting line the afternoon before by Tanner and Jasper, at which time they'd secure the chairs and mount the umbrellas.

Darcy, Coralene, and Coravelle would arrange craft baskets, fuss with bunting, and generally ensure that four pallets and a riding mower would suitably transport six little old ladies through the middle of town.

Lo and Glad had grumbled that they would be gathering right at the time that respectable people eat lunch and suggested they bring sandwiches. Leonora didn't like the idea of the ladies eating while they rode their float down the street, but Glad would not be dissuaded.

"If we get too hungry," Glad had declared with a patronizing tone, "then we'll get weak, and if we're weak and out in the heat – to stay nothing of being elevated above the street – we could fall plum off the float. It just follows that we'll need something to eat. I would've thought you'd think of that."

Darcy, who intended to walk alongside the float, and perhaps score a cookie from a first grader, had tried to assuage Glad's concerns. "If you fall off," she'd said, "I'll catch you before you actually hit the street." Glad had only grumbled further, and Leonora had no doubt that a bag of sandwiches would appear.

~ ~ ~

Darcy – who was quite skilled at convincing total strangers to give her what she wanted – managed to sweet-talk a clipboard-laden parade steward into letting her drive the Pinto to within a few dozen paces of the float. Donald, it appeared, had a similar talent. Leonora was relieved when all six women appeared at approximately the same time. She'd feared that Donald would need to park a mile away and corral Hy, Lo, Glad, and his own mother-in-law through the crowds. Had that happened, Donald's herd of old ladies would have missed everything but the fireworks.

The guild ladies, Darcy, and Donald admired the float where it stood in the queue, between a 1929 Model A and what appeared to be a growing contingent of poodles.

Chairs were secured to the float floor, three on each side. Red, white, or blue umbrellas were attached to the chair backs, and each chair swiveled, so should they choose to, the guild ladies could twirl themselves 360 degrees to delight parade-goers on both sides of the street with no end of scrubbies, pot holders, and corduroy turtles.

Jasper had built a portable set of stairs with a railing attached so that each guild lady could climb aboard into the seat of her choosing without suffering the indignity of clawing over the bunting. In Leonora's case, such a feat would have been impossible.

It was a moment before Leonora noticed what was perhaps the most thoughtful gesture she'd seen in an age. The chairs had seat belts. Surely Jasper's handiwork. Suddenly this entire circus – old ladies, stuffed turtles, office chairs, umbrellas, sandwiches, and God knows what else – became a tolerable event. Maybe even a happy one. For weeks, Leonora had worried. How would she sit securely for the hour it would take to travel through downtown Hanley? What if she stumbled getting on or off? What if she keeled over, right in the middle of Center Street? But she'd agreed to this, and she'd see it through. Surprisingly in this moment, standing between her best friend and her favorite grandchild, Leonora could picture herself on the float, buckled in, and perhaps even enjoying the ride.

Jasper and Coralene wouldn't be accompanying the guild. Coralene's responsibility for the junior high school kitchens required that she, Jasper, and Coravelle set up a hot dog stand at the end of the parade route. It occurred to Leonora that the hot dog idea was ripe for mishaps. Too many cooks in the kitchen. But if anyone could pull off the distribution of hot dogs to legions of parade-goers, it was Coralene Johnson.

As for Tanner, he'd proposed that he be responsible for a task more noteworthy than dolloping hot dogs with corn relish. Tanner had asked, had practically begged, to ride the mower that would pull the float. His pleas might have gone unanswered had Jasper and Coralene been the ones to decide, but Tanner had appealed to Cora. As grandmothers are known to do, Cora had stood her ground, confirming that Tanner taking the wheel would be an appropriate reward for the work he'd done on the float and his track record of responsibility as a carpenter's apprentice. Besides, who else was going to drive it?

Leonora was mortified that this important detail had been overlooked by all of them, including Darcy. When Olive had enlisted Donald to shuttle the ladies to the parade, she'd crowed that Donald would be the perfect mower driver, given his experience driving his new van and all. But Tanner had prevailed. So Leonora was more than a little peeved that when it was finally time for the parade, Tanner failed to show.

CHAPTER TWENTY-THREE

LEXIE

SUNDAY, JULY 4, 1976

"THIS IS A marvel of organization. I'm impressed." Lexie stood with her hands on her hips, admiring the taco salad stand.

Artfully twisted red, white, and blue crepe paper streamers looped along the stretch of folding tables, which were, thank God, perfectly positioned in the shade. From one end to the other, they were encased in red butcher paper, crisply creased at each end, sealed up like some oversized Valentine. Small white balloons filled the gaps of each crepe paper loop. It all looked exceedingly festive. This would not have been Sheila's doing. Sheila wanted everything just right but even on a good day, festive was not Sheila's natural state, and Sheila would not be having a good day today. No day had been a good day since the death of Ralph Blatson.

Lexie had decided against wearing her denim cutoffs, thinking perhaps Sheila wouldn't approve. Lexie liked the idea that she'd be representing the school district, or at a minimum her alma mater. She'd opted for her seersucker skirt. It was perfect for the toned-down outfit she'd put together: white skirt, sleeveless navy blouse, and a red bandana to hold back her hair. It was the bicentennial, for heaven's sake. She would've loved to go wild: pump up the celebration with beads, bows, and bells. But she was here for Sheila, who was struggling to be here at all.

Not surprisingly, Sheila's outfit was like many others Lexie had seen on hundreds of Friday nights: a brown cotton shirt dress, its short sleeves the only nod to the July weather. There was no nod to the holiday. Red, white, and blue were as absent from Sheila's outfit as if she'd dressed for a funeral.

Lexie gazed across the stretch of tables, catching Sheila's attention and those of her two cooks. "I bet y'all do this kind of assembly line thing all the time, yes? It looks terrific."

"That we do," Geneva Green piped in. Geneva had replaced Sheila as head cook at Norlin Hanley High, Lexie's old school. A few yards from Geneva, Tammy Peterson, head cook at Lake Sylvester, paused to wipe a forearm over her already sweating face.

The women were friendly enough but Lexie sensed irritation from Tammy, who had a strained, scratchy voice. "There's a lot to get done here," she said, scraping the words across an invisible rasp. "We've been at it a while." Tammy was tall and exceedingly thin; her hairline left her forehead exposed in a way that was unusual on a woman. No wonder she was wiping sweat off her brow at 11:00 in the morning.

Geneva was the opposite of Tammy in every visible way. Neither short nor tall, Geneva had a perfect figure. Her skin was smooth and brown, bringing to mind the glossiness of maple syrup. She was older than Tammy, early fifties was Lexie's guess. Tammy, Lexie figured, had only recently reached her thirties.

Lexie felt a pang for Tammy; this woman had never been pretty. Never would be. She'd donned a black hairnet which flattened her dirty-blonde curls and left her looking as if someone had shaken a brush in her direction, spattering her head with countless specks of black paint.

Next to her, Geneva's dome of black hair shaped her face like a perfect oval frame. It would be a shame to contain that afro with a hairnet.

Introductions over, Sheila turned away. Ignoring Lexie, Tammy and Geneva picked up the discussion they'd been having regarding the pros and cons of Hanley's bicentennial celebration.

"Hanley doesn't hold a candle to East Coast cities," Tammy was saying. "Or maybe I should say East Coast rivers."

"What are you talking about?" Geneva scowled and Lexie sensed an underlying disregard between the two women. "What's the matter with our river? It's the Mississippi, for goodness sakes. It can hold its own with any river on the east coast."

"Not as far as festivities, it can't," Tammy said. "At least not here. They've got tall ships on the Hudson from all over the world. All sailing right through the middle of New York City."

"Sounds like a recipe for disaster. No thank you."

"Maybe. But in Boston, they've got their orchestra playing outside. Outside! Can you believe it? That's the one I'd like to see." Tammy's cranky words had turned to whines. "What do we have?" she murmured, so low that Lexie could barely hear. "What do we have? We have taco salads and Shriners in clown cars. A bit of a disappointment, if you ask me."

Geneva was wrangling plastic wrap, attempting to quash an unruly mound of shredded lettuce. "I wouldn't want to be in the middle of those big-city crowds," she said. "This is more my speed." She waved her arm toward the mild-mannered masses gathering on Center Street. "We'll have fireworks tonight. That's what we'll have on our river. Off a barge, I think. That's enough for me."

Tammy was waging her own battle with a pan full of shredded cheddar. The two women triumphed at the same moment, and as if performing a dance move, turned on their heels to slide the trays into the refrigerator positioned behind them.

Lexie did a double take. There was a refrigerator? Well of course there was. Sheila had arranged for a generator. There would be no glitches today, Lexie doubted that there ever were on Sheila's watch. Any risk of parade day food poisoning had been checked off the list. As if conscripted to the cause, the generator, refrigerator, and a squat warming oven stood in precise formation under an oak tree. Each had been leveled on the rough terrain with 2x4s and an assortment of wood shims.

Paper bowls, paper napkins, and plastic forks had been neatly stacked in pans at one end of the tables. Serving spoons, laid out at intervals, would soon be assigned to chopped lettuce, taco-seasoned hamburger meat, and grated cheese. There was a large lidded bin full of Fritos. Lexie assumed a few of those would be sprinkled atop each salad. The only thing missing was the salsa.

Promising to return around noon, Geneva and Tammy wandered off. Lexie was relieved that they were out of earshot; she walked over to stand next to Sheila. "Have you heard from him?"

"Hell no. Not a word. Not a goddamn word. I should've known better. Why would he want anything to do with this whole operation? For that matter, why would you? I can't believe I fell for his baloney. 'I'd like to think I could be useful' he says? Useful my ass."

"Let's not go down that road, okay?" Lexie said gently. "Not as it relates to me anyway. You know why I'm here. Same reason Tom will be here too. It's probably a parking problem, don't you think? Or maybe the restaurant didn't have the salsa ready. Knowing Tom, if there was a screwup, he's tracking down salsa at the Piggly Wiggly this very minute."

Sheila's expression didn't change. There was a vagueness in her voice this morning, and her face had a foggy cast. It had been just over two weeks since what Lexie thought of as *obituary night*. The Sheila she'd seen since, and the Sheila who stood beside her this morning, barely resembled the Sheila Lexie knew.

Sheila was handsome; the incongruous descriptor suited her. Or it had. Now, Lexie wasn't sure how she'd describe Sheila. "Sad" or "lonely" were insufficient. This Sheila was like fraying cloth, as unlikely to return to her original state as the hems on Lexie's cutoffs. Fraying such as what Lexie saw in Sheila's face, and deep in her eyes, would never be repaired.

Lexie shook her head, as if trying to understand a mystery that was beyond her. "In case you were thinking I blew it," she said, "I reminded him to be here at 11:00. That's what you said on Friday and that's what I told Tom when I saw him last night."

"It never crossed my mind that you blew it."

From babes in arms to every size and shape of old person, Hanley's citizens had descended on downtown. Fathers carrying children on their shoulders and mothers with squirming toddlers on their hips mingled with parents who'd already had enough. They were the ones squeezing small arms and scolding their youngsters to keep up. The hodgepodge of Hanley humanity was filling every available inch along Center Street, pouring into view like water from a broken pipe.

Every possible article of clothing – tee shirts, shorts, bowler hats, maxi skirts, and bikini tops – showcased vivid red, white, and blue. Stars and stripes were everywhere. Images of the Statue of Liberty, Uncle Sam, fireworks, Liberty Bells, and replicas of timeworn copies of the Constitution filled store windows. Children clutched teddy bears that were in turn clutching American flags. Older soldiers, who had served in an earlier time, wore uniforms as pressed as age would allow. Younger soldiers stood among them, their backs straight, their uniforms still crisp. In other clusters along the street, young men who might have been soldiers, or who might not, stood along the parade route with American flags draped around their shoulders.

Some parade-goers lugged lawn chairs; others sat on the curb. The curb sitters kicked debris into the street and used their shoes as dust brooms in futile attempts to remove grime before planting their rumps and taking in the sights. Some people made decisions in the moment, claiming spots as they happened upon them – causing others to accordion behind them – before sitting down or joining the rows of people standing in zigzag lines like some makeshift choir.

Across the street, four teenage boys had managed to climb onto the striped awning of Doubles and Bubbles Hardware Store. They dangled their legs over the sidewalk below, pitching peanuts in the general direction of anyone under the age of twenty. Lexie couldn't watch. What would happen if that awning gave way?

There were vendors everywhere, peddling popcorn, American flags, and God knew what else. They crossed back and forth across the street, dodging parade-goers cautiously, given the weight of their loads and the number of children darting about. Lexie remembered childhood parades when she and her sister likewise ran in the street from which they'd typically be forbidden. "Hold Wendy's hand," her father would remind her. "Be careful with her, Lexie. Don't let her out of your sight."

~ ~ ~

Not once had Lexie let Wendy out of her sight. Not once had she or her father needed to panic. Never had their guileless, vulnerable Wendy slipped away at the park, the grocery store, or the beach. Never at the parade. Wendy was not one to pull away her hand, and Lexie and her father had not been ones to let go.

Instead, "Don't let Wendy out of your sight" became just one of those things her father said. It had been as comforting to Lexie as any kiss on the forehead, any smile, any heartfelt "Atta girl." They'd tended to Wendy together. By the time Wendy was three years old, Lexie barely missed the mother who'd become unhinged upon Wendy's arrival.

Her mother couldn't abide the baby she and Lexie's father had excitedly awaited, so many years after Lexie was born. Lexie understood that what her mother had craved was another Lexie. She'd wanted to care for another Lexie. Raise another Lexie. Show off another Lexie to the church ladies and the bridge club. She hadn't asked for a Wendy. Eventually Lexie's mother chose freedom from Wendy over tending the ties that bound her to Lexie or Lexie's father. She'd driven off on a Tuesday afternoon.

Wendy's needs were simple ones, easily met. Her sister's innate sweetness soon filled the vacuum left behind at her mother's departure. For Lexie, her father and sister were more than enough.

Mrs. Gaard, the kind, pudgy widow next door, had watched Wendy when Lexie was in school. Hour after hour, Wendy hung laundry in the sun, walked Mrs. Gaard's dog around the yard, or climbed onto the kitchen counter to hand Mrs. Gaard the teacups from the highest shelf. She learned to weed the garden – discerning between the tall, thin leaves of quackgrass and the first frilly tops of carrots and parsnips.

Mrs. Gaard's front room knew no dust, her rugs knew no crumbs, her bathtub never once had a ring. Keeping things clean was Wendy's job, and she took to it with enthusiasm, and, over time, some considerable skill.

It was Mrs. Gaard who had discovered Lexie's father in the driveway. He appeared to have parked the car, gathered his keys and briefcase, and set out for the front door. He never made it to the porch.

The medics said the heart attack had been quick. Probably painless. There was nothing Lexie could've done, they told her. And certainly nothing she could do now.

Lexie's last year of high school had been spent with Mrs. Gaard, who'd guided Lexie through the business of her father's death and did what she could to fill the vacancy in Lexie's heart. With Mrs. Gaard's steadying hand at her back, Lexie sold her family home and used the money to find a place for Wendy. A safe and happy place, not too far away. Then Lexie started down the road on which she still found herself. She moved with her friend Grace into an apartment on Northeast 14th Street and went to work at Denny's.

As for Mrs. Gaard, she moved to Eden Prairie to live with her daughter and sent Spritz cookies and cardamom bread every Christmas.

It had been that simple. Lexie understood simple. She'd never dreamed of a complicated life.

~ ~ ~

Once the parade was over, the next round of Hanley's celebratory activities would begin down by the river. The bandstand in the park would burst forth with every patriotic song that Lexie had learned in kindergarten.

At 7:00, Hanley's mayor would dig a hole – with the real muscle coming from the Public Works Department – and bury a time capsule in Riverfront Park. As president of Hanley's First National Bank, the mayor had insisted that a safety deposit box be used as the container, the bank's name emblazoned for all time across its lid. Hanley's residents were evidently fond of securing their valuables for posterity; the mayor offered up the biggest box available. It was – according to Hanley matrons who remembered such things – bigger than a bread box.

Time capsule contents had been on display at the public library since June. Hanley lacked imagination. Lexie had read about a man in Nebraska who'd enshrined a car. Nothing so bold here. Instead, the twelfth-grade American History classes had selected random items: a 1976 yearbook; a copy of the *Hanley Herald*; a toothbrush and a tube of Crest; a tie-dyed tee shirt; family photos contributed by the mayor; packages of Pop Rocks, Pringles, and Ho Hos; an electric knife; a fondue pot; a floating candle; a mood ring; a pet rock; Malibu Barbie; a cassette tape of *Goodbye Yellow Brick Road;* and a Doubles and Bubbles key ring. Such a mediocre effort.

To Lexie's delight, the children's librarian had intervened to boost the overall quality of the capsule. Leaving the high schoolers to stand by their dull offerings, Hanley's youngest book lovers had voted to include a few of their favorites: *The Wizard of Oz, Charlie and the Chocolate Factory, Where the Wild Things Are, The Snowy Day,* and the book Lexie knew Wendy slept with under her pillow: *Pat the Bunny.*

It occurred to Lexie that perhaps the Earth Sciences

teacher should have been consulted as well, before the decision was made to bury the capsule only twenty feet from the river bank, deep into Mississippi mud.

Fireworks would begin at 9:30, and throngs of teenagers would kick up benign mischief well into the night. Lexie loved the Fourth of July, this one more than most. The noise, the floats, the bands, and the mishmash of people folded together like meringue into cake batter. Her city, her people, this community she adored, were amassing for one hell of a party. These sentiments were safe in her heart; she was intent on relishing every minute of the day. But still, there was a taint. How could Tom just not show up?

Lexie had a sixth sense about when people were only late, and when they weren't coming at all. Tom Downlane was not coming.

CHAPTER TWENTY-FOUR

Coralene

Sunday, July 4, 1976

CORALENE WASN'T PARTICULARLY drawn to Janet Pettigrew and Peggy Stamm. Jan had been Peg's assistant cook at Sinclair Lewis. When Coralene's head cook spot became available at F. Scott Fitzgerald, Jan had handily taken it on. Jan and Peg were White, both in their thirties, and both exuding a vigor that Coralene found not off-putting necessarily, but unnerving, or just plain odd. Both women opted out of the polyester dresses that were the standard cooks' uniforms, choosing instead to wear white nurse pants and half-zip polyester shirts that Coralene had to admit were appropriate for the work they did.

Jan was a head taller than Peg, with straight blonde hair that she wore short. The skin of her left cheek was cloudy and taut, evidence of a grease fire she'd endured in a school kitchen outside Duluth.

Peg was a pixie, with a pert haircut that showed more

style than Jan's but was similarly short. Her skin was as smooth as powdered-sugar icing. She reminded Coralene of that Romanian gymnast on TV.

On Friday afternoon, Coralene had met with Jan and Peg in the kitchen at Fitzgerald for a dress rehearsal of sorts. It probably hadn't been necessary; she wasn't worried. Her cooks were competent. The plan was a solid one. Not a show-stopper, but practical and doable, and one which Coralene believed – and Jan and Peg agreed – made sense on many levels.

Hot dogs. For heaven's sake. What could possibly be more appropriate fare for a bicentennial celebration than hot dogs? They might as well have "All-American" written in ketchup on the top of the buns. The buns would be soft; the hot dogs would be hot; ketchup, mustard, and corn relish would be plentiful. Provided there was a sufficient supply of paper napkins, the junior high schools' hot dog stand would do itself proud.

Jan and Peg had enlisted their assistant cooks to keep those hot dogs coming, along with a few junior high girls to work as runners. Serving utensils, trash disposal logistics, and table layout had been covered in less than an hour.

Coralene was eager to put this entire event behind her. Crystal referred to the schools' parade participation as the "big whoop-ta-do." Coralene didn't go in for sarcasm, but in her mind she cheered on Crystal's candor.

Coralene had told Jan and Peg about the hospital guild float, explaining that while the hot dog stand would have her full attention, she'd have the distraction of worrying about Tanner, who was slated to be behind the wheel of a riding mower as it set off down Center Street with its cargo of little old ladies and stuffed turtles.

Questions had been asked and answered on Friday, so Coralene was alarmed by Saturday morning's call from Jan. Was she sick? Was her husband sick? Did she even have a husband? Jan bore no dire message other than telling Coralene that she'd be in the neighborhood in twenty minutes and could stop by to pick up the corn relish and stow it in the Fitzgerald refrigerator on her way home. This, Jan proposed, would leave one less thing for Coralene to worry about on Sunday morning.

It was a thoughtful gesture. That didn't make it a welcome one. Her private life was precisely that; Coralene had no interest in opening her home to her co-workers. Adding insult to injury, when Coralene answered the door it was not only Jan showing up to provide needless transportation for the corn relish, but Peg too.

"Oh," was all Coralene could say as she opened the door. Both her composure and her manners faltered miserably. "Oh, my goodness, you're both here. No need, really. We could've brought it along in the morning. There are eighteen jars, which should be more than enough, but I don't think it'll take both of you to carry them."

"Oh golly no," Peg said, as if standing in her supervisor's doorway was the logical place for her to be at 11:00 on a Saturday morning. "Jan and I were playing tennis. You know, at the courts down by the river? Jan had the smart idea to swing by and fetch the relish. Help out a bit, you know? There was a pay phone right there, so I pulled out my little black book, found your number, and here we are."

The women were as high-spirited as they were sweaty. Peg wore a yellow tennis skirt with a yellow and white striped tank top and blindingly white tennis shoes. Jan was in a navy-blue tennis dress with red trim along the skirt. Her shoes were identical to Peg's. The two of them could've played endless games of tennis in the dark, by the light of their shoes alone. Just the thought made Coralene want to sit down.

"Perfect day for tennis," Jan said. "We couldn't resist. Had to hit the ball a bit before it got too hot. It's not bad out though. If this weather holds, we should be alright. We don't want clouds tomorrow, but we don't want to swelter either."

Jasper appeared, unbeckoned, carrying a cardboard box of corn relish jars, packed as tightly as Spam in a can. He sidled up, as if Coralene's discomfort had been communicated to him along some invisible spousal wavelength.

"Perfection! Thank you," Jan said, taking the box from Jasper as she introduced herself and Peg. "We work with Coralene. She's the greatest, just the greatest. You're a lucky man."

Coralene should have handled introductions, for heaven's sake. But she'd lost her footing at the sight of her tennis-garbed cooks on the front porch, and now she just wanted them to leave. Still, they were colleagues, and she was their supervisor and a Christian woman; it wasn't in her to be inhospitable. "Would you like to come in?" she asked.

"Oh no, but thanks. We need to get a move on," Peg said, "so Jan can buy me a milkshake." With a grin toward Coralene, Peg explained, "The loser buys, which means it's usually Jan pulling out her wallet on a Saturday."

Coralene forced a smile. "Sounds tasty," she said.

Nudging Jan playfully, Peg stepped off the porch. Jan followed with the box of corn relish which she stashed in the trunk of the Dodge Dart parked at the curb, while Peg opened the driver's side door and climbed in. With a jaunty wave, the women were off in pursuit of milkshakes. Coralene leaned gratefully against Jasper, as they stood for a few moments on the porch.

~ ~ ~

Jan and Peg were huddled beside the stretch of tables being decked out for hot dog fans, while a trio of junior high girls squatted over butcher paper that was spread across the Fitzgerald Junior High parking lot. Felt markers were scattered like tinder on a campfire as the girls drew red and blue stars and colorful splotches of what Coralene assumed were fireworks.

"Thought we'd have the girls decorate a banner so we could use it to cover the tables. Looks great, no?" Peg had bounded over as Coralene got out of the car.

"Great idea, but please, just a sec…" Coralene tried to keep panic from her voice. "Have you seen my nephew?"

"Tanner? The one who's going to tame the wild bull of a riding mower?" Catching Coralene's expression, Peg stepped closer and put her hand on Coralene's arm. "What's up? Is there something wrong? Jan and I have been here a couple hours; we thought we'd get a jump on things. In fact, we're almost done. Haven't seen Tanner though."

Jan handed the girls some masking tape before joining Peg and Coralene. Jasper, who had parked the car in the fac-ulty lot behind the school, joined the women by the table, Coravelle in tow.

Coralene shook her head. "They haven't seen him," she said to Jasper. "Oh my good Lord. Even from Tanner, I didn't expect this. He knows this is important. He's been doing well the last couple months. Been on his game."

"How can we help?" Peg asked. "Do you think he's here? Along the parade route somewhere? Do you want to go look for him?"

"I don't know." Coralene's disappointment in Tanner was weighing her down, making it impossible to think it all through. "When we talked last night, he was feeling upbeat about helping his grandmother with the float. He's young, so he had to keep it cool. But I know he was excited. Then this morning, his friend Craig came by, and the two of them took off in Tanner's truck. That was hours ago. He wouldn't mess this up, I just don't think he would."

"We don't know what he'd do," Jasper said, his eyes only on Coralene. "That's the truth. We never quite know."

Coravelle leaned against her father. "I agree with Mom," she said. "Tanner can be a knucklehead, but he's not stupid. I don't think he'd disappoint everyone on purpose. Especially not Grammy."

"I don't know where to look." Coralene's frustration seemed to form a canopy under which they all now stood. The day was going to be warm; heat was already emanating from the pavement. She wanted to be anywhere but here. "I don't know what to do," she said, looking at Jasper. "Maybe you should go down to the beginning of the parade route. Maybe he's down with the guild float. Could be he's messing around with the mower or some such thing. I thought we'd agreed to get work done here first, but maybe he forgot."

Coralene tugged at the collar of her bright-red blouse, shaking it in an effort to cool off.

From far down Center Street, noise from a nattering assortment of horns and drums shoved its way into Coralene's brain, as if all the bands were practicing at once. "I can't think," she said. "I can't think with this noise. But I know something's wrong. I know it."

Jasper brought over a folding chair from the table. "Sit, Cory," he said. "You think better when you sit."

The inertia was suffocating. She wasn't an alarmist by nature. If anything, Jasper was more inclined to forecast troubles that didn't materialize. Hadn't Tanner told Jasper he'd be back? That he had a surprise? But if that was true, then she had all the more reason to be concerned. He wouldn't have been specific about returning, about some surprise, if his intention was to drop the ball. Not that dropping the ball was something one did with intention, but the conversation Jasper had described didn't seem like one that was leading up to foolishness. Coralene was familiar with Tanner's foolishness. This felt different. This felt menacing. And what about Craig? Tanner hadn't been alone, so where was Craig? Maybe Craig's mother knew where the two of them had gone.

"Let us handle this, Coralene," Jan said. "Please, just let us handle this."

"What?" Coralene's voice was icy. What was the woman talking about? This was a family matter.

"Let us handle the hot dogs," Peg clarified. "The whole show here." She waved her arms to include their entire setup. "This is a great idea you had. The hot dogs, the relish and all that, but it's not rocket science. We're lunch ladies, for God's sake. We can cook up hot dogs and hand them out. We can do it with our eyes closed. You go do what you need to do. Please. Let us handle this."

Coralene reached out to Jasper, who steadied her as she stood. "What do you want to do, Cory?" Jasper asked. "I agree with Peg here. Let them manage things. I can go on down to the guild float. If that excruciating noise is any indicator, the parade'll be starting up soon. All the ladies will be there, including your mother. She might know something."

"You do that. I think that's the right next step. Velly, I want you to wander around. You might have a better idea where young people would be hanging out. Or maybe you'll see a crowd that Tanner got himself sucked into."

"What are you going to do?" Jasper asked.

"I'm going to go to Crystal's cookie stand. Find Lola, Craig's mother. She might know something. Maybe Craig's with her. Maybe Tanner's with her too. It's the only think I can think of."

The girls had finished their lavish drawings of stars and fireworks and taped the butcher paper along the front of the tables. The hot dog stand looked appropriately celebratory. Instead of the thin white paper napkins, ubiquitous in school lunchrooms but useless for containing any actual mess, Jan and Peg had supplied towering stacks of red and blue ones, such as might be found at a birthday party. Much more suitable for condiment-laden hot dogs. A glint of daylight snuck into Coralene's dark thoughts. This was under control. Jan and Peg had it under control. So, let them.

Jan watched Coralene take in the scene. "Go," Jan said. "We've got this. Maybe he's down by the guild float right now. Jasper can cuss him out, pop his behind on the riding mower, and y'all will be back here before the throngs hit the hot dog table." Jan winced. "Sorry," she said. "Perhaps that was too blunt. Sorry, Jasper."

"No apology necessary," Jasper said. "When I find him, cussing him out is likely what I'll do. You're not far off." Jasper glanced from Jan to Peg and back as he reached for Coralene's hand. "Thank you," he said. "Cory's lucky to have you. Hopefully we'll all be standing back here in no time."

The parade route was only six blocks, maybe seven; Coralene couldn't remember. Scanning ahead, it looked twice that. The crowds had yet to part to their respective sides, so navigating from the parking lot up to the starting line was slow going. Memories pounded her brain: Tanner, brushing her cheek the morning they'd had breakfast at the Pancake House; DeCora, on her death bed.

Every day, Coralene felt the urgency of the promise she'd made: to smooth Tanner's path, and to keep him on it. He'd made some stupid choices as a teenager, gotten himself in trouble more than once. But when he'd moved back home, wiser choices, pragmatic choices, showed themselves more frequently. He'd been putting his shoulder into it, seemed to be clueing in to what it meant to be an adult.

Ignoring the blister building on her right heel, Coralene trudged ahead, pumping her fists in front of her as if knocking back a mound of risen dough. Oh dearest God, had something happened to the truck?

Children were everywhere, many too young to be running about so freely. If she wasn't careful, she'd trip over them. But even in her rush, Coralene cupped her hand over the back of any child's head she could reach. "Thank you, Jesus," she murmured aloud. "Thank you for these beautiful children. Please keep my child safe. My Tanner. My sweet boy."

Within two blocks of where she expected to find Crystal, Coralene saw the mayor's Corvair convertible proceeding down Center Street at a glacial pace, ensuring that every Hanley citizen had ample opportunity for waves and accolades. Spectators stepped out of the street, thickening the crowds on the sidewalk. It was impossible to build speed, each step had to be calculated, lest she press her face into the back of a total stranger.

The Boy Scout honor guard barely escaped being clipped by the Corvair's front bumper. The American flag should've been parade-goers' first sight once the procession began. Spectators who weren't already standing rose quickly, removed their hats, and placed their hands over their hearts. But the Corvair was relentless. The sight made Coralene think of Moses, who perhaps the mayor wished to emulate, as he parted the dutiful Boy Scouts, and the majesty of Old Glory, to be first down the street.

For all his pomposity, the mayor was quickly forgotten by the arrival of the high school marching band. Students from Norlin Hanley and Lake Sylvester roused the crowd with a respectable rendition of John Philip Sousa's "The Thunderer." Behind the band came tractors – corn stalks adhered to every exposed surface – driven by more farmers in overalls and straw hats than Coralene could count. They appeared to be performing some combination of road rally and tractor ballet. Next up was a float sponsored by Doubles and Bubbles, which she didn't pause to decipher.

Craig stood beside his mother, peripheral to the bustle of activity at the cookie table. Even from a distance, Coralene could see that his clothes were filthy. Behind him, as despondent as Coralene had ever seen a person look, was Tanner.

Running through the crowd was impossible, but Coralene forced herself forward. People absorbed in floats and marching bands pivoted, as if intuitively making room for her to pass. "Thank you," she mumbled to one after another. "Thank you. Thanks so much."

Coralene's eyes filled seeing Tanner standing so wholly alone. She watched as he drew his hand over the crown of his own head, back and forth, as if stroking a beloved cat. As if seeking tangible comfort.

"Tanner!" The words squeaked out. She was too breathless for any volume. "Tanner!" she tried again, successful this time, but in a voice she didn't recognize. "Tanner! Over here, sweetheart. Tanner!"

Seeing her, Tanner's eyes filled. He was sobbing by the time Coralene took him in her arms. "Tanner," she whispered, kissing the side of his head. "Tanner, sweet baby. You all right?"

It was over a minute before his sobs subsided. Tanner took a step back and Coralene shuddered at the sight of his puffy eyelids and his face smeared in mud. She put her hand to his wet cheek, her gaze urging him to speak, but Tanner only settled his head back on her shoulder and folded awkwardly into her arms, losing himself in the body she held against him.

From nowhere, Lola appeared with a folding chair. Coralene eased Tanner into it then stood behind him, leaning down to clasp her hands over his chest and lay her cheek against his. "Shush, baby," she whispered into his ear. "You're okay now. You're okay."

"I'm going to take Craig home," Lola said, taking a step closer. "I told Crystal. Cookie distribution is underway. The other gals can handle things without me."

"But what happened?" Coralene asked. Keeping her arms firmly crossed against Tanner's chest, she looked up at Lola. "I haven't gotten a word out of him."

"They've had a shock," Lola said, her voice low and grim. "The boys, they've had a shock. But this isn't the place to talk about it." Lola shifted her eyes toward Crystal and the other women at the cookie table. "Not the place," she said again.

Lola put a hand on Coralene's shoulder. Leaning over, she grasped Tanner's arm, giving it a squeeze. "Call me later," Lola told Coralene, "if you want." Straightening, Lola returned to Craig, wrapped an arm across the back of his neck, and steered her son away from the parade.

Bent over Tanner's shoulders, Coralene encircled him in her arms, like a wool blanket in winter. Suddenly Craig was back, tapping Coralene's knees from behind with a second folding chair. "Here you go, Mrs. Johnson." Then to Tanner, he said, "Call me later, man."

Coralene positioned the chair so she could lean in toward Tanner, knees to knees. "I'll sit here until you're ready," she said. "I'll sit here long as you need."

Coralene could hear the souped-up engines of what she suspected was an impressive gathering of vintage cars, and yet another marching band in the distance. She rested her hands on Tanner's knees as he began to speak.

"He was dead," Tanner mumbled, raising his eyes to meet Coralene's. "He was dead."

CHAPTER TWENTY-FIVE

THE THREE COOKS choreographed cookie distribution with a knack that Crystal lacked. Although each of them had hand-selected their cookie ambassadors in June, it simply had not occurred to Crystal that Betsy, Lola, and Midge would expect to manage the children on parade day. Thank God they did.

Crystal's idea, which of course hadn't been her idea at all, was that thirty-odd elementary children would appear at the cookie table on time. They would accept the cookies they were given to distribute with no regard for cookie flavor or the nature of the drawings on their cookie bags. The children would certainly not quarrel over which floats they were assigned to accompany. Wouldn't the reverent and reserved VFW float be every bit as enticing as the rambunctious troupe of Rotary Club clowns? Surely, no children would drop their cookies in the dirt or allow their bags to tear. And didn't it go without saying that every child would arrive with clean hands? Crystal was confident that not even Ada had considered the possibility that a few of these cunning children would decide to taste test the cookies in their bags before putting them in outstretched hands along the parade route.

All of these eventualities, and more, had occurred to Betsy, Lola, and Midge. Well ahead of time. Crystal watched in amazement as the lunch ladies from the Hanley elementary schools navigated major disasters as adeptly as they did minor disruptions. While the setting in which the ladies took on their tasks bore no resemblance to a clattering school kitchen, no one observing the scene would have had cause to wonder who was in charge, or what each of these women did as a day job.

Soon enough, each school's cookie brigade was lined up single file, facing their respective lunch lady. Dirt-laden or torn cookie bags were replaced with clean, full ones. No child from Prescott who'd arrived at the parade intending to distribute chocolate-chip cookies was required to distribute the oatmeal-raisin cookies that were the purview of those kids over at Alicia Park. This satisfied the Alicia Park kids just fine, given that they in turn had no wish to hand out the boring sugar cookies that were the pride and joy of every cookie ambassador from Hastings. Children who just couldn't abide drawings of cheerful suns on their bags were allowed to carry plain ones instead, or to choose from among varied depictions of fireworks.

All the children immersed their hands in a bucket of soapy water which appeared out of nowhere. Each was allowed to eat one cookie of their choosing before the big cookie handout began. "Always know your product," Betsy told them. Only a few of the children understood what Mrs. Becker was talking about, other than the part where she said they could each have a cookie.

But when it came to parade partner assignments? Which children would walk beside which floats, bands, or miscellaneous celebrants? Negotiations stopped. As did griping, pouting, and bellyaching of any kind. Not a peep would be tolerated. At least not from any child who hoped to pass out cookies today, or to remain in the good graces of the lunch ladies when school resumed in the fall.

The lunch ladies' message was unambiguous: every float, band, and group; every little old lady with a potholder; every man with a funny hat and a tiny car; every single person the children saw here today was a neighbor. It was a birthday party to which everyone had been invited. The children who walked alongside the VFW float should get to know those men; they'd earned the attention they were getting today. As for business owners who'd dressed up as a bunch of clowns? Well, grownups can be silly that way. The children? They deserved to be here too and they had a job to do: represent their schools, their families, and their country. So, as the lunch ladies made clear before handing children into the care and company of their parade partners, there would be no whining. Absolutely. None.

Ada was the first to see the poodles. "Well, would you look at that," she said, prodding Crystal, who was still recovering from the sight of her grandmother and the guild ladies flaunting their crafts as they were pulled by a riding mower.

Crystal was stunned. "Well, knock me off my chair. See that guy in front? That's my boss. That's my boss, Ada. The one with the big black poodle."

"Looks like a nice dog," Ada said. As Ada would. "Does he ever bring him to the office?"

"Oh hell no," Crystal said too quickly. "Oops, sorry there," she recovered. "Didn't mean to sound snotty."

Ada clucked and patted Crystal's arm. "You're my friend, dear. I'm never going to assume that you're being snotty. Or being anything else, for that matter. Nope, if you want to get rid of me, you'll have to try harder. You'll have to actually say so. You know, say something like, 'Ada, I don't want to be your friend anymore.' You say that, I'll listen. Otherwise, you're stuck with me as a best pal. Just stuck, stuck, stuck." Ada leaned forward in her folding chair, straining for a better view.

Crystal, who really wanted to carry on about Gordon and his poodle, was speechless. Words such as Ada's were uncharted territory. She tried to take them in. A shield against hurt feelings had protected Crystal for as long as she could remember; she kept it close at hand. That a sharp word would be met with kindness, and with the assumption of kind intent, was a new one. Sharp words were handy barbs to keep the riffraff at bay. What Ada was suggesting? This was simply not how Crystal's world worked.

Ada – built like a penguin and with a heart of gold – sitting next to Crystal at the big whoop-ta-do. Cheerful as a game show host. Chipper as a bluebird. Ada had staked her claim with Crystal. Said it out loud. Once again, Crystal was out of her depth, but for the first time in memory, she eased her shield down. It was time to quit wondering if she'd ever have someone special to talk to. Because now she did; she had Ada. So swat that fly dead.

Ada was squirming gleefully, waiting for Crystal to say more about the poodles. There were a dozen of them, in four crisp rows of three, walking obediently down the middle of Center Street. Gordon was in the first row, on the side closest to the cookie table. He was wearing white tennis shoes and a pair of stiffly pressed navy pants. A red collared shirt was tidily tucked by a wide white belt. Gordon's uncharacteristically dapper ensemble included a red baseball cap, with writing in white script which Crystal couldn't quite decipher. Gordon Hund. In a baseball cap. Now wasn't he the dashingly turned out citizen? Leading a shipshape assemblage of like-minded poodle lovers in the Fourth of July parade. This was something to see. Napoleon, as close to Gordon as a motorcycle side car, sported a powder-puff tail and gleaming red collar and leash.

"I don't know quite what to say." Crystal tried to rein in a stellar inventory of sarcastic responses that came immediately to mind. "We all know about his poodle club, or poodle shows, or whatever. He mentions them in every memo. Dogstravaganza this, blue ribbon that. I thought there were more dogs involved than just poodles. Can't decide if that's the saddest thing in the world or sort of sweet. He's a strange bird, our Gordon, so I guess," Crystal paused. Ada wasn't listening.

Instead, Ada let out a sweet little squeak and popped out of her chair. Betsy and Midge, who had yet to sit down, stepped in next to Ada and Crystal and leaned on the table.

Lola had mumbled something to Crystal, before leaving with her son for reasons unknown.

"Isn't that, you know, isn't that...?" Midge fumbled for Gordon's name.

"You betcha, that's who that is," Crystal said. "Mr. Gordon Hund, Department Manager for Nutrition Services in the Hanley School District. My boss." Crystal smirked. "So, your boss too."

Ada squeaked again. Horrified, Crystal realized Ada was trying to draw Gordon's attention to the cookie table, its bins of cookies, its stack of paper bags, and its enthralled array of lunch ladies.

"Here we are!" Ada shouted, jumping up and down. "Here we are, all the elementary schools, and lots and lots of cookies!"

In seconds, Betsy and Midge were waving too. Ada's squeals caught Gordon's attention, and perhaps Napoleon's. Did that dog just add a spring to his step? Crystal was out-numbered. The other women were waving at Gordon as if he was Jesus Christ himself marching down Center Street. With a poodle.

"It's great, don't you think?" Betsy said, her voice rever-berating in Crystal's ear. "All the festivities Gordon helped create? Dogs. Cookies. It's a party! I love this."

Midge was waving and smiling. Betsy was beaming and, oh no, Crystal saw that Ada was staring right at her. This must end, and soon.

"A little slice of whoop-ta-do heaven is what we've got here," Crystal said, hoping to divert attention back to the poo-dles, but Ada didn't waver. The mother of six, the grandmother of fourteen, the honorary lunch lady, and Crystal's friend had Crystal ensnared in a look that could only mean one thing.

Without breaking eye contact, Ada tipped her head in Crystal's direction. *Oh no I won't*, Crystal thought, knowing that Ada would not let this one go. Crystal raised her hand slightly off the table, mentally urging Gordon and all the other poodlers to move it along. A band of some variety was gaining on the poodles, it couldn't be long now.

Ada shifted her gaze to Crystal's arm, as if to levitate it. At the slightest shake of Ada's head, Crystal raised her hand higher. She held it beside her cheek; that should suffice. But Ada would not be rebuked. The woman could glare. Crystal pushed her elbow a few inches higher and allowed her wrist to twist, just a bit. With that, Ada gave an approving nod.

Crystal tried to avoid looking directly at Gordon and Napoleon, but this whole encounter had pulled her in, like the sight of roadkill along the highway. In the most minute human exchange she could remember – and she, Crystal, was an inordinately experienced people watcher – Crystal saw Gordon smile. No teeth, thank God. Nothing unseemly. Just a smile, from a colleague who was walking his poodle down the middle of the street on a Sunday afternoon. Crystal wiggled her wrist once more, and, pursing her lips tightly over her teeth, smiled back.

"Move along, little doggies," Crystal said with a twang as the poodles cleared the cookie table. "Yeehaw."

"Oh for heaven's sakes," Ada said. "You can be quite the pill."

"That is true," Crystal said, "it's just that…"

"Look! There they are!" Ada was squealing, yet again.

As the poodles pranced on down the street, the next spectacle filled the void. *A bad dream in daylight*, Crystal thought, *here it comes. An oompah band.*

"Oh, this is wonderful. I really wanted them to come!" Ada's voice was quivering. "I heard them over at the German Club last week when I went there for dinner. My son John? His wife's family is German. Lovely woman, named Adelheid, can you believe it?"

The parade wasn't even half over, but Crystal was done in by Ada's enthusiasm. Additional caustic comments came quickly to mind. She let them go. Instead, she smiled benignly at Ada, who was, in turn, grinning like a school girl as six men with bellies beyond what their lederhosen were ever intended to accommodate, paused in front of the cookie table and lifted their instruments.

"The oompah band!" Ada squealed with the exuberance of a square-dance caller. "Look, Crystal! It's the oompah band."

As he puckered up, Crystal saw the tuba player give Ada a wave and wink. In seconds an accordion player, two men with trombones, and two more with clarinets were belting out music that made it impossible for onlookers to stand still. Hands clapping, toes tapping, a gregarious crowd was swept up by the music, their bodies urging the rhythms forward. Swinging heads and bobbing chins.

What's next? Crystal thought. *Teamsters dressed as Lady Liberty? Chickens pecking out John Hancock in the dirt?* No doubt Ada had deserted her chair for the parade's duration, but Crystal sat back down and reached for a cookie.

CHAPTER TWENTY-SIX

SHEILA WOULD HAVE thought it impossible to feel more deadened than she had for the last two weeks. No. Erase that. Tom Downlane had no influence on her state of mind. He'd made no contribution toward the incinerator which had blazed in her chest since the fourteenth of June. He hadn't added fuel. He hadn't doused flames. He was irrelevant.

The salsa was as trivial as Tom himself; dishing out salads would be easier without it. One less step. Sheila didn't really need to think about it to make it happen. Planning was over. Geneva and Tammy were in place. Hell, Lexie was in place. Sheila would raise a serving spoon like the rest of them and turn out as many salads as this preposterous production required. *I'll feed these morons*, she thought, *then I'm done.*

The parade-goers who lined up at the taco salad stand could have been in any church, on any Sunday. They waited quietly, and if not reverently, then close enough. Proceeding along the tables' crisp papered edge, no one questioned the servings they were given. No doubts were expressed about the proportion of lettuce to meat, or meat to cheese. No one asked for additional chips. No one mentioned the absence of salsa.

Napkins and forks found their way to garbage cans. Bowls were scraped clean, but not a single person returned in search of a second helping.

Sheila, Geneva, and Tammy were drill sergeants, and Hanley citizens in pursuit of taco salads were unwitting recruits. File through the line, give a respectful nod, move along. With nothing more than a raised eyebrow or the cluck of a tongue, the lunch ladies dominated their patch of Center Street with the comportment of General Patton.

Lexie had kept to the side, making herself useful by refilling pans, restocking bowls, and replacing full bags of trash with new plastic liners. *One more reason to appreciate Lexie,* Sheila thought. *She knows when she's out of her league.*

Eventually the queue shortened, and then disappeared. Adults and children meandered past, digging their hands into childishly decorated cookie bags, or fumbling for popcorn in paper cones printed with thirteen-star American flags.

Teenagers in gangly clusters proceeded down the street holding cans of 7-Up, or Coke, or Orange Crush, leaving behind a trail of metal pull tabs, like breadcrumbs in the woods. They were pulled into the wake of the final float, which was the showpiece of Hanley's Girl Scout troops. Their float deck was covered in pine and cedar boughs and dotted with pup tents, from which girls stuck out their heads and waved American flags.

Younger children, with the frenzy of wind-up toys, pulled their parents and siblings up and down the street, likewise bringing up the rear, or returning to the parade's launching point to salvage candy from the bounty which still littered the streets.

There had been no Tom. And so what? He had never been remotely necessary. Now only cleanup remained, which Sheila would handle with her typical dispatch. She knew Lexie had continued to scan the crowd, on the lookout for a chubby retiree in a baseball cap. Didn't happen. Of course it didn't.

Declaring interest in this undertaking had been a stunt for him, and had left her playing the fool. No wonder there are estranged ex-wives, alienated children. The man must leave wreckage in his wake as a matter of course. Some people do that; they step in, then just as quickly step back out. Why had she made herself a patsy for the disregard of Tom Downlane?

"Everything's in apple-pie order," Tammy said, announcing, not subtly, that she was ready to leave. Sheila had unplugged the generator and bundled the cords on each appliance so they'd be easy for the school district's maintenance team to load onto a truck. Tammy and Geneva had broken down the folding tables, which now leaned against the tree. The area resembled base camp for a massive Boy Scout hike.

Lexie struggled to straighten and fold the butcher paper Geneva and Tammy had used to cover the tables. At her feet was a mound of tangled crepe paper and a dozen white bal-loons which looked like blisters ready to pop.

"Oh for pity sakes," Sheila said. "Stuff that in the trash. We're not going to reuse it. No need to fold it; jam it in there. I bet you reuse wrapping paper, don't you?"

Lexie abandoned her efforts, collapsing the expanse of grease-stained paper against her shirt before forcing it into the overflowing trash can. "Of course I do. Birthdays, Christmas, you name it. You're never going to get a gift from me in brand new paper. I consider it a challenge to see how many times I can reuse it."

"Admirable," Sheila said. "But no need today."

Tammy made no move to help, but Geneva gathered up the streamers, cramming them into the trash on top of the crumpled red paper. "That leaves the balloons for you," Geneva told Tammy. "Want a pin?"

"How about a paring knife? There's one of those around." Locating her weapon, Tammy stabbed each balloon, leaving what looked like a pile of used tissues atop the other trash.

Sheila was ready for Geneva and Tammy to be gone. She appreciated their efforts today; she couldn't have done it without them. She'd told them so, but without the fanfare they seemed to expect. "Thank you, ladies," she'd said, as the last taco salad eater had tossed his empty bowl and wandered off. "This all went smoothly. Thank you."

"Well, this was quite the production," Tammy said now, puffing up a bit as she admired the overflowing trash can. "Good thing all three of us were here," she said to Geneva. "Don't you think?"

Geneva rolled her eyes and nodded. "It was definitely a

production. Heck of a lot of work. But actually there were four of us here." She turned toward Lexie. "I'm sure Sheila appreciated you being here too," she said, her tone patronizing. "I'm sure she'll thank you too."

"Oh, she's thanked me," Lexie responded quickly, keeping annoyance out of her voice. "Plus, I thought it was fun. Saw the parade from another perspective. I liked that. We had a good view."

"Wasn't about the view as far as I'm concerned," Tammy said. "I'm tired out. Done for the day. Ready to go home."

"Well, we'll be off then," Geneva said. "You're welcome, Sheila. Right, Tammy? Sheila's welcome?"

"Oh most definitely. You're very welcome, Sheila."

An awkwardness emerged, for which Sheila had no patience. What the hell? The two women retrieved their purses from beside the tree and stepped off the curb into the parade crowd that was winding its way toward the river.

Stores along Center Street had reopened for business. Across the street, a middle-aged man in red pants, a vivid blue shirt, and a white straw hat emerged from Doubles and Bubbles, carrying a broom. Grasping the bristles in both hands, he poked the broom handle straight up into his striped awning. One of the two teenagers still splayed above yelped and scrambled toward the roof, one hand on the back of his thigh. The other boy didn't wait for the broomstick to strike again. He clambered up after his friend and disappeared from view.

Lexie's eyes were closed when Sheila sat down beside her on the curb. "I'm considering taking a trip," Sheila said, startling her.

Lexie stammered, caught off guard. "You are? That's great." The response was disproportionately enthusiastic, but Sheila let it go. "Where are you going?" Lexie asked. "And when?"

"I'm not sure of the answers to those questions. But it occurred to me that perhaps I should give you a key to my house. Just in case."

"Umm, okay. Sure. I can take in the mail and the news-paper, water the houseplants, whatever you need," Lexie said. "I'm guessing you have things pretty organized. And I mean this nicely, but you don't strike me as someone with a house full of African violets."

"I'm not. I just have one." For a moment, the air was heavy between them. "My niece gave it to me six years ago," Sheila said finally, "when my brother moved his family to California. It's lovely. Blooms all the time. Perfect little purple flowers with ruffly edges. Purple and ruffles, those were Connie's favorite things at the time. It helps remind me of her. We used to talk every Saturday at noon. Last few months though, her activities have taken off. She's in high school. It's to be expected. She's a wonderful girl. Just wonderful."

Lexie knew about Connie; there'd been passing refer-ences over the years. "You must have the perfect spot for it," Lexie said. "All my thumbs are brown. I'd have no chance of keeping a houseplant blooming."

"It's on my nightstand."

"Well, when you decide to go, you can tell me exactly what you need. I promise not to kill it. Won't leave your mail in the box or the newspaper on the porch either." Lexie's chatter was falling flat. "Maybe I could come by? You could show me the ropes?"

"That's not necessary. There's no secret to taking in mail or watering a plant, and I don't take the newspaper." Sheila sat motionless for a few moments before turning to Lexie with the saddest eyes Lexie had ever seen. "Thank you though," Sheila said. "I appreciate you being willing to keep an eye on things."

"Happy to. Any time. Just let me know when you're going and when you'll be back."

"I've got the key in my purse." Sheila pushed herself to a stand and reached out to help Lexie up. For only the second time the women grasped hands, before Sheila released her hold and fetched her purse from under the tree.

"Here you go," she said, handing Lexie a single key. The key ring was a giveaway from the Doubles and Bubbles Hardware store. Lexie had a few just like it in her sock drawer.

"Are you going to go find Coralene or Crystal?" Lexie asked. "Compare notes on today?"

"No. We'll compare notes at work tomorrow. We'll work one day, then we'll be on vacation until mid-August."

"That sounds lovely. I've always envied your summer schedule. I'm glad you still come to see me on Friday nights."

Lexie's words seemed to make no impact on Sheila, who had closed her purse and was scanning the scene, making sure nothing had been left undone. "I'm off," Sheila said.

"You sure? I'm going to stick around. Wander down to the river and see what all's going on. Then I'll drive out to get my sister and bring her back for the fireworks."

"Not me," Sheila said. "I'm going home."

"I'm sorry about Tom," Lexie said quickly, before Sheila could step away. "I can't imagine what happened. I just can't."

"Nothing for you to be sorry about. It's certainly not your fault."

"I know it's not my fault. Doesn't mean I don't feel bad, because I do. I'd pictured the three of us having a good time today. I truly believe he was picturing that too."

"Obviously not." Sheila put a hand on the back of her neck. She needed to leave. Discussing this with Lexie was a waste of time.

"Kind of a double whammy for you," Lexie said. "Finding out about Ralph, I mean, and then having Tom do a disappearing act."

"There is no comparison between Ralph Blatson and Tom Downlane," Sheila snapped. "No comparison at all."

"I didn't mean that," Lexie said, her voice even. "I meant that you had one huge shock a couple weeks ago, and then to me it feels as if Tom kicked you when you were down. I mean, he didn't, obviously. He didn't know about Ralph. And I know he annoys you, but, oh, I don't know how to say it. Or what to say." Lexie paused. "I hope you know what I mean. You're my friend. And you've hit a bad patch. That's what I'm sorry about. Just that."

Once again, Sheila found herself crying in front of Lexie. "Goddammit," she said. "Just god damn it all." She wiped a forefinger under both eyes. "God damn everything. God damn everything but you Lexie Clark, you wonderful girl."

Before Lexie could respond, Sheila was off the curb. She sidestepped through scatterings of people in the street and disappeared from view.

CHAPTER TWENTY-SEVEN

DONALD HAD DONE a fine job. Leonora had feared that once the six of them were seated with scrubbies and turtles at their feet, umbrellas over their heads, and seat belts around their middles, the float wouldn't move. She'd doubted that horsepower sufficient to pull a parade float lived in the motor of a riding mower.

Badger would've been able to diagnose such a situation; Badger had been good with motors. Had he poked around, Badger would've found that Oscar, the post office's mechanic, had replaced the factory motor with one that had exponentially more oomph, and which was never intended for the purpose to which it was put on the Fourth of July. But Badger wasn't there, and Leonora wouldn't have known how to check. As for Jasper? He wasn't talking.

Jasper had appeared unexpectedly as the float set off, searching for Tanner. The underarms on Jasper's shirt were visibly damp, and his expression bore none of its typical charm. Unsuccessful, he hadn't lingered, but Leonora knew he'd promised Cora that he'd find her the minute he knew all was well and had asked that she stay with the float.

Even with smooth sailing – smooth mowing? – under Donald's sure hand, Leonora was blue. She cared for Tanner, because Cora cared. Cora, who was perhaps the best friend Leonora had ever had.

Leonora had watched Tanner's life from a distance. He was a beautiful young man. Although he might wish otherwise, he had never outgrown his goofy childish grin. It had lit up his face like a movie marquee when he was a youngster playing in Leonora's back yard, while good-naturedly tolerating Cora and Leonora's extended discussions of rhododendrons.

The grin did dim as Randy Deveraux ambled in and out. And it disappeared for a while after his mother's death. But in the years that followed it resurfaced, in moments replete with family life during his years with Jasper and Coralene. According to Cora, it even came into view when Tanner was "up to no good," accompanied, to hear Cora tell it, by a "variety pack of ne'er-do-wells."

Cora and Leonora had spun half-heartedly in their office chairs, waving bibs, potholders, and stuffed turtles at bemused onlookers, wishing mightily that it was Tanner, rather than the affable Donald, at the wheel of the riding mower.

Two adorable second graders had walked alongside the float, reluctantly extending cookies. The girls' sense of duty was evident, but enthusiasm for their task was nonexistent.

"What are your names, girls?" Cora called down after she and Leonora observed them for the first block. "Wouldn't you rather ride up here with us?" Cora mustered the trademark grin of a grandmother. "It's great fun."

There'd been no need to ask twice. Nancy and Kristin had scrambled onto the float's deck and positioned themselves, cross-legged, in front of Cora and Leonora. Leonora mindlessly stroked Nancy's hair as the girl waved corduroy turtles at the crowd with the intensity of an airport flagger landing a 747.

There was no news of Tanner when the float reached the end of the route. Cora descended briskly from her perch, and with a nod to Olive and the sisters, left to find her family.

Leonora was exhausted.

"Let's get you home." Darcy positioned the set of stairs in front of Leonora's chair.

"Yes, let's."

"Was it fun?" Darcy held Leonora's elbow as her grandmother eased her way down. "Or just tedious?"

"Fun, I suppose," Leonora said. "And yes, tedious too. I'm ready for a nap. A snack and a nap. I tell you, I couldn't have gone another block. Even with the umbrellas it was getting warm up there. And I'm hungry."

"But you turned down one of Lo's sandwiches?"

"Of course I turned down one of Lo's sandwiches. I don't know what the sisters were doing on the other side of the float. Once I had Nancy at my feet, I couldn't spin. But I doubt I would've been happy seeing them eating up there."

"No. You would not."

"Did we all look ridiculous? Cora and I were glad the little girls showed up. Kept us from completely adopting the crazy-old-lady look."

Darcy had finagled a parking spot ten yards from where the guild's float was now parked. Her Pinto blocked the road, causing a vintage Buick and a cornstalk-bedecked tractor to maneuver around it. As usual, Darcy's charm, validated by the little old lady clasping her arm, engendered kindness from total strangers.

"Let me get the door there," offered a short man in a red baseball cap. He appeared out of a crowd of similarly attired people and color-coordinated dogs, holding the leash of a tall black poodle, which seemed unfazed by tubas, tractors, and all variety of parade debris that clogged the street.

Once in the car, Leonora asked again, "So did we? Look completely ridiculous?"

"No. I really don't think you did. The float was clever. The riding mower was actually good for a chuckle, but not in a bad way. I have to say, the sisters were whooping it up. I'd never seen them like that. Waving and giggling. Winking at old soldiers. It was delightful. Really. Made me wonder what all we don't know about them. Decades and decades together, you know? What's gone on in their house over all these years? A lot can happen. Happy stuff. Sad stuff. Hurt feelings. Forgiveness. Don't you think?" Darcy turned to Leonora. "Don't you think so? That a lot must have happened in their house over all these years?"

"Yes," Leonora said, almost too softly for Darcy to hear. "Every imaginable feeling comes home to roost over decades spent in the same house."

In the last few hours, Darcy had given little thought to her grandmother's health or state of mind. But in bringing up the sisters, she'd opened a can of worms. Grandma also had jaw-dropping tenure in one place. Grandpa Badger had been gone long before Darcy was born. Decades and decades? That was precisely the verdict Leonora had endured. Alone, and yet not, surrounded as she'd been with children and grandchildren who needed to be raised.

Why hadn't she found someone else? She was self-reliant, eminently lovable. Would loving again have been so impossible? Yes. Yes, it would have. Because Grandpa Badger still lived on Vermillion Avenue. He would have needed to move out. Would have had to agree to be dead. Fully dead, and completely gone. Neither Badger nor Leonora would have ever accepted that. Badger had stayed put, entwined with his wife until they left their home together.

"Want me to stick around this afternoon?" Darcy asked. "I could make dinner while you nap. Could even spend the night. You've had lots of company today; it might feel lonely to be by yourself all of a sudden."

"Darcy. Sweetie, really? Being with those gals is precisely the reason I'll need this evening to myself. They wear me out. Well, not Cora, but the rest of them. It was a tiring day. I'm going to take one of my little pills. They're prescription," Leonora added quickly, muzzling any objection. "Then I'll settle into bed. I want to eat something when we get home, but then my nap will probably become my good night's sleep. May skip dinner altogether."

Leonora laid her head back against the passenger seat. *Alone. Please*, she thought. *The sooner the better.*

"Want me to stop at the store? Get something to eat? We could load up the fridge."

Darcy was hanging on like grim death. "No," Leonora said. "I want to go home. There's plenty there to eat. Besides, it's a Sunday and a national holiday. No grocery store will be open today. I'll be happy with cream of chicken soup and some oyster crackers. That'll stick to my scrawny ribs, then I'm off to dreamland."

It wasn't until she'd heated the soup and joined her grandmother at the kitchen table that Darcy clued in on the tightness in her own chest. The months-long focus on the guild's float was finally over. Now what?

Outside the kitchen window, Darcy noticed the foxglove in its pink splendor along the side-yard fence. Oh good God, foxglove? Weren't they poisonous?

"More soup?" Darcy took her own bowl to the stove and waved the ladle in Leonora's direction. "I think I'll have a tiny bit more." With theatrical slowness, she dipped the ladle into the pan and dribbled soup into her bowl.

"No need to dawdle," Leonora said. "You go ahead. None for me. I'm going to go brush my teeth, then I'm done. I'm just done." Leonora eased herself up from the table, gripping its edge, as she'd come to do. Steadying first on the table, and then on the counter next to Darcy, Leonora pulled Darcy into an embrace.

They weren't a demonstrative family, so the urgency of the hug only added to Darcy's distress.

"Thank you, sweetie," Leonora said when she pulled away. "For everything. For today of course, the float and such, but just for everything. I'm proud of you. I appreciate you so much." She grasped Darcy's arm, rubbing her hand up and down, from elbow to shoulder. "You go do whatever you and your friends have planned for tonight. I'm sure you have a party to go to. Don't you dare miss it on my account. I'm done, sweetie. I'm done."

CHAPTER TWENTY-EIGHT

Darcy

July 4, 1976

"I CAN'T DROP in on her tomorrow. Dropping in is not what I do." Crystal sounded tired. "Besides, I have to work."

Calling her cousin had been a long shot, but one that Darcy felt she had to take. "Problem is," she told Crystal, "I have to work too. We'll do a review on every aspect of today's events. What we did well, where we flopped. I can't miss it."

"Well, spoonbread. That's what I'll be doing. But what's got your tea kettle whistling? I didn't know you visited Grandma on Monday nights."

"I don't. But I swear, Crystal. Something's going to go wrong. I just know it. I'm afraid something massive is going to go wrong."

"Like?"

"Oh good God. I can't believe I'm saying this, but I'm afraid she might hurt herself. I know she doesn't feel well. More than that, I'm pretty sure she's actually sick. Seriously sick. There's foxglove in the side yard."

"So…?" Crystal dragged out the word. "You're thinking she's going to cook up some poison or something? Not a chance. Not her style."

"How would you know?" Darcy was instantly angry. "How the hell would you even know?"

The silence between them was long and painful. Darcy wondered whether Crystal would hang up. If Darcy apologized, she could pull the conversation back from the brink. But apologizing would mute the urgency she needed Crystal to feel. Finally, it was Crystal who spoke.

"Burgers?" Crystal asked.

"What?"

"Burgers? Want to do burgers? It usually works when we arrive with burgers. Want to do that tomorrow? I could pick you up instead of the other way around. I have the Fairlane out for the summer. Then we could arrive with burgers. Sit in the backyard. Admire the flowers, well, except the fox-glove. Perhaps we ignore that." Darcy didn't react. "Come on, spoonbread," Crystal said. "I'm trying here. Would burgers make you happy? If so, let's do that."

Darcy didn't want to cry in front of Crystal. Not even on the phone. But it was going to happen anyway.

"Darcy?" Crystal said. "Come on, Darcy. Come on, my little spoonbread. It'll be okay."

Now there would be no muffling tears. Darcy gave in to them. It was several minutes before she could speak. As she tried to pull herself together, she heard Crystal's breathing. Not impatient. Not huffy. Just steady.

"I'd like it if you'd pick me up," Darcy said finally, her voice small. "I'd like to be the one who's picked up."

"Then that's the plan. I'll be there at 5:00. Tell me again which building? I'm not sure exactly where you work."

"4:30?"

"4:30."

There was another long pause before Darcy gave Crystal the address for her office. "I'll see you tomorrow," Darcy said, trying unsuccessfully to reclaim a breezy tone.

"It will be alright," Crystal said. "I'm sorry, spoonbread. I'm sorry you're so worried."

PART SIX

"We become who we're going to be early on. The child we are when we're young is not that different from the child we still are the day we die. Childhood doesn't age."

PEARL CARMICHAEL

1914-1948

MEMO

TO: Nutrition Services Employees
FROM: Gordon Hund, Nutrition Services Manager
DATE: Monday, July 5, 1976
RE: Bicentennial Celebration: appreciation and
              congratulations, and other topics of interest

Ladies: Please accept my heartfelt appreciation for your excellent work prior to and during yesterday's Bicentennial Parade, and your impeccable representation of the Hanley School District and the Nutrition Services Department. I offer unconditional congratulations to the three of you for a job well done.

From my vantage point in the delegation of standard poodles, I was able to observe the enthusiasm, efficiency, and teamwork which were hallmarks of your efforts at each of our three food stands.

In a brief conversation yesterday with my uncle, Mayor Dooley, I confirmed that Nutrition Services will make participation in Hanley's Fourth of July Parade an annual event. I look forward to discussing plans for the 1977 parade when we all return to work on August 16, 1976.

I have secured four front-row seats at the August 7, 1976 statewide Dogstravaganza in Minneapolis. Napoleon and I would be honored to have you join us for the festivities of the day which we hope will result in winning a blue ribbon as best in show.

CHAPTER TWENTY-NINE

Crystal

Monday, July 5, 1976

"BURGER BILL'S OR McDonald's?" Crystal waited while Darcy buckled her seat belt, before pulling the Fairlane back into traffic.

"Burger Bill's," Darcy said. "Or I was thinking we could stop and order from Denny's."

"Nah, breakfast is what Denny's is good at. I've never eaten a hamburger there. Let's stay with Burger Bill's. No need to rock the burger boat."

"Fine. I just want to get to Grandma's. I tell you, Crystal, I'm worried. I thought about stopping by on my way to work this morning, but I didn't have time. I tried to call during my lunch break, but she didn't answer."

"Maybe she had her ear trumpets turned down and didn't hear the phone," Crystal said.

"This isn't funny." Darcy's voice cracked. "It isn't funny, Crystal. Besides, she doesn't wear hearing aids. Hearing isn't her issue, but everything else seems to be. She has so many pills. There were four bottles in her nightstand. Four! And she had another in a separate drawer, like it was a secret or something."

"A secret? You don't think you might be reading too much into this? Don't you keep things in separate drawers? And…" Crystal drew out the pause. "One might ask, what were you doing in her drawer anyway?"

Darcy groaned. "I don't keep the same things in different drawers. No, I don't."

Leonora's house on Vermillion Avenue was only two miles from Darcy's office at Hanley Electric on Bullman; Burger Bill's was on the way. Crystal let Darcy stew for a few blocks. This was a whole lot of huffing and puffing. That's what this outing would turn out to be: a whole lot of huffing and puffing. As they closed in on Burger Bill's, Crystal glanced over at Darcy's soft profile. "We'll grab dinner," Crystal said, finally. "We'll grab dinner and go check things out. I'll even pay. You go in; I'll pay."

Crystal backed the Fairlane into a spot in front of the restaurant where she could watch people come and go, and handed Darcy a ten-dollar bill.

"It won't be this much," Darcy said.

"I know, but go wild. Get Grandma whatever you think she'll eat, get what you want, and get me a double with extra cheese. No lettuce. The lettuce gets slimy."

"Anything else?"

"Yes. Large fries, and a strawberry shake."

Crystal had barely stopped the car on Leonora's gravel before Darcy leapt out and dashed up the front walk. With no chance of matching Darcy's speed, Crystal moved as quickly as she could, trudging toward the house with the bag from Burger Bill's.

Darcy had left the front door ajar. The lights were off inside, but why wouldn't they be? It was July; no need for lamps at 5:00. With her back to Crystal, Darcy was standing in the doorway between the dining room and kitchen, gripping the doorframe. Crystal poked her head over Darcy's shoulder; the kitchen was empty. Leonora's table was in its usual spot against the window, overlooking the side yard. Dozens of foxglove were in full bloom, in what appeared to be an undisturbed garden bed.

There was no evidence that anything had recently been cooked or eaten. The counters were clean. The sink was empty. Darcy flung open the refrigerator as if expecting to find their grandmother inside. She was not. *Score one for Grandma*, Crystal thought.

The back door was open; the screen door was closed, but not locked.

"We have to check her bedroom." Darcy's voice was tense, as if uttering her own cry for help. "Move, Crystal. Please." Darcy pushed past her cousin and disappeared. Crystal knew Darcy would be taking one more peek in the living room: checking behind the sofa for their motionless grandmother. Then she'd stop at the bathroom to find Grandma drowned in the tub, before moving into the bedroom where she'd trip over Grandma's lifeless body in a heap on the shag carpet.

Crystal went out the kitchen door, down the back steps, past the foxglove and into the backyard.

Crystal's shadow caused Leonora to shield her eyes and

look up. "What on earth are you doing here?" Leonora was reclined on the low metal-framed chaise lounge. Its floral cushions appeared to be sliding toward the patio, but otherwise the scene was shipshape.

"Do you mind?" Crystal asked, as she reached for Leonora's iced tea and sat down in a wrought-iron chair. "I'm parched. Darcy's having a bit of a crisis today."

Leonora sat up, bracing herself on the table from which Crystal had just lifted the tea. "Where is she?" Leonora scrunched up her face in concern. "What's the matter? Is she hurt?"

"She's fine. She's currently scampering through your house looking for trouble, but she'll be out here any minute. I have the burger bag."

"You have what? What's going on, Crystal? I mean I'm glad to see you of course, but you never come without Darcy. And now you're telling me she's in a crisis? What do we need to do?" Leonora had shifted her feet off the chaise and was leaning over to retie the laces she'd loosened on her tennis shoes.

"No crisis. No crisis anywhere to be found." Crystal said. "Unless it's the crisis of having perfectly good hamburgers get cold."

"Oh my God! There you are." Darcy swept past Crystal to squat in front of Leonora. Unbidden, Darcy reached to tie the shoelaces. Leonora swatted her away. "I'm glad you're okay," Darcy gushed, not seeming to have noticed the reprimand. "I'm just so glad. You scared the crap out of me."

"What are the two of you talking about?" Leonora's affect had become one of annoyance, which Crystal was amused to see directed at Darcy as well.

"Hey, spoonbread," Crystal said. "Go get some napkins and bring out another patio chair from the basement. Make it snappy. Cold fries are worse than cold burgers. I'm not going to pay for dinner and then postpone it for the anti-crisis."

Surprisingly, Darcy did as she was told. Crystal shimmied uncomfortably before resigning herself to her metal chair.

"She's all in a dither," Crystal said, facing her grandmother. "Darcy. She's all in a dither."

"About what? Poor thing, she must still be tuckered out. I didn't expect to see her today. She had a long day at the parade yesterday."

"So did I," Crystal said.

"Pardon?"

"So did I. Have a long day at the parade yesterday."

Leonora eased back onto the chaise and stretched out her legs. Again, she cupped her hand over her eyes to look square on at Crystal. "I bet you did, honey. As we rode by on the guild float, I saw a gaggle of children and an impressive collection of paper bags. Did everyone have fun? Looked like there were several women there with you. Did you all have fun?"

Crystal couldn't remember the last time she'd so fully let out a breath. It made her dizzy. How long had it been since anyone, anyone at all, had asked if she'd had fun? Had taken any interest in what she was up to?

"We did," Crystal said, sarcasm gone from her voice. "Have fun, I mean. My friend Ada helped out. She's, well, she's a lot of fun."

Leonora sat quietly for a moment, taking it in. "I'm

glad, honey," Leonora hummed. Her face was flushed as she looked toward Crystal. "I'm very glad. Now, can you please tell me what's up with Darcy? I'm a bit confused by the activities. I'm happy. Don't get me wrong, but having you both appear with so much fuss and bother, I'm taken aback is all. Fill me in."

"Ask Darcy," Crystal said, sounding snide in a way she didn't intend. "Ask Darcy," she repeated, softening her tone. "She's in charge of fuss and bother. She'll fill you in."

Sunset was still several hours away, but the backyard on Vermillion Avenue held a tranquility similar to the close of day. The mosquitos weren't bad yet, but they'd be showing up soon to make nuisances of themselves. Crystal thought to suggest that the three of them move up to the screened porch, but in a way she didn't quite understand, that seemed the wrong thing to do.

There had been very few times such as this when she'd been growing up in this house. Had she missed them or avoided them out of hand? Gazing around the backyard and into the faces of her grandmother and her cousin, Crystal felt as if some treasure trove of memories had been placed in her lap. Problem was, the memories weren't hers. Sitting here with her tiny family, as intimate as they'd been at any time Crystal could remember, she wondered how hard she'd have to wish, how outside her typical self she'd have to step, to invoke the other lives that had been lived here: her grandfather's, her aunt's, and her mother's.

In this yard, in this moment, listening to her grandmother talk, Crystal missed her mother more than any time she could remember since she'd been grown. Layer after layer of emotional steel protected her from exposing her grief to air. Should it seep out, it would overwhelm her; it would take shape. Still, she ached to hear her mother's voice, or to feel a comb being worked through her hair, as it had on hundreds of mornings before Crystal left the house for school.

"Have fun today, Crissy," her mother would murmur, as she conquered Crystal's tangles. When she finished, she'd put down the comb and use her fingers to wrap sleek brown curls around Crystal's ears, over and over, as gentle as a whisper. "There's no one like you at school, my love. There's no one who sees the world quite like you do. No one with your insight, your humor. No one whose soul is quite so deep. You carry those things with you, all the time. They're gifts, but they're burdens too. Step away from yourself sometimes, Crissy. Just have a little fun."

Silence had descended in the backyard once Leonora stopped talking. Licking salt off her fingers, Crystal wadded the wrappers from her burger and fries and stuffed them into her empty milkshake cup. Darcy had finished her meal, but rather than balling up her burger wrapper, she smoothed it out, folded it into a square, and inserted it into her soda cup as if she was filing a valuable document. Half of Leonora's burger and many of her fries sat ignored on the little table, next to a barely touched milkshake.

Crystal reconsidered the idea of moving up to the sunporch. There was nothing comfortable about this chair. The only padded option was the chaise lounge, which Leonora wouldn't be vacating any time soon. It was time to dispose of the trash and either find a softer place to land, or head home. Still, she was reluctant to disrupt the rarefied air.

It was Darcy who finally spoke up. "Thanks for explaining what's going on, Grandma." Her voice was uncharacteristically squeaky. "I've been so worried." Darcy paused as if needing to gather steam. "And yes, I apologize for snooping. It didn't feel like snooping at the time, not really. I just felt like I should know what was going on over here. Figured it would be me who'd need to know at some point. I'd be the one who'd need to help out, or deal with it, or whatever." Darcy paused again. Crystal knew she was trying not to play the martyr. *There you go, spoonbread*, Crystal thought. *Good job*.

"And I love you," Darcy continued, "so I used that excuse too. But I am sorry for taking nosiness too far. I feel better now, knowing what the doctor says." Darcy turned to Crystal, as if it was her turn to speak, but Crystal felt no need to add to all the words that had already been said. They were piling up at a frightening pace. After a moment, Darcy continued. "So it sounds like maybe the doctor's optimistic?"

"Sweetie," Leonora said, "you can spin it any way you like. I'm content. Which must sound odd, but it's true. That's all I can say. I'm not too physically miserable, mostly tired. I can live with that." Leonora grimaced. "No pun intended."

Leaning back against the chaise, Leonora stared up at the fading blue of the summer sky before turning a contemplative look toward Darcy and Crystal. Crystal felt swallowed up by her grandmother's gaze. Leonora closed her eyes before speaking again. "The women who raised the two of you? Your mothers and me? It's safe to say that all three of us expected that you'd learn to take charge of your own lives. We tried to teach you that. Everyone needs to do that. And not just the two of you, me too. Taking charge means different things to different people. For me, it means I'll decide what I want to do. Decide when I want to do it. Decide what that might look like. But," Leonora breathed in and was motionless for a long moment before letting the breath out, "enough of this now. Let's not go through it all again. I won't be wanting another heart-to-heart next week, or the week after that. If you two need to keep talking, you go right ahead. Do it over pancakes. But leave me out of it. Which doesn't mean that I wouldn't love to have many more evenings with my two girls in the backyard. Please. I'd like that very much."

Crystal nodded. "Your milkshake has completely melted," she said. "Still good though, can I finish it?"

"Of course, honey. You're welcome to it. I have half a burger left. You're welcome to that too."

"No thanks. Just the milkshake." Crystal slurped the last drop before speaking again. "I don't work for the next six weeks. No making meals on summer vacations, now that we've wrapped up the big whoop-ta-do. Except for one day in August when I'm going to Minneapolis with Ada, I'll be around. I can drive you to an appointment or two. Might be a nice change from taking a cab. I can be scintillating company."

There was no missing the look of surprise on Leonora's face. Crystal didn't call her on it.

"Well, you know," Leonora said, flustered. "That would be a nice change. Thank you, honey. I'll take you up on it."

She appeared to ponder her next words carefully. "But I don't want to be fussed over, Crystal. I don't want that."

Crystal blew a puff of air out her nose. "Well," she said, "then you're in luck."

CHAPTER THIRTY

Coralene

Monday, July 5, 1976

PERHAPS BECAUSE IT was summer, or maybe riders were stretching their holiday into Monday, but for whatever reason, the #17 up Palisades Avenue was less than half full. Coralene had boarded the bus alone. Crystal had driven her car as she did in good weather, and left early. No matter. The work of the Nutrition Services Department was complete for the 1975-1976 school year. It was a blessing to be done. Come August 16th, Coralene, Crystal, and Sheila would return to their office, Gordon would return to his supply closet, and the nutritional needs of the students of the Hanley School District would once again be center stage. But for now, Coralene was antsy to get home.

She was of two minds about this morning's meeting. Given everything that had happened yesterday, she'd spent very little time thinking through Nutrition Services' work on the parade. The hot dog stand had been a hit, a huge hit, to hear Jan and Peg tell it. What would she have done without them? The Lord continued to bring blessings into her life, surely Jan and Peg fit that bill. Not how she would've thought she'd feel, but she did.

Crystal's review of the elementary schools' cookie stand had been brief. Crystal was many things, verbose was not one of them, although her mastery of the cryptic comment was impressive. Still, it had appeared this morning that perhaps a new Crystal was emerging.

Crystal's description had struck only positive notes. She'd mentioned how helpful her cooks had been and that they'd shown up early with their bounty of cookies and their husbands in tow. She'd mentioned another woman, someone named Ada, who must be a friend Crystal had recruited into cookie distribution. That Crystal had such a person in her life pleased Coralene. Perhaps an answered prayer. Crystal had made no mention of Lola stepping away to tend to Craig. Classy move. Only once had Crystal uttered the words "big whoop-ta-do." She'd concluded her report with a nod to Gordon: "Nice-looking poodle you had there," she'd said, before swiping her hands together once again and reaching for her coffee cup.

But Sheila? Lord have mercy. She'd been barely recognizable. Her eyes were sunken and the dark circles below them seemed to have overtaken her entire face, as if the very structure of her, the flesh and bones intended to scaffold, were no longer up for the job. There had never been anything showy about Sheila, quite the opposite. But she'd always presented herself professionally; she was intelligent and articulate. That Sheila was not the one who'd shown up today. "Nothing to report," was all Sheila had said. Asking questions, probing for a few details as Coralene would typically do, had felt tantamount to cruelty this morning. Instead, silence had suspended over their table like a swarm of bees. When Coralene had reached out to pat Sheila's hand, she'd been horrified by its chill.

As usual, Gordon had contributed little. It had taken months of frustration for Coralene to make peace with her boss' behavior. The man was simply not capable of engaging in conversation. Likely the mere thought was terrifying, thus the execution would be impossible. So he wrote memos. Memos upon memos. His final missive had been left on each of their desks at the end of the day. Coralene had put it in her purse on her way out; she'd get to it later. In this moment, her every fiber was focused on getting home to Tanner and Jasper, and hearing about their visit to the Hanley Police Department.

Tanner was in the kitchen when Jasper and Coralene walked in. He produced a fresh box of Nilla Wafers, which he opened and offered to Coralene while Jasper poured coffee. This time together around the table felt momentous. Tanner would remember yesterday's events for a long time. But, while meaning no disrespect to the dead, it was Coralene's job, and Jasper's, to see that Tanner didn't get mired in the memories of what he'd been through.

"Thank you," she said, reaching for a second handful as Tanner once again offered her the box. "Now, tell me everything that happened. Everything. You got there at 10:00 and then what? Was Craig there too? How long did it take? What did they say?"

Jasper snagged his own Nilla Wafers before putting his hand over Coralene's. "Tanner can tell you," Jasper said. "Let him finish that mouthful he's got, then he can tell you all about it."

Coralene forced herself to lean back in the chair and wait for Tanner to speak.

"They asked a bunch of questions," Tanner began. "They wanted to know how me and Craig had found the truck. Had we seen it from the road, or had we just happened to climb down the bank? I don't know why they'd think we were been climbing around. I told them we were in my truck, but that we saw tire tracks going off the side of the road, so we stopped to check it out. But then they wanted to know had we touched anything. Asked about our shoes, so they could tell whose footprints was whose. But there hadn't been any-body else there. I told them that. One officer, he was a real nice guy. Gave me a Coke. But the other guy, he made a lot of noise. Really gruff. Like it was our fault that the guy in the truck drove off the road and hit a tree. Like we were the ones responsible. I think he wanted it to be a big crime scene or something. I think he wanted to catch a criminal, but the other guy knew we weren't criminals. The mean guy knew it too, he was just being that way because he could. Strutting around and stuff. He must've been new because the other guy, the nice one, got irritated and told him to sit down, so he did."

"And you were with him the whole time?" Coralene addressed Jasper.

"No, Cory. I wasn't there when the officers talked to him. Tanner's twenty years old. He talked to them alone. I sat outside with Bruce Berg, Craig's dad. They had the boys come in one at a time. That part was sort of stupid, if you don't mind my saying so."

"You didn't say that to them, did you?"

"Of course not. I talked to the one officer. The one Tanner says was the nice guy. I know him, but only by name. Jimmy Blanchard. His brother's a supervisor at the post office. Good man."

"We aren't boys," Tanner said.

Coralene squinted at him. "What?"

"No disrespect, but we aren't boys. Uncle J said 'they had the boys come in one at a time.' We aren't boys. Sorry, Uncle J, it's just that –"

Jasper cut him off. "My mistake, son, you're right. I'll try not to do that anymore."

"You've handled this as young men," Coralene said, brushing cookie crumbs off the table. "We're proud of you. But I'm glad this part is over. Did you find out who the man was? The one you found in the truck?"

"We didn't find out much," Jasper answered the question while Tanner stacked his Nilla Wafers into a tower. "I talked to Jimmy for a couple minutes before we left. He said the man had identification in his pocket, but they hadn't tracked down next of kin yet. They need to make those calls before they release the name. He did say it must've happened Saturday night. Said the fellow had been there a while." Jasper raised an eyebrow at Coralene, indicating her coffee cup. "Refill?" he asked.

"In a minute, thanks." Coralene looked down at her own cookie tower. "Now," she said, catching Tanner's gaze and holding it. "Now, I want to know the rest of the story. You didn't want to talk last night, and I gave you that. I expect you've probably filled your uncle in on the whole backstory, but now you need to tell me. What were you and Craig doing on Sunday morning? You knew we had the parade. And you were going to drive the float. Where were you going?"

A grin was not what Coralene expected to see. "Craig's got an aunt who lives out by Lake Sylvester." Tanner said. His voice was unexpectedly light. "She has a giant garden and grows these big flowers. They're called dahlias. Craig told me about them, said they can get big as plates and that they're really pretty. In vases and stuff, on tables, you know? So we got this idea that they'd be nice on the food tables. Your table, and Craig's mom's table that the elementary schools were doing. For the parade, you know? His aunt said she could give us red and white ones. She didn't have blue ones. We went out there first thing in the morning. She said we could cut as many as we wanted, and she gave us vases. So we did. They looked real nice."

Coralene caught her breath. "That's where you'd been? Getting flowers for me and Craig's mom?" There must be words for how she was feeling in this moment, but Coralene had no idea what they were.

"Yes, ma'am. They're still in my truck. But they're all dried up. We were on the way back from getting them when we saw the tire tracks off the road. Craig saw them first. So we pulled over and looked down the bank. Like we told the police. It was right there. The truck, I mean. No question about what had happened. It smacked right into a huge maple tree. One of those big ones that grow up by Lake

Sylvester. It was a nice-looking truck, although I guess that's bad to say. But when we climbed down there…" Tanner's voice caught and he paused the retelling. Coralene watched Tanner grind his jaw, pushing back tears. She didn't know how he felt about his breakdown at the parade, but she was certain he would not want to cry again today.

Tanner took two cookies off his stack, chewing them slowly before he continued. "When we climbed down there, the guy's head was on the steering wheel. We couldn't see his face, but there was blood on the side of his head. Lots of it." Tanner paused again; when he spoke, Coralene could barely hear his words. "It was bad. Really gross. Sorry to say that, but it was. His hands were on the wheel and they were bloody too. The front of the truck was banged up. It wasn't that steep, but he must've hit that tree real hard."

"That must have awful for you and Craig," Coralene said tenderly. "Just awful."

"And you were bringing back flowers for your aunt and Craig's mom," Jasper stated quietly. "That was thoughtful there, son. Tragic what happened. Absolutely tragic. You were doing a good thing. A kind thing. I'm sorry it turned out sour."

"It did. It really did. I'm sorry I wasn't there for Grammy and the old ladies," Tanner said. "It was such a horrible day. I don't really want to talk about it anymore, at least not for a while."

"That's fine. No reason you have to. But if you find that it's making it hard for you to eat, or sleep, or work, you tell me or Uncle J. Okay? Eventually you might want to talk to the pastor. Talking to him can be helpful." Coralene took a

Nilla Wafer off Tanner's stack. "Did you have any trouble getting the time off today? To go down to the police station?"

"Nah, the foreman was cool about it. Or at least I thought so at first. I told him I'd witnessed an accident and had to make a report, so I thought it'd be all good. But then he told me I'd have to make up the time. Can you believe that? He told me I'd have to work this Saturday. Saturday!"

Tanner stood up to get the coffee pot. Holding it above Coralene's mug, he repeated his question. "Can you believe he wants me to work on Saturday?"

Coralene nodded. "Yes. Yes I can. There's still work to be done, even when terrible things happen."

"Real world, son," Jasper said, as he raised his cup for Tanner to fill. "Sometimes the real world can knock you flat. And when it does, you get back up."

CHAPTER THIRTY-ONE

SHEILA

WEDNESDAY, JULY 7, 1976

THERE WAS LITTLE left to be done. Sheila watered the African violet, knowing Lexie might not get to it for a few days. The last of the lasagna had been thrown out; the Pyrex was clean and back in the cupboard with Sheila's other baking dishes. Milk, half and half, orange juice, and a half-full can of V8 had all been poured down the kitchen drain. A nearly empty jar of mayonnaise, three remaining eggs in their cardboard carton, and the nub of butter on the plate by the toaster had been dumped in the can under the sink. Wiping her hands on the dish towel, Sheila surveyed the kitchen for anything else that might start to smell. Assessing her purge complete, she took out the bag of trash and left it in the can in the alley.

She hadn't expected the letters would take so long, but she'd needed to make her intentions clear. Two envelopes were now the only items on the kitchen table.

She didn't crank up Motown. That had served its purpose at the time; now there were no songs left to play. Sheila told herself that Tom's absence had been only that. No more relevant than a student who'd stayed home with a cold. She doubted he'd had a cold, but if he had, so what? Still, Tom's disregard, layered atop the unbearable loss of Ralph, left Sheila with nothing. What would she contemplate now? Why on earth would she bother? There was only one place she wanted to be, and she needed to get there before a fickle summer wind would no longer conjure the departed.

The sun warmed the back of Sheila's neck as she stepped into the lake. The mud between her toes was as familiar as the chair, table, and empty bed she'd left behind. She waited and listened as a breeze stroked her cheek. It was the slapping on the water that she heard first, but once Ralph hollered her name, Sheila swam out to meet him.

CHAPTER THIRTY-TWO

Lexie

Friday, July 9, 1976

LEXIE HAD LEARNED of Tom's accident from late-night local news on Wednesday. There was no way to know if Sheila had heard. Regardless, Lexie hoped they could speak a few kind words in Tom's memory tonight, once Sheila arrived for her Friday dinner.

~ ~ ~

After work on Wednesday, Lexie had made a grilled cheese and poured herself a glass of milk. Her new roommate, Beverly, was out for the evening, allowing Lexie welcome solitude in the small apartment she and Beverly shared.

It was late, and the walls in the building were thin, so as usual, Lexie kept the TV volume low. Her only interest at this time of night was having something to eat and catching the weather report. Fingers crossed for a weekend forecast that wouldn't be too hot. Come Sunday, she'd visit her sister, two towns over, in Aurora. Lexie would arrive with a picnic lunch, something Wendy always loved, and the two of them would spread out a blanket and eat together, on the vast lawn of the care home where Wendy lived.

Waiting for the weather report, she'd been only half listening, so it had taken a moment to tune in to the newscaster's account:

"The Hanley Police Department reported today that there was a fatal accident Saturday night on the highway that borders Lake Sylvester. There was one casualty, a man who has now been identified by his grandson as Thomas John Downlane. Mr. Downlane's truck went off the road on a curve at the northern tip of the lake. Skid marks in the opposite lane provided evidence that an oncoming vehicle had been approaching at high speed. Investigators surmised that Mr. Downlane may have been blinded by the other vehicle's headlights, which caused his truck to leave the road and descend the bank, resulting in a collision with a tree. The medical examiner has determined that Mr. Downlane likely died instantly. Tire tracks left by Mr. Downlane's vehicle were noticed by two young men who were driving in the area on Sunday morning. It was a considerable time before another vehicle appeared, at which point the young men flagged it down and the incident was reported to local authorities. Thomas John Downlane recently retired from Hanley School District, where he worked in the maintenance department for thirty-one years as a journey-level plumber, a trade he took up upon leaving the army after the war. He is survived by two ex-wives, four children, and nine grandchildren."

Stepping through the sliding glass door onto the balcony, Lexie looked down at the traffic on Northeast 14th Street. She shuddered at the terror that must have struck Tom – sweet Tom, Tom of the corny quips, Tom who would surely have showed up with the salsa – the absolute terror of an oncoming car. Was it okay to want the newscaster to be right? That Tom had died instantly? Yes. Yes, it was.

Lexie pulled a crumpled napkin out of her apron pocket, with no idea whether it was clean. She used it anyway, to wipe away tears at the loss of such a fundamentally good man. Her father had been such a man. He'd also been lost too soon. The thought of not seeing Tom in his usual booth come Saturday made Lexie unbearably sad. Poor Tom. Poor, sweet Tom.

She stayed on the small balcony for over an hour, until the crying was done. She owed her tears to Tom. People deserve tears when they die. They deserve smiles and kind words when they're alive, and tears when they die. It is no more complicated than that. Lexie thought of Sheila. Sheila, for whom every human emotion was inexplicably complicated. Would Sheila be able to muster a kind word for Tom in light of the accident? Tom had not abandoned the salsa. He had not abandoned the taco salad stand. He had not abandoned Sheila.

~ ~ ~

Sheila didn't show. She hadn't missed a Friday night at Denny's in years. Years. When Lexie was still the hostess, she'd seen Sheila in her booth. Even before Lexie came to work at Denny's, theories had abounded about the brooding woman who sat alone by the window. Everyone knew Sheila. And nobody did.

There was no one Lexie could call. Sheila's office at the school district was closed for the summer; there would be no possibility of tracking her down there. The only person Sheila spoke of was her niece, Connie. Lexie knew no way of locating Connie, plus that seemed an odd idea, even inappropriate.

Lexie had the key to Sheila's house. Why hadn't she also gotten Sheila's phone number? It was not in the book. Having an unlisted number was such a Sheila thing to do. Perhaps she'd fallen? Or had the flu? The first might warrant an immediate visit, but the second did not.

Had it been daytime, that would be different, but an uninvited visit late in the evening? No. Lexie knew Sheila was distraught over Ralph. Her world had not righted. Maybe hunkering down was what she needed. That was also a very Sheila thing to do. Waiting until next Friday felt irresponsible, not the actions of a friend. Tomorrow, in the light of a Saturday morning, Lexie would go see Sheila, make sure there'd been no catastrophe, and help, if she could, to get Sheila back on a Sheila-version of even keel.

Had she not known the house number, Lexie would still have successfully identified Sheila's house from among an assemblage of similar structures due south of Denny's, on Northeast 35th Street. Sheila's was single-story, tan with black trim, and nondescript in a way that reflected Sheila herself. A knee-high box hedge hugged the house under the two windows that faced the street. The hedge was interrupted by the front walk, a dozen paces from the sidewalk up one low step to Sheila's front door. The porch light was on. A little hedge trimming was called for, but there was no need to cut the lawn that had already surrendered to the summer sun.

Curtains were closed in both front windows, which Lexie assumed must be the living room and a bedroom. In the sunshine of early morning, it was impossible to tell if lights were on inside. Lexie felt no call to wander down the fence line on either side, which would surely reveal additional windows and lead to the backyard. Standing on the porch gazing toward the still-quiet street, the answer was in the air. Sheila was not here.

Unlocking the front door, Lexie paused on the threshold, expecting to find some essence of Sheila in the empty house. It was clear she wasn't home. But more than that, Lexie would've said it was also clear she'd never been home, or not in a very long time. True, there was evidence of a recent inhabitant and that inhabitant had surely been Sheila, but the house felt no more home to a living, breathing, vibrant being than did a backyard tool shed, or an empty bird's nest.

There were two envelopes on Sheila's kitchen table: one with Lexie's name, one with Connie's. No. This was too much. The lump in Lexie's throat made it difficult to swallow. Losing Tom was awful, but life could be that way. Sorrow and loss? They deserve their day. People need to go through that. But this?

Holding the unopened envelope that bore her name, Lexie considered just leaving it be. Nothing about who she was, or who Sheila had been, suggested that she, Lexie, should be in this kitchen, with little doubt about what she'd find when she read Sheila's letter. Why hadn't Sheila made this someone else's problem? She had a brother. Let him discover suicide notes in an empty house. Lexie could keep the curtains closed, forsake the African violet, and leave the key on the table. Or she could put the envelope in her purse to be deposited, unopened, in a trash can somewhere. She could leave Connie here, alone.

Sheila's bedroom was spotless, and spectacularly unadorned. The African violet was not yet dry. An ancient chenille spread covered Sheila's bed, which was pushed against one wall. A highboy was on another, and a dressing table on a third. There were no photos. No books. Not a vase, or tray, or strand of beads to be found. There must be evidence of daily life, decades and decades of it, tucked into drawers or in boxes under the bed. Lexie had no interest in learning more. What she knew in this moment was all she cared to know.

Returning to the kitchen, she sat for a long time letting the silence of the house pound in her ears before running her thumb under the unsealed flap of the envelope that bore her name, in the precise script of a former English teacher.

Dear Lexie,

I am sorry I've disappointed you. Disappointing others was never a behavior of yours. You are the opposite of disappointment. A true and honorable young woman, loyal to those who don't deserve such loyalty. I know I offered you no such grace. I'm under no illusion that our Fridays replenished any empty vessels in your life, as they did in mine.

I know you've offered this same care to others, including Tom Downlane. I bear Tom no ill will, and I do hope, oddly enough, that he retains your regard. I can't say that I wish him well, but neither would I say that I do not.

I'm leaving you my house. It's paid for, in respectable shape, and on a respectable street. I know I never asked about your sister. I've tended to avoid questions to which I can provide no more response than a nod. Perhaps you'll choose to bring your sister here and that will lighten the load you never let anyone know you were carrying. A wise young woman once told me that lightening the load is what friends do.

My revised will is in my nightstand drawer. It should provide all the documentation you need. I've included a small monthly allowance to help cover expenses should you choose a different path than the one on which you find yourself.

To feel anew the loss of Ralph Blatson is more than I choose to accept. Choices are always ours to make; I'm content with this one. I cannot be a swinger of birches, for indeed my wish is to be snatched away and not to return.

I have left my financial assets to Connie. You'll find her telephone number below. Please ensure that she is made aware of my wishes, which are outlined in the letter I've left here for her.

Sheila

Tears for Sheila would have to wait. It was not as if Lexie had an endless supply. The tidy package Sheila had presented was anything but. Her gesture, intended as generous, landed instead as misconstrued, and provided no comfort for all this. Lexie remembered enough from AP English to recognize the Robert Frost references Ralph and Sheila had each strewn in their wake. On Lexie's tongue, the words were sour.

Still, she'd see this through. She'd call Connie. From one abandoned young woman to another, Lexie would extend a hand to Connie, ease the way, if she could. But understanding Sheila's choice? Acknowledging her right to make it? Grieving, truly grieving in such a way that would lead to peace in Lexie's own heart? That would take time. A great deal of time. Because it was not grief Lexie was feeling, it was rage.

CHAPTER THIRTY-THREE

Leonora
Tuesday, July 13, 1976

"THANK YOU FOR driving and everything," Leonora said. "Picking me up. Taking me. Taking me home. I appreciate it."

"I think we've covered all that," Crystal said. "Swat that fly dead."

"What?"

"Let's be done with the nonstop thank yous."

"Fine by me," Leonora said. "But –"

"No buts."

"Okay."

"Doesn't mean I'm not glad the appointment went well," Crystal said. "I am. I can bring you back in two weeks. Write it down."

"Will do. Thank…" Leonora cut herself off. Instead she leaned back against the passenger seat of Crystal's Fairlane and considered a quick nap. A nap would not elicit any comment, which left Leonora with a murky mix of feelings: some combination of relief and pride. There was no question that having Crystal play chauffeur had taken the edge off, reducing the fatigue that typically accompanied days such as these.

It was nearing noon. Perhaps Crystal would stick around for a sandwich when they got home. Leonora kept her pantry and fridge well-stocked with favorites of Darcy's, but it had been years since she'd considered laying in food for Crystal. But pulling together something for lunch wouldn't be much of a lift. Pleased at the thought, she nodded off.

"I'd like to make a stop on the way home," Crystal said.

It took a moment to center herself when Crystal's voice punched a hole in the gauzy air of her nap. Leonora righted herself and rolled down the window. "Pardon?" she said.

"I said I'd like to make a stop."

"Let me guess: burgers." Leonora's sarcasm rang in her own ears, startling her. "Ugh, I didn't mean to sound that way. What I should've said is, would you like to stop for lunch? I'm happy to buy."

"You had a good snooze there," Crystal said. "Nah, nothing to do with burgers, although that would be okay. I'm talking about a stop at the animal shelter."

Leonora felt her good mood snap. The animal shelter? Engaging Crystal had been a mistake. "Excuse me?" Leonora said. "Why? It's been a long morning, Crystal. Let's skip your shenanigans. I don't want to stop. I'm ready to go home."

Leonora waited for a response. Too harsh? Probably, but she couldn't ignore this reminder that Crystal always made things difficult. Still, here they were together on a beautiful summer day. Leonora held her breath. She looked at Crystal's often opaque profile. Oh dear. In this moment, Crystal's state of mind was as transparent as glass.

Leonora started to speak, but Crystal lifted her index finger off the steering wheel, as if hoping to quiet her.

"Shenanigans?" Crystal said softly. "No. No shenanigans. My cat died. The cat I've had for the last few years. Good little cat. Thought I might get another one." She sighed, running her hands up and down along the circumference of the steering wheel. "I've had enough of death."

Leonora knew there was more to be said here, but it felt as if a bubble had burst inside the car, as if she'd lost her opportunity to blow fresh air toward her granddaughter, to revive her somehow. Bringing them together, even in this small space, felt impossible.

"Tell me what you mean, honey," Leonora asked cautiously. "Tell me what you mean about being tired of death. I know you didn't ask me, but maybe I'd understand."

Crystal was silent for a long time. She waited through a long red light before making a turn onto Bullman, driving past Burger Bill's.

"A burger would be fine, really," Leonora said. "I was just teasing. And it wasn't very funny. I'm actually a little hungry. Although those burgers are huge. I don't know why they make them so big. I can never eat a whole one."

"Nah," Crystal said.

As Crystal drove on, Leonora realized that they were indeed going to the animal shelter. She held her tongue for several miles until Crystal pulled into the lot and parked the

Fairlane close to the shelter's double glass doors. The building was long and low, brick along the bottom and dark-stained siding above. It would not have looked out of place as a house in the suburbs. There were a few other cars: two small pickups, similar to the one Cora had bought for Tanner, and a bland, beige Corolla. As Crystal turned off the engine, Leonora put her hand on Crystal's arm.

"I'm sorry about your cat, honey. Do you have lots of cats?"

"Do I what?" Crystal used that uniquely Crystal tone that Leonora remembered so well. The one that had built walls between them through much of Crystal's adolescence.

"You love animals," Leonora said tentatively. "I thought maybe you had more than one cat."

"I live in an apartment, Grandma," Crystal said. "It would be a sanctuary of stink if I had more than one cat." She paused. "I just had the one," she said. "Its name was Terry. I found it down by the river a few years ago and brought it home. Good little cat. Sweet cat."

"I'm sure losing Terry does make you tired of death," Leonora said lamely.

"That's not what I meant. But it's okay. We don't have to talk about it."

"But we can."

Silence descended on the car again. Leonora was too hot. This was not the time of day to be sitting in a parking lot in July. She opened her door to let in a bit of air, fearing that Crystal would make a move to get out. She didn't.

"Like I said," Crystal's voice had an unfamiliar twinge of vulnerability, "I found my cat down by the river. I used to go down by the river a lot to find cats. Once I found Terry, I was done with that. With helping cats, you know. But then I started something else. A different kind of helping thing. But I need to stop that now. I can't do it anymore."

"Do you want to tell me about it?"

"Not really," Crystal said. "Sometimes you do things that make sense at the time. And then all of a sudden they don't make sense anymore. Someone I know died. I didn't really know her. She wasn't a friend or anything. But her dying made me decide I'm done thinking about people who've died."

Leonora reached for Crystal's hand again. She gave it a quick squeeze, and just as quickly let go. "Sometimes it's hard not to think about dying," she said. "I'm not morbid, not fatalistic, not really. But I do think about it all the time. Most of my friends do too."

"I figured you must," Crystal said. "I know Darcy thinks you do. It's your right. You're old."

Leonora chuckled.

"That sounded bad," Crystal said.

"You've always called things as you see them. And you're right. I am old. But I'm still here, at least for a bit."

"I'm done with death as a hobby," Crystal said. "Other people's deaths aren't going to be my hobby anymore. I need to find a new one. I can be pretty creative as far as hobbies are concerned."

"I'm sure you can."

Crystal opened her own car door before shifting in the driver's seat to face her grandmother. She nodded in the direction of the building. "I'm going to get another cat here today. I want another cat. We could get two; you could have one. Do you want a cat? They're good company."

Leonora wanted to go along, to preserve the moment, but she was not at all sure she wanted a cat. "I don't know," she said. "I've never thought about it. Maybe. Let's go in and see."

THE END

ACKNOWLEDGMENTS

I've worked with many lovely people as I've written this book, who have informed and inspired my efforts. Thanks go to Eva Lesko Natiello for her wise publishing and marketing guidance, to Arielle Eckstut and David Henry Sterry of The Book Doctors for answering questions I didn't know I had, and to Carol Edelstein for her thoughtful review. Thank you also to Proof Positive for their meticulous final read, and the team at Damonza for their creative insights on *Lunch Ladies'* cover and interior. And a huge shout out to Zoe Mitchell, for her magnificent sketches.

Thanks to all who came to know *Lunch Ladies* as advisors and readers: Lauralee Thompson who, by being one of the first to visit Hanley, ensured that other readers had a clear path; Roslyn Dawson Thompson, whose vision and wisdom were invaluable in ensuring the book was the best it could be; and Judy Jablon, who's had her hand to my back from the beginning. To my wonderful second-round readers: your suggestions and encouragement sharpened my writing and my thinking, and helped me believe that *Lunch Ladies* would find its place. Much gratitude to Erin Havens, Juleen Vache and Cathi Bibby.

I believe that we are what we do. My life is an overflowing cup of friends who do – or like most of us, *try* to do – the best that can be done. Their acts of kindness, wisdom, humor, and love sustain me; they make me a better writer, and a better human. Thank you to my treasured friends: Kimberly Mitchell, Julie Chappell, Lori Hardwick, Beth O'Donnell, Anne Arnold, Kristie Kauerz, Judy Jablon, Robin Boland, Joelle Wheatley, Brenda Blasingame, and Ann Dickensheets. And to Gretchen Noble, who by caring for the creatures I loved, helped me get here.

When the pandemic was sufficiently behind us, I made the *now or never* decision to write full- time, because, as has been said by many who are wiser than me: "If not now, when?" Around the same time, I found Chet, and Crystal Creek Farm. Without the last two, I'm quite certain I would never have accomplished the first. So from the bottom of my heart, I thank Becky, Dave, Ditto, and Peaches Bishop. The wonderland you've created lifts my spirits every time Chet and I arrive. (Which we know is *all the time*!) I would wish such blessings for every dog, and every dog owner. And to Becky's partners in fun: Julie Betts, George Chaney, and Katie Morrell, thank you.

With the farm, have come incredible friendships. I love my dog people, and their dogs. Your interest, support, prolific texting, and sourdough bread have kept me balanced and focused: clearing my mind of ricocheting characters and plotlines, if only for an hour. You're the best: Cathi and Theo Bibby; Christine and Esme Walker; Colleen, Riley, and Henry Freedman; Debbie and Lacey Carley; Denise and Franny Trogdon; Erin and Max Havens; Jan, Chai, and Hoss Beers; Juleen and Bonnie Vache; Katie and Monkey Otto; and Diane Schultz, Baker, and Nero.

Thank you to my family: Rex Thompson and James Baker, who are in leagues of their own, and we're all the luckier for it. To my mom – my beloved, transcendent mom – who never insisted on steadying the boat when I chose to rock it. And to my brilliant and beautiful daughter, Raleigh. Bunny – I'll know I've arrived as a writer when I find the words to describe how much I love you.

BOOK CLUB DISCUSSION QUESTIONS

1. Does Hanley, Minnesota remind you of anywhere you've been? How would you describe it as a town and as a community? What elements of the story helped paint the picture for you?

2. What were your thoughts about Crystal when you first encountered her? How did your impressions of her change over time, or did they?

3. Leonora continued to talk with Badger after his death in 1928. How do you imagine the conversations between Leonora and Badger might have played out at different times in Leonora's life? What might Badger have had to say about the discussion among Leonora, Crystal, and Darcy in chapter 29?

4. What words would you use to describe Coralene and Jasper's marriage?

5. In chapter 17, Darcy studies Crystal over the breakfast table and realizes: "…*how badly she wanted to slide out from her side and go over to Crystal's, lay her head against Crystal's shoulder, and say out loud*

what she'd never said: that she, Darcy, had lost her mother too. That Crystal didn't have exclusive rights to the grief that had shaped her into who she was: sarcastic, peculiar, and out of reach when Darcy needed her most." What did Darcy want from Crystal, and how did her relationship with Crystal shape the woman Darcy became?

6. Sheila had curated a solitary life for herself with two exceptions: Lexie and Connie. Why do you think Sheila was drawn to Lexie initially, and what are the characteristics – Lexie's or Sheila's – that contributed to their continued relationship? Why do you think Sheila maintained such a devotion to Connie?

7. What do you make of the friendship between Crystal and Ada? How might Ada have influenced the person Crystal became by the end of the book?

8. In Leonora's musing in chapter 22, she reflects that: "*… There are days when people know they have been less than they should be. In those lesser moments, we are people we don't recognize. And then there are days – and Leonora understood that there were more of these now – when the only thing we recognize is what we look back on, who we used to be. We have lost ourselves, and going forward we will never truly know ourselves again.*" What does this passage tell us about her? How does it resonate for you?

9. Crystal, Coralene, and Sheila took different approaches to deciding on parade food. How did

their choices align, or not, with their personalities? How important were the assistant cooks, and Gordon, to the success of the school district's food tables?

10. How did the characters differ in their thoughts and actions related to illness, aging, and end-of-life? Were there characters you particularly related to?

11. Why do you think Tom was so persistent in his efforts to connect with Sheila? How might what we know about Tom help us color-in what we don't know, such as how his second marriage ended, his relationships with his children and grandchildren, and his Saturday night dinners at Denny's?

12. Grief and loss touched each of the primary characters, and they responded in very different ways. Discuss how various characters' loss of loved ones shaped their choices and relationships. Why do you think some people are able to cope, or even flourish, following a traumatic event? And others are not?

13. How do you picture Lexie's life a year after the story concludes?

ABOUT THE AUTHOR

Jodi Thompson Carr is a University of Washington graduate and a third-generation Seattleite. This is her first novel.